# Sing Me An Old Song

Morgan James

# Also By Morgan James

Promise McNeal Mysteries

Quiet The Dead

Quiet Killing

**A Novel**

# *Sing Me An Old Song*

Morgan James

**Published by
The Malabar Front
Atlanta, Georgia**

ISBN: 978 0615782935

ISBN: 0615782930

*This story is in part inspired by Spooky The Cat, who would rather nap in the warm California sun than whine about what she's lost, and by Chris and Ansley, who were brave enough to give her a chance.*
*I'm proud of all three of you.*

# Mavis Anne Banks Book

*September 5, 1911 – April 11, 1986*

*I will lay you down beneath a sigh of newborn grass*
*Where water tumbles lazy at your feet.*
*Sunshine to kiss your closed eyes,*
*And rosemary to whisper goodbye.*

# One

Shading her eyes against the crystalline, mid-day Atlanta sun with her left hand, Mavis steps from the porch out into the front yard. Explosions of light fly from the diamonds of her wedding rings and play across the stucco façade of 24 Cherokee Place.

*Well, here I am again. I have to say I'm a little surprised. You would think dead is dead. Oh, look at that. My azaleas are blooming. Do they have a fragrance? I'm not sure.*

Once her eyes adjust to the sunlight, she lowers her hand and follows the purr of a well-maintained, big-V8 engine approaching. Presently, a maroon Cadillac drives slowly up the street. *Must be old Terry Spiegel out for errands.* She waves to her neighbor and lets her eyes wander with the car as it prepares to make a left turn onto Ponce de Leon Avenue. Without hurry, she catalogues the houses from her porch to the intersection, recalling the character and colors of each. Finally, she visualizes the landscape, down to the last pink crape myrtle as Ponce de Leon meanders east to the Atlanta suburb of Decatur or west to Peachtree Street and downtown.

Because her old friend Terry is a creature of habit, she knows the Cadillac will make a right off Ponce onto Briarcliff Road and soon arrive at the nearest grocery. There, wheeling his buggy filled with the usual milk, eggs, oatmeal, and other quick meals packaged for a single, older gentleman whose cooking interests are minimal, Terry will splurge on two chocolate croissants for his breakfast. He will also take advantage of the weekly sales on California wine. The transmission groan of an Atlanta city bus, brakes whining with relief as it stops to gain or lose passengers, diverts Mavis' attention. Then, as she listens to the complaining bus, its singular voice joins a hum of afternoon traffic and becomes part of the song of the city. It is familiar. It is home.

But if number 24 Cherokee Place was not your home–if you were a stranger–and you walked along Mavis' still fashionable street, you might pause in front of her house, uncertain if the ambient scent was blooming gardenia or newly poured Amaretto liqueur. Then you might let your eyes linger on the single-story Italianate structure, with its floor-to-ceiling arched windows, and terracotta-tiled porch, and yawn inexplicably. You might stand in front of the house a while longer than necessary, and remember clean, sun-dried sheets, love in the afternoon, and a deep after sigh. Truly, Mavis' house was a house that revived the senses, and promised more imaginative stories, more excitement, than its more staid neighbors of rectangular, red brick Georgians. Mavis had felt this revival herself the first time she'd stood in front of the ivory stucco bungalow, and had that day fallen in love.

Some said the 1920's house had a romantic, European villa flavor. Others called it tacky, nouveau riche, and out of place on the conservative, old money street. All agreed that the façade, creamy white during full sun, was magical when deepening afternoon shadows mutated the color to a pearlescent pink. Then the house came alive, as theatrical as a Caribbean coral reef. Mavis loved every eccentricity about the house. When she was in her fifties she married the owner, Dr. Martin

Book, and he deeded the house to her–a gift he said–a small expression of his great love and devotion. From then on, in her heart of hearts, Mavis cherished the house all the more, knowing that unlike every other thing she had owned in her life, she had not worked for this generous gift.

But that was then. This is now. And it is spring in Atlanta, 1996. Mavis bends to sniff the crimson azalea blooms bordering her front walk. She sniffs a second time. Life is exuberant around her–white dogwood limbs hang low, heavy with flowers, yellow forsythia pillow on leafy bushes, daffodils rise from pine straw banked beds–yet Mavis smells nothing. Nothing at all. *Too much to ask, I suppose,* she grumbles, and then stands to right an errant strand of light auburn hair into her French twist.

From an old habit, Mavis looks across the street to the small neighborhood park, its open grassy lap spotted with massive oak and pecan trees, themselves young when her house was new. She recalls marking the years by the flocks of noisy blackbirds returning through gray November skies to assemble in the trees–their frantic wings ruffling dry fall leaves, their high pitched cries sounding for all the world like a thousand excited runaway children bound for anywhere that was far away. When the years turned from two, to ten, to twenty, it was the vagabond blackbirds who, when they flew away, had carried with them memories of the Mavis before she owned Cherokee Place, until she lived without a thought of the earlier years. Until near the end, that is.

But on this fine spring day Mavis inhales with a clear heart, enjoying her nostalgia, conscious that each breath is not labored and shallow. She feels rested. She feels young. Being here, enjoying the warm day is a lovely turn of events. Though, not wanting too much sun on her arms, she turns away from the park and the open yard, and steps back onto the porch to face her mahogany front door. *I do hope it isn't locked.*

There is a crinkle sound from under her expensive, high-heeled, ivory leather pumps. Mavis looks down. She is standing on a newspaper. Gingerly, she moves to the side to read the banner across the top: The Atlanta Journal. Covers Dixie Like The Dew. Wednesday, April 11, 1996. Mavis releases a peal of laughter that sends a squirrel foraging for pine nuts in the azalea for cover. *Well, would you look at that? Ten years to the day. How time does fly. God, if there is one, must have a strange sense of humor.*

Mavis looks back at the newspaper. The headline reads: Israel Begins Massive Attacks on Lebanon. *Oh my Lord, are those people still fighting? Terrorists, retaliations, more bombings, more killings.* Below the Lebanon story is another headline: Atlanta Prepares for Summer Olympic Games.

Before she can read the article, Mavis is inside the house, standing in the foyer facing familiar blue, yellow, green, and red Birds of Paradise hand painted on the wallpaper. A small mountain of suitcases huddles neatly on the white Carrera marble floor. It would be impossible to walk through the foyer, unless you navigated around the well worn, slightly scuffed, black leather cases. *Lovely. If I am not mistaken, Jack is home.*

Mavis turns around when a key tumbles in the lock. The front door opens and a woman–not a beauty, though rather pleasant looking–comes through. She is whistling an unrecognizable tune, bobbing her head to-and-fro as she hits the notes. Mavis smiles and moves aside to give her more room in the cramped space. On one hip the woman balances a large black plastic pot; a crewel worked handbag, large enough for a weekend trip, hangs heavy from one shoulder. Protruding from the pot is a three-foot tall, brown stick affixed with ten or so pale pink blossoms opening into fuchsia hearts. As the woman shifts her weight and pushes the front door closed with one foot, black dirt escapes from weep holes in the bottom of the pot and drifts onto the foyer floor. One of the few elongated leaves from the stick brakes off and floats down. While still balancing the pot, she picks up the fallen leaf and stuffs it in her pants pocket.

The woman is not as tall as Mavis, not as thin, and the ragged cut of her in-between length curly hair offers no hint of style. Her white canvas shoes are stained, more suited for cutting grass than playing a set of tennis, and in her kaki cotton slacks and soiled blue tee-shirt, she looks as ordinary as the older woman beside her does elegant.

Mavis presses her cream silk shirtwaist against her flat tummy and checks the foyer mirror to make sure she wears lipstick and foundation. Absentmindedly, her left hand goes to the earlobe where the matching pearl and diamond earring should be. She is sad to find it still missing and checks the pockets of her dress to make sure she hasn't dropped it there. One clean folded Kleenex. No earring.

The woman holding the pot removes her sunglasses and leaves them, along with her car keys, on the carved Chinese table standing below the mirror. Mavis bends closer to her. *Niki? Is that you? You look like a farmer, dear. To be the last of the Banks' women, you surely don't favor any of us. Of course, there's nothing wrong with that. You're your mother's child and she was beautiful in her own right. I am glad you have your daddy's freckles, though. He got those from my daddy. We all did.*

Mavis steps back, and takes in the whole of the woman's face. The past ten years have been kind. *You seem more rested than the last time I saw you. That's good. Our skin must be protected by plenty of rest and a quality moisturizer, especially after forty. I'm sure I told you that many times over. No makeup? No matter, the natural look is very in, I hear. I'm very glad to see you. But Niki, dear, allowing your pretty, strawberry-blond hair to go gray? I'm not sure about that. Let's talk about that hair later on. And what is that stick in the pot you're carrying? Well, for heavens sakes. You've brought home a peach tree. Whatever for?*

"Oh crap," Niki says aloud. "Just look at this pile of stuff in the foyer. Now why would Jack dump his suitcases here? Are there no hotel rooms in all of Atlanta? Wonder which war he's en route to this time." She maneuvers around the suitcases, kicking at the leather-bound pile to make more walking room, and heads for the kitchen at the back of the house. Mavis' house—or was Mavis' house. Mavis follows and watches Niki haul her pot bearing the peach tree out to the back garden where she moves the fledgling tree three times before she is satisfied the spot had sufficient sun. Then with a cursory slap at the dirt on her shirt, Niki returns to the house, brushes by Mavis in the kitchen, and goes through to the bathroom for a shower.

Mavis waits, going about touching the familiar, white tile countertops, opening the cupboards to note what she remembers, and enjoying the music reaching out from the radio nesting on top of the refrigerator. She sings along. *Kiss me once, kiss me twice, and kiss me once again. It's been a long, long time. I love that old song. Wasn't it Bing Crosby who recorded it first? Or was it Louie Armstrong? I liked his arrangement better. More emotion. I loved Louie's sweet gravelly voice. I know the song was released at the end of World War II. I remember that much. All the boys coming home. It was such a relief.*

*Ellis was gone for eighteen months, stationed on some Pacific Island—the name escapes me at the moment—cooking for the army. Can you imagine Ellis as a cook? Maybe a chef, but not a mashed potatoes and spam cook. I managed the house fairly well while he was gone.*

*We were good partners, Ellis and I. Too bad Brother Frank didn't get drafted—4F he said, whatever that meant. If he'd been out of my hair during the war years, life would have been less stressful. But we made it through. Of course, now that I think about it, things really never were the same after the war. Our men were changed, like children afraid the dark would steal everything. What am I talking about? Wars always change everything. Innocence is gone. Nothing brings it back.*

Mavis' memories are interrupted by the news on the radio. She listens as a BBC journalist reports, "In retaliation for rocket attacks two days ago on northern settlements, Israeli planes and helicopters have attacked Beirut, the capitol of Lebanon, and bombed suspected Hezbollah strongholds. At least five are reported dead."

She reaches to turn up the volume on the radio. *I wonder if Jack is on his way to Lebanon? Usually, he's first in line after the bombs drop.*

Niki returned to the kitchen barefoot, her curly hair still damp, and wearing a white loose fitting blouse over a long cotton skirt of graduated shades of green. After she turned the radio down, she poured an iced tea and sat down at the table.

Mavis smiled, deciding her niece looked a bit more put together after a shower, then focused her attention on the back yard beyond the kitchen windows. Someone had pruned the white spirea bushes down to toddler height. Still, they bloomed profusely. Her goldfish pond was dirt filled to accommodate a patch of vegetable garden.

*Niki must have taken up gardening. The yard looks like a Jackson Pollock work in progress. What has she done, tried to buy one of everything Pike's Nursery sells? It's just as well, I suppose. Some neighbor's cat was always skulking around the pond eying the goldfish. And I'm sure Niki has a master plan for her crazy quilt landscaping. At least I hope she does…*

When Mavis realized that she was viewing the yard through white organdy curtains–curtains certainly not hanging there the last time she'd stood at these windows–she slid the fabric back along the rod for an unobstructed view.

Niki, busy separating papers at the kitchen table, stood up and closed the curtains.

*Oh, for goodness sakes,* Mavis fussed. *What harm can a little light do?*

Niki offered no answer to her question. Mavis opened a curtain panel on the adjoining window. Niki rose again, closed the curtain, and sat down.

*Well, this is a bloody waste of time,* grumbled Mavis. She gave up the fight and stood behind Niki, content to read over her shoulder. *Looks like papers from my desk. Why in the world would you save all those useless pieces of paper?* On top of the pile was a paid Rich's charge account statement from 1984, addressed to Mrs. Mavis Banks Book, 24 Cherokee Place, Atlanta, Georgia. The statement read: one pair ivory silk pajamas, one matching robe, one pair Bernado ivory leather pumps, size eight. Next was a non-descript white envelope with two tickets to a Neil Diamond concert for May 16, 1982. *Why didn't we use those tickets? Jack must have been called out of town.* She hummed a few bars of "Sweet Caroline." Niki opened another envelope, a letter.

Mavis felt a flutter of unease and moved a step away from Niki's shoulder. *Oh dear, that's the letter I wrote to her. I can quote it by heart. Well, actually there were two letters. The first one I wrote began: Dear Niki, Early in my life I realized my tomorrows were wrought not by luck or by the gifts of others, but by my own choices. Perhaps not a profound realization for some, but for me it brought power. Now, late in my life, another truth is clear: the heart is encased, imprisoned, a moth in a spider's web, by the secrets we keep. After a time the heart sleeps, dreaming only of what is concealed.*

Mavis sighed and crossed the room to stand in front of the windows again, thinking about secrets, and why we keep them. In the back garden, a squirrel ran from a hole he'd dug in the soil surrounding a row of newly leafed spinach. She watched him leap into a nearby pine tree and bounce from one bushy bough to another. She remembered that she'd torn up that first letter to Niki; decided it was too pompous. A second letter was written that same afternoon. Mavis returned to look over Niki's shoulder. She was reading the second letter. Mavis followed along.

*Dear Niki,*

*I regret not telling you more about your father over the years. Truthfully, I wasn't sure what to say, didn't believe I could explain your father. And then too, your mother wasn't comfortable with me talking about him. Nevertheless, I should have told you more when you asked, if for no other reason than to offer you something other than the sketchy half- memories you have of your childhood.*

*I realize your father was a disappointment to you, and to your mother. I certainly understand why. Most of us can stop with one drink, or two. Your daddy couldn't. I don't know why. I suspect just having Brother Frank for a father made it more difficult for him. Frank was… well, the word formidable comes to mind. It was always his way, or no way. Your daddy was not an evil man. He was smart, did well in school, and could be charming and very attentive. I think he was just not tough enough to break away from Frank, or his own weaknesses. Most of us weren't tough enough. In the end Frank usually beat us with our own cowardice.*

*Niki, the point is that your father always had choices in what he did. If we are lucky, we have choices. Most of us are not victims. We raise our hands.*

*As for my own life, it has been what it has been. Nothing more. Nothing less. I make no apologies; don't ask for forgiveness. I did what I felt was necessary, was always determined not to live my life by default.*

*You are my only niece: the last of the Banks' girls and the last to remember Brother Frank. You are also the first who can live her life independent of his shadow. Forget him. Forget your daddy. Forget all of us. Choose your own destiny.*

The letter was signed: *Love and Happiness, Aunt Mavis*

Reading the letter again, after so many years, Mavis was embarrassed. Today it sounded just as pompous as the one she'd discarded, and offered little helpful information to Niki. She waved her hand into the air, as if to clear away the memory, and wished she'd never mailed the letter. Then she crossed the kitchen and opened the door to let in a breath of fresh air. *Oh well, spilled milk*, she said to the spring afternoon. *Can't put it back in the jug again.*

When the door yawned ajar, Niki looked up from her reading thinking: old house, door must be out of level. After she returned the letter to its proper envelope, she got up and closed the door.

Mavis left Niki alone in the kitchen and wandered back into the foyer to relive that Sunday afternoon in 1986. She wondered how that day could have been ten years ago, but knew that it was. The Atlanta Journal on the porch proved that fact, and in truth, today seemed very different from that Sunday. On that day she had been in her bedroom, at her desk. After signing, sealing, and stamping Niki's letter, she had held it lightly between her fingers, tapping it atop a thick stack of typed pages on the desk as she would a six of spades, debating whether or not to play the card. So many secrets, she had pondered. What do they matter to anyone else? The others are dead now with only me to name the names. Who knows if what I remember is actually what happened?

Mavis recalled how she ill she had felt that Sunday, so sick. She had dragged the portable oxygen canister closer to the desk chair, and then using it to steady herself, she stood. She had adjusted the thin clear tube extending from the container to her nose, and had slowly made her way from the bedroom down the hall to the foyer. Standing in this same spot, she recalled placing her letter on the Chinese table. Jack would mail it for her.

Now, today, Mavis turned toward the bedroom and imagined herself sick and weak, coming from the bedroom and standing here. She remembered being out of breath from even the short walk, and leaning against the frame of the mirror hanging over the Chinese table. With her right hand she had caressed the body of a bird carved in mid-flight on the wood, then traced ribbons of gilt held in the bird's mouth to where the pattern merged with mirrored glass. The mirror is eighteenth century, English, Mavis reminded herself. One of Martin's favorite finds—an auction in Charleston, lovely town. On that day, ten years ago, an old woman had stared back at her from the mirror.

Mavis remembered the typed pages stacked on her desk that Sunday, and also remembered what she finally did with them. Today, that memory seemed a little odd, a little off somehow. Had she done with the papers what she meant to do? For weeks, she had worked diligently, pushing through the sickness to finish the papers. Why had the finishing been so important? She whispered to the carved bird on the mirror.

*For years I willed myself not think about yesterday, or last week, or last year. That worked quite well for a very long time. Then, for no discernible reason, all the yesterdays returned, filled my mind, expanded like balloons inside my body until I could barely breathe. After that, I wanted desperately to sleep and dream of more than yesterday.*

Mavis put away the sorrow of that time and came back to the present. Today marked ten years since she'd slipped away to rock beneath a calm sea, listening to whales sing, and to sleep. She left the shadows of the foyer and returned to her kitchen. In the delicious sunlight of this moment, she felt fresh, could breathe easily, and walk anywhere without fatigue. That Sunday afternoon in 1986 seemed far, far away, and today the memories lacked the razor sharp edges they once had. For that, Mavis was grateful.

Niki, immersed once more in reading the papers stacked on the kitchen table, did not look up when Mavis breezed by to turn the radio up again.

# Two

Niki looked up when the kitchen door opened. Mavis smiled, left her niece's side where she'd been reading over her shoulder, and flew over to swing the door wide. A dark-haired man of about Niki's height, wearing a tartan checked flannel shirt, sleeves rolled to the elbows, pressed jeans, and brown Docksides, came through carrying several grocery bags. Jack. Mavis stepped out to hug him, but he moved aside to back his weight into the door to close it. Mavis frowned at missing a hug, but then recovered her smile and flitted across the room out of the way, though close enough for a ringside seat.

Jack dumped his bags on the counter and unpacked groceries. "Hey, Niki. What a surprise. Long time no see. I didn't know you were here."

"Catherine."

"Catherine?" With his back to her, he shook his head and smirked dramatically as he put yogurt, half-and-half, and a jar of black olives into the refrigerator. "Okay. Whatever. Catherine Nicole Banks." He stacked the remaining non-refrigerated grocery items on the counter. "I always called you Niki. Aunt Mavis called you Niki. Your mother called you Niki. When were you not Niki?" He stopped his grocery stacking to turn around and give her a wicked little smile. "Oh yes,

I remember now. Wasn't it your first husband? What was his name? I don't remember."

"Lyn. His name was Lyn"

"Oh yes, Lyn. He was the one who insisted Niki wasn't suitable, right? Not classy enough? I remember he called on the phone every fifteen minutes before the funeral. Reassurance that you were coming back to him straight away, I suppose. Poor sod, must have been bloody insecure."

The one taboo subject with Niki was the dissolution of her first marriage. "Why would you bring up Lyn? God, that was years ago."

"Because you insisted on correcting me with the Catherine thing. Lyn just came to mind. By the way, I tried to call your apartment in Roswell. The phone's disconnected."

"I know. That's because I'm here. I wrote to you at your apartment in London, and your office. Didn't you get my letter?"

"No, I've been traveling."

"Of course you have. You're always traveling–never a lack of wars to photograph. The last time we saw each other you were traveling."

"Yes, that's what I do. As I recall we ran into each other in early February 1993. I'd been stateside to cover the World Trade Center bombing and was flying out to Sarajevo. You were flying to Palm Beach to marry Lyn's successor, I believe."

"You make it sound like I had no right to be getting married again."

Jack grimaced. His raw nerves were showing and he didn't like that. Time to back up. "I didn't mean anything by it. Bosnia was a bitch, that's all. Bad memories. Murdered women and children. Their own countrymen…made you want to stay and fight the bastards."

Niki's breath caught in her throat. "Children? They killed children?"

"Jesus wept." Jack shot back at her. "Doesn't anyone actually read the entire magazine article? What world have you been living in, woman?" He noticed her eyes were wet at the corners. Tears? Oh shit, not tears. He quickly held up his hands as a sign of peace. He hadn't the strength for this today, certainly not if it involved a woman's tears. His leg hurt like a son-of-a-bitch; he needed to lie down. "Forget what I said. I'm sorry about your first marriage, and your second marriage. I take it that didn't work out?"

Niki sniffed back her tears. "No. As a matter of fact it didn't. I assume you're still single? Not even a pet rock to hold you down."

Jack leaned against the kitchen counter and tried to remember when he'd taken the last ibuprofen. Could he take two more now? "Yes. I'm smart like that, brilliant, actually. So what happened with the Palm Beach marriage? You didn't say."

Niki straightened her back to relieve a kink that had just that very second developed. "Why are you ragging me? Is hello not sufficient?"

"I'm not ragging, but I think you started it with the haughty *Catherine* thing. I'm just interested in what happened. The guy seemed nice enough. Mr. Personality. All smiles as I remember."

The kink tightened. She reached around to rub it. Couldn't quite get to the spot. "Yes, all smiles–a laugh a minute. I hadn't laughed in a long time. Too bad I confused entertainment with love. My mistake. Turned out marriage wasn't such a good idea, after all. Only lasted seven weeks."

"You left the guy after seven weeks?"

"No. He left me. Went back to his former girlfriend."

Jack ran his hand across his mouth to keep from laughing. "He dumped you? You're joking. That must have been humiliating as hell."

Niki couldn't believe they were having this conversation, but oh well, why not? She stood and raised her arms up and over her head until they touched, palm to palm, held the pose for a few seconds to relax the kink, and then sat back down. "Humiliating? I guess it was. For about five minutes. Then I realized he did me a huge favor. He had to pay for the divorce. He's old history. Can't even remember his middle name."

"Really?"

"No, I remember his middle name. But it doesn't matter. I'm happy he left. I made a mistake. We both did. No regrets on the divorce. So now that I've confessed my most foolish life decisions to date, you want to grill me about anything else?"

Jack cocked his head to one side and tried to read the expression on Niki's face. He wasn't good at the more subtle emotions below the terror and fear that he usually photographed as a journalist. He gave up. Niki's look was inscrutable.

"Sorry. Didn't mean to grill you. I'm just surprised to see you here, and I'm jetlagged from flying London to New York with a four-hour layover, and then New York to Atlanta. I'm not even sure what day it is. Why did you write me a letter?"

Niki shifted her weight in the chair and stretched her bare feet out in front, noticing as she did that she needed to repair the red toenail polish. "The letter was to tell you I was giving up the Roswell apartment and moving into Cherokee Place."

Jack's ears began to hum with rising anger. He shoved the rest of the groceries into the nearest cupboard and turned back to Niki. "You can't do that. Why didn't you call me? You have my cell number. You called me last summer when we needed to replace the AC unit. And two years ago about the termites.

And when the tenants moved and we decided to leave the house vacant for a while to do repairs, you called me then. Why didn't you call me now? You can't just move in."

"Why not? I can take care of the repairs, just like I usually do, since you are usually in London, or somewhere. We own the house fifty-fifty. I'll pay you rent for your half. You'll come out the same as if we had it rented to someone else. Why isn't that fair?"

He reached over and held on to the back of one of the kitchen chairs for support. This was a major complication to his hope for a little peace and quiet, a place to heal and plan what to do with his life. After closing his eyes for a second and reaching into a nearly depleted reservoir of patience, he answered, "Because, I was trying to call you to tell you that I was en route to Atlanta. I've given up my London flat. *I'm* moving into the house."

From her perch on the counter top, Mavis clapped her hands. This was going to be even better than she'd anticipated. Niki and Jack both looked up at the ceiling. Was that thunder?

"What?" Niki blurted out loudly. "I doubt that. Have you seen the evening paper?" She unfolded *The Atlanta Journal* to the headline of Israel bombing Lebanon and waved it in front of him like a flag. "There's another war heating up. Your magazine probably wants you to cover the bombing and bloodshed."

Jack took a moment to scan the article. Nothing new. "I heard the news on the radio. But I'm out. No more jumping from low flying helicopters and dodging bullets. I've packed it in–retired. I'm fifty-two years old. I've had enough."

Niki eyed him suspiciously, thinking leopards don't shed spots quite so easily. "Umm. Well, that's terrific. Congratulations. But can't you be retired somewhere else? I've already moved out of the Roswell apartment. Didn't you see the furniture in the foyer when you dumped your suitcases?"

"No. I was more concerned with getting groceries. And I don't want to be retired somewhere else. I lived here with Aunt Mavis and Dr. Book for years after they married. Besides the Baker Street house, this is the only home I know. You were a just a visitor."

"I did too live here, several summers at least, and after Mama died, for a while. You were away at boarding school and then college, so you've forgotten."

Mavis waggled a finger at Jack. *Well, she's right about that, Jack. You were having a stellar time at college in Florida. I remember you hardly came home during those years. Naturally, I understood the need for a boy to party a little, but honestly, I did worry sometimes if you weren't overdoing. Then when I learned you'd been working after classes for the Tallahassee newspaper, I was crushed you didn't tell us. Knowing you, you were afraid the job wouldn't last. It wouldn't have mattered, dear. Martin and I would have been proud either way. I'm always proud of you.*

Tossing the newspaper down on the table with a whack, Niki raised her voice ever so slightly. "Didn't we go over this already, about ten years ago? I know you aren't happy with the terms of the will. I have no idea why Aunt Mavis left us both the house. But she did, so here we are."

Jack stepped away from the chair and took a step closer to Niki. "Didn't you see my bags in the foyer? I've brought everything I own from London. *Everything.*"

"Everything? Are you telling me your entire life of the past thirty years is contained in that leather bound pile of suitcases in the foyer?"

"What's wrong with that? I travel light."

"Nothing. It'll make it easier for you to move somewhere else. My furniture, and Mavis' things are moved in already.

Like I said, furniture in the foyer, furniture all over the house. You will note we are standing in a kitchen equipped with a table—Mid-century style—gray and white enamel over metal, four shiny red upholstered chairs. My table and chairs."

"Okay, okay. I hear you. No need to be sarcastic. I guess I forgot the house was emptied when we rented it out. I told you I was jetlagged."

"Well, the house is not empty now. I've moved everything back."

"You mean in ten years you haven't sold anything? You've kept it all?"

"Well yes. Why should I sell? I like Mavis' antiques. A few newer pieces are mine, to fill in what you and I agreed to sell from the estate. I'm sure you remember getting your half of the proceeds. Nice check as I recall."

Jack opened his mouth to say something else, but thought better of it. Arguing was not doing his headache or the pain in his leg any good. "Of course I remember; I'm retired, not senile. Can we call a cease-fire for a while? Sort this out later?"

Niki felt a tinge of compassion at the fatigue in his voice and turned away to look out the window to the garden. There was her new peach tree, hopeful in the gathering shadows of late afternoon, waiting for a permanent home. "Prunus Persica," she said. "Did you know peach trees are members of the rose family? They were cultivated in China before 200 BC and brought to Europe by Alexander the Great."

Jack had no idea where her comments came from, but took them as a positive sign that the argument was deflating. "I'll make coffee," he offered, and then added, "but you're Niki, not *Catherine*."

"Coffee? Oh good. Did I see you bought half-and-half? I was out. By the way, good move to shave off the beard and mustache. They made you look villainous."

Jack reached for the Don Pablo coffee beans and the grinder. "I'd forgotten you suffer from Tourette's syndrome."

"And I'd forgotten you are so witty."

Mavis listened to the exchange. Smiling. Delighted. *Well, I have to agree with Niki about the beard, Jack, though you could have left the mustache. A mustache would give you a little Errol Flynn drama.*

She rubbed her manicured hands together and congratulated herself on the decision to leave the two of them her beloved house. *What fun. Here they are, trapped like two cats in a burlap bag. I wouldn't have wanted to miss this. Not for all the peaches in China.*

Mavis' laughter rang like sleigh bells awakened by a frisky horse, rattling the coffee cups Jack was taking down from the cupboard, and sending crackles of static from the radio on top of the refrigerator.

# *Three*

Sometime during the wee morning hours Jack woke, either from the pain in his leg or from the memories that stirred in the house. Was he dreaming, or did he hear the old song Mavis was fond of singing as she went about the house? *Kiss me once, kiss me twice, and kiss me once again. It's been a long, long time.*

Once awake, knowing from experience that sleep wouldn't come again, he put on his robe and walked as silently as possible down the hall past Mavis' room where Niki slept, across the living room, through the French doors, to the screened porch beyond. He sat in one of the wicker chairs, now slightly damp from the dew, and listened to a night bird complain—*jon-kill, jon-kill, jon-kill.*

He couldn't get his mind off the news about Lebanon. What time was it in Lebanon? Who did they have covering the action? Grant? Maybe Tom Peabody? He shifted his weight in the chair and stretched his bad leg out in front, hoping if he righted the knee, the throbbing would ease. No point in thinking about it, he told himself. Two pounds of ricocheting mortar shrapnel on the Khobar Road has taken me out of the game. I need to shift my gears to something else, like how I'll set up a photo studio here and use what I know to continue to work. Or how I'll get that annoying Niki out of my house. God, no wonder she's been married and divorced twice. She's so twitchy. Two glasses of wine with her dinner and she was still wound tight like a Swiss watch spring.

He rubbed the upper part of his leg where metal had chewed bits of flesh away like a weed-eater. Could have been worse. I've still got the leg. Mavis would tell me to pamper myself for a few days then make the best of it. *Spilled milk, sweetheart,* she would say. Jack allowed himself a slight smile. There will never be another like her.

His thoughts went back to Niki. I wonder if she remembers it is ten years to the day. She seems so concerned with herself, she's probably forgotten. I remember. I was here, between assignments. Home is where I always came to rest, recharge, get out of the crazy life for a dew days and let Mavis' calmness wash me clean.

As he sat in the darkness of the screened porch and let that night of ten years ago re-play in his mind, Jack recalled being back in Atlanta for about two weeks: a long hiatus for him in those days, and already he was anxious to get back into the excitement of the "war of the week," as Mavis called it. At about three a.m., in that silent, nether time of darkness between starred sky and returning day, he woke to the faint but unmistakable smell of burning paper. Why in April, he had wondered, would Mavis make a fire?

Jack recalled he had stumbled sleepy-eyed into the hall, and quietly opened the door to Mavis' lamp lit bedroom, expecting to find her asleep and the half-spent logs she'd ignited with newspaper cooling in the fireplace. Instead, he found the French doors to the patio ajar and night air whispering encouragement to a flickering stack of typewriter paper at the hearth's edge. Mavis was lying on the bed atop her satin coverlet.

Jack remembered she wore her ivory silk robe and was turned on her side facing him, and the open door. Though it was the middle of the night, her red hair was combed away from her face and styled in a carefully done French twist. Had it not been for her open eyes and bluish lips Jack would have thought her beautiful against the clean white lace pillowcase. One diamond clustered pearl earring, the size and shape of an almond and the color of fresh given cream, hung from her right ear lobe. Its match had fallen on the carpet beside the bed. Her right hand clutched the satin lapel of her robe. Her left hand was outstretched over the bed's edge pointing down as though to signal the location of her pearl treasure. Her oxygen canister, its plastic lifeline coiled on the carpet like a skinny snake, was over on its side, about two feet from the bed.

Jack's eyes had rested on Mavis' face. Her mouth was slightly open, as if her soul had been jerked outward in the middle of a spoken word. Jack knew death well enough to know it was useless to check for a pulse. Uganda, 1985, rushed his mind like rank air escaping from a garbage can. Catch a hop to Paris, the editor had said. Here's your ticket to Kenya. You'll hook up with two guys there who've covered the area before, they'll get you over the border and as close to Kampala as possible. That's where the action is. Photograph what you can in two days and get the hell out. Word on the street is the whole place is about to…*about to what?*

Jack couldn't remember what else the editor had said, but he could never forget Uganda. Nothing had prepared him for massacred bodies propped against banana trees or for child soldiers thrusting Soviet made rifles in his face and demanding money in exchange for not shooting him. The military controlled refugee camps were the worst of it. Lines upon lines of dead bodies, ripe with decay under the unforgiving African sun, attended only by the flies that crawled over them.

Jack recalled most of what he'd photographed was never published. Too graphic, the magazine decided. So many murdered, ashen-faced men, women and children, life blown away by land mines, hacked away by machetes, oozed away into the Ugandan soil. And he was standing over the bodies with his camera, taking photograph after photograph. Jack was sure those were the longest two days of his life.

For a few, very long seconds, Jack didn't think he could step farther into Mavis' bedroom. He waited for the remembered stench of spilled, warm blood to fill his nose so he could retch and get it over with. But it didn't come. There was only the cool April night breeze blowing across his sweaty face, the familiar gardenia perfume of the room, and Mavis, dead. Finally, he forced himself to swallow, took a deep breath, and walked into the room to close Mavis' eyes and mouth. "You got what you wanted," he said to her. "To die here, no hospital. I don't know where your soul went, but I wish you peace wherever you are." He had pinched the bridge of his nose to fight back tears, picked up the dropped pearl earring from the carpet, and turned away from the bed to call 911.

After the call was made, Jack surveyed the bedroom. Except for the unseasonable fire in the fireplace, everything about the bedroom was as it should be. White furniture framed by ivory walls, chairs in pale creamy moiré, off white carpet, billowing loose drapes of the same color—all in order. Back issues of Antiques magazine neatly stacked in the basket beside the desk. On the desktop, the plastic case of Mavis' Olivetti typewriter was snug in place. No cold cups of half-drunk coffee or brandy glasses strewn about. Mavis' canary, Abelard, was asleep in his cage, covered for the night.

Suddenly Jack felt like an intruder into the most private of acts. Part of him felt he should tiptoe out of the room. The other part would not leave her alone to the emptiness. He circled around the bed and crossed the carpeted floor to close the French doors. As he passed in front of the fireplace, he took the brass shovel leaning against the marble surround and stooped down to rake the smoldering mass well back into the firebox. Black, burn- pocked sheets of paper caught fire again and curled upward like cupped hands. Jack bent on one knee to get a closer look.

"Well, I'll be dammed," he had whispered and turned to Mavis. "You decided to burn it all? Worked day and night writing, then just lit a match to it." For no reason he could imagine at the time, Jack dragged the papers back to the front of the fireplace and tapped out the flames with the shovel. Smoke trailed up the chimney like pointing fingers.

With no idea of what to do next, Jack had sat at Mavis' desk to wait. He picked up the familiar filigreed silver framed photo of three women. Sisters, photographed years ago, descending the wide staircase at the house on Baker Street—a time long before Mavis married Dr. Book and owned the Cherokee Place house.

Mavis, sedate and mysterious in a forties-style suit with slim skirt and waist fitted jacket, her long auburn hair confined to a tight bun at the nape of her neck, was forever caught in time on the higher step. She gripped the turned handrail casually as though she would slide her right hand down the polished wood more for effect than support. The camera was acknowledged simply because it was there. She held no pose, no charming smile, and no flirtation. She could take it or leave it.

The other two women, dressed for a costume party in flapper dresses and feather headbands, smiled playfully and leaned over the rail showing plenty of cleavage for the photographer.

Each sister was beautiful in her own way, though one might not guess they were related. Marie screamed sexuality, though lacked Mavis' refinement and restraint. Where Mavis seemed willow tall and elegant, Marie was all curvaceous breasts and hips trying to escape the skimpy dress. Marie was ready for any party. The other flapper, Baby Fern, her sisters called her, was shorter, much younger, and stunningly beautiful.

Light from the camera's flash appeared drawn into Fern's face, illuminating hers more than the others. Yes, the face—that hungry, fetching, china-doll face—framed by thick tendrils of soft brown hair, a smile that promised the world, but gave nothing. Jack had held the photograph closer to the desk lamp and concentrated on her eyes, waiting for some stir of connection. None came.

He noticed Fern was not really looking at the camera. She was looking beyond the photographer, over his shoulder. Jack remembered she was always looking somewhere beyond. Did anyone else notice that?

His memory jumped from that night ten years ago to a time when he was a child playing on that same staircase, running up and down, clomping loudly as his little-boy boots jumped from one wide, wooden step to another. Another woman, not a Banks sister but a hired cook, called from the kitchen, "Jackie Rainwater! You wake them girls and they is gonna be hell to pay! Get off them steps and come out here and help me make the cinnamon rolls. Hurry up now and you can cut 'em out with the jelly jar."

Jack smelled the warm yeasty kitchen of the house on Baker Street, and smiled.

That night, when Mavis died, when the doorbell rang announcing the ambulance, Jack had walked from the bedroom, closed the door, and carried with him the faint fragrance of

White Shoulders perfume into the hallway. They were alone again, the dead woman and her dreaming canary, perhaps listening to the hissing from the fireplace and the lingering echo of a life.

A truck grinding through its gears out on Ponce de Leon Avenue brought Jack back to the screened porch, and 1996. His thighs were cold against the damp wicker. He stood up, paced a few steps to the end of the porch to warm his legs, and noticed morning light gradually filling the darkness between the pecan branches in the park across the street. He was glad to be home, even if home lacked Aunt Mavis and meant dealing with Niki.

Ah yes, Niki. Jack shook his head, thinking: bat-shit crazy woman. We cannot live together in the house. Impossible. I hate having a roommate. There was a click when the automatic timer switched on the sprinklers. Water splashed against the screen at his feet. Jack flexed his toes in his now soggy slippers and cursed, "Damnation."

"Why are you standing out here in your robe? It's barely daylight."

Jack turned to see Niki framed by the doorway into the living room. "Is standing on the porch before seven o'clock not permitted?"

Niki's shoulders slumped. "Please. Let's not claw at one another again. I thought you might be sick. You seemed to have a headache or some sort of pain last night."

Jack shoved both hands into his robe pockets. "Me? I'm fine. Just watching the sunrise over the park. Beats smoggy London any day of the week."

Satisfied he'd diverted Niki's attention from any discussion of his injured leg, Jack noticed her worn jeans, long sleeved shirt, brimmed straw hat, and naked feet. "Are you up for raiding the bee hives? If so, you may want to collect your shoes."

Niki looked down at her outfit, momentarily confused by his remark. "Oh, shoes, yes. I mean no, not bees. No bees. I've put in a small garden out back and want to weed before the day gets too warm. My gardening shoes are in the utility room." She paused and then added, "Speaking of shoes. You do realize your slippers are totally wet?"

Jack balled his fists inside his robe pockets, wondering if strangling such an annoying woman would be justified.

# *Four*

Mavis was out in the garden inspecting the young tomato plants when Niki arrived, loaded down with a shovel, hoe, trowel, gloves, watering can, and a bag of 10-10-10, fertilizer. *Good Lord child. Is all of that really necessary? I do hate to tell you this, but the rabbits will eat anything you grow. Have you noticed they've already munched on the spinach you put in?*

Niki pulled on her gloves, knelt in the newly turned dirt, and began to work the fertilizer into the topsoil. Carefully, she went down the row on her knees and tended to each new planting. Tomatoes, spinach, kale, red leafy lettuce. Sweet peppers in yellow and red would go in next. Mavis stood behind her, mindful to stand far enough away to keep her new high heels out of the soft dirt. An early morning breeze lifted the tail of her silk shirtwaist, and she turned to feel a kiss of wind on her face.

*I guess not. No matter. I suppose spinach can produce more leaves. You know, Niki, I was thinking about your father, and about Brother Frank. I'm sorry Frank Jr. didn't take after my daddy. He was a man to admire. You would have loved my daddy.*

Another row fertilized and weeded, Niki stood up and stretched her back before she began the next. She was thinking about a disjointed dream she'd had about her father the night before, and hoping she would lose the threads of the dream permanently in her purposeful digging. Thinking about her father was never a good thing. Better to concentrate on the task at hand. She puzzled why, of all times, would she dream about her father, whom she hadn't seen in over forty years, rather than about her mother, who struggled to raise her, and was her only family aside from Aunt Mavis?

Poor Mama. Was she ever really happy?

Mavis caught Niki's sadness and sighed, wishing that she could tell her niece that she understood dreams about the past, understood how easily they could sneak into sleep and leave behind a kernel of uneasiness. She decided to change the subject.

*Niki, I want to tell you about my daddy. Perhaps if there had been women friends in my life, sitting over coffee, heads leaning inward, voices quiet to hold the world beyond, I would have said it all before. But how can you be friends when you can't see yourself in the other's eyes? No, women have always fallen into categories other than friends for me. That wasn't the way I planned it. It was just the way it was.*

Mavis bent over Niki's shoulder and spoke softly in her ear. *I loved my sisters, of course. One always needy, the other a beautiful fire, paining everything she touched. But they were my sisters and required my care. I have no doubt love existed between us, but friendship was not part of the bargain.*

*I thought your mother and I might be friends after she left your daddy. I admired your mother. When she'd had enough of his behavior, she was done. No looking back. No whining. But she didn't seem to warm to me. I think she only tolerated me and the relationship I kept with the two of you because she felt you needed some contact with your father's side of the family. I don't really blame her. The Banks family of Baker Street was probably a little much for her small town sensibilities. And what of my Baker Street girls? Well, what can I say? They were part of another bargain. You know, if one crosses that fine line defining psychological distance, business does not run smoothly.*

*Mind you, I am not complaining about the lack of friends. I have been fortunate. Ellis was my friend. A true and dear friend. To the best of his ability, my husband Martin was also my friend. He gave me his respect, his counsel, and his love throughout the time we were together. Had he lived longer, we would have been friends in our old age.*

*But of course, these are both men. I have missed the familiarity, the sameness, and the mirror of understanding I would have thought only another woman could give. I'm rambling, I know. I only meant to speculate that having women friends might have satisfied the need to tell my story. I would have told it over and over to a friend and thus worn it out in the telling. As it is, the past roves my head in rabble bands of voices, broken pieces of memories with no particular order.*

Mavis sighed and settled in to tell her story.

In those last days I felt a need to close the circle on those recollections. Ah yes, the unbroken circle. A long time ago my daddy sang, "The circle will be unbroken, by and by Lord, by and by..." I forget the rest of the words. No doubt they had something to do with dying and the grace of God. Most of the old songs did. God's grace? My dictionary defines grace as: the unmerited favor and love of God. A fascinating concept. Apparently, you don't earn grace, or pay for it. It just *IS*. How can that be? I understand cause and effect. I understand consequences. But grace? I can't imagine such a thing. What I can imagine is being a small child, hearing my daddy sing that old song, and feeling the thumping rhythm he counted with his foot as I pressed against his leg.

You see my daddy, Theron Banks, was a mountain man from Cokercreek Tennessee. In my mind he is always dressed in his Sunday suit of black thigh-length woolen coat and trousers, a clean, white, starched shirt, and a narrow black ribbon tie carefully bowed at his neck. He is cradling his beloved fiddle in the crook of his left arm and searching for his hat, eager to be off somewhere to play foot-stomping dance tunes or to sing lonesome melodies recalled by his Appalachian heart. When I was a child, my daddy's tenor voice could lift me up from our mean little porch in Atlanta, and set me walking foggy mountain roads found only within the songs he sang.

He was six-four, a giant in those days, and so thin I remember his leather belt always puckered the extra fabric at his waist. Not that he didn't eat; Mama was a good cook, and whatever else we may have lacked, there was always plenty of cornbread and pork fatback on the table. Sister Marie inherited Daddy's sad smile. I got Daddy's red hair, his height, and his mother's name, Mavis. Brother Frank inherited Daddy's honeyed voice and his ability to drink a quart of corn liquor and still walk a straight line.

Daddy's face was as angular as his body, tanned and leathery, as you would expect of a man who spent his life working outside. I remember his face as a smiling surface of sharp cheek ridges, deep set eyes, and a chin with a cleft serious enough to bury my little finger. When I was young I was endlessly amused by tracing his face with my hands just to feel the in and out hardness of it, and to see if I could make a sandpaper sound from his stubble beard.

Daddy said he brought Mama, their two-year old daughter, Alice, and Brother Frank, to Atlanta from Tennessee on a mule. Everything they owned was tied in two gunnysacks and hung across the mule's back. He and Brother Frank walked most of the way so Mama and the baby could ride. I've retraced their journey by car and it seems inconceivable to walk such a distance. But I believe Daddy's story. Theron Banks was an even-tempered man—slow to anger and even slower to forgive—who did not lie.

He told me that when they neared Atlanta, Baby Alice died from summer fever. They buried her on a hot twilight evening lit by fireflies and a half-moon. She was sent to glory, Daddy told me, behind a Holiness church in Smyrna, Georgia, by a preacher whose named he couldn't remember. Mama, he recalled, said The Lord's Prayer and he played "In The Garden" on his fiddle. The preacher prayed long and hard over Alice, and then refused to take one of Daddy's five remaining dollar bills for the burying. Daddy recalled they camped that night in Smyrna on the edge of the cemetery, and at dawn he saw three crows pass over Alice's grave to ferry her home to Jesus. When they were back on the road, Brother Frank, then nine years old, vowed he would never walk anywhere again if he could "figure a way" to ride. I believe Frank made good on that promise.

Daddy, Mama, and Frank ended the trek from Tennessee by settling in Atlanta on Moody Street, a neighborhood of shotgun, pine-board houses near Oakland Cemetery and the Fulton Cotton Mill. I have photographs somewhere of the old neighborhood. It was spare and devoid of any appurtenance not necessary for survival. All the houses were pretty much alike, duplexes really, built front to back, one room behind the other. Outhouses squatted in the mud yards behind every other house, and cats staked out their turf underneath rickety front porches raised off the ground by squat columns of blood red Georgia bricks.

You could lie on the kitchen floor with an eye pressed against the pine floorboards and count Mama's chickens scratching sand under the house. When the wind turned our way, soft coal soot from the nearby railroad yard combined with the ever-present cotton lint drifting from the mill and stuck to our windows like filthy gray snow.

For some reason, Mama loved the house on Moody Street. She was comforted, she said, by having close neighbors in times of trouble and by the fact that the house was in no danger of being carried away in spring by Tennessee floodwaters. I think it was only a few days after they settled on Moody Street that Daddy found work laying brick pavers for the front patio of the new, eleven-story, Georgian Terrace Hotel on Peachtree Street. As did many men in the neighborhood, Daddy also worked a shift at the cotton mill to feed the family. He told me he felt very fortunate to have work.

Marie and I were born on September 5, 1911, the same year Mama and Daddy moved to Moody Street. Mama said we were the only twins she knew born into the Banks family, and concluded God meant to bless her twice for the baby girl she lost on the way to Atlanta. *Mama was forever the optimist.*

# Five

Mavis paused her story, gathering her thoughts. She noticed Niki had stopped her digging, taken off her gardening hat, and sat down in the grass. An errant curl dipped down on her forehead and Mavis bent to blow it back off her face. Niki felt the cool breeze lift her hair and absentmindedly combed the curl back into place with her hand.

*You seem tired, dear. Not sleeping well?* Jack's footfall distracted Mavis and she drifted onto a limb of a nearby Bradford pear tree, resplendent with April blossoms.

Niki looked up. Jack stood before her, two coffee mugs in hand. "Thought you might be ready for a coffee break. Double cream in yours, right?"

"Yes, that's right. Thanks."

Holding both mugs in one hand, Jack offered his free hand to Niki. Instinctively, she took his hand, closed her fingers around his and allowed him to help her up. *Odd, she thought, all these years and this is the first time I can remember Jack touching me. Even at the funeral, I don't remember so much as a handshake. Wonder why he's being so helpful?*

Jack handed Niki a mug. "Tell me again what you've planted. I'm not a gardener."

Niki took a welcomed sip of coffee and pointed to the end of the rows of vegetables. "I'll name them for you starting

from down there: kale, red leafy lettuce, spinach, and tomatoes. This next row, the one with just tiny sprouts showing, has
Blue Lake green beans and snap peas. Peppers go in next."

"Very impressive," Jack offered. "Why such an ambitious
garden?"

"Ambitious?" Niki repeated the word as though it held
new meaning for her. "I didn't think I was being terribly ambitious. It's just that gardens aren't possible in an apartment, and
I thought it would feel good to grow..." Her voice trailed off
when she realized she had brought them around to the elephant
that sat between them: namely that each wanted the other to be
somewhere else, rather than the Cherokee Place house.

Jack picked up the subject. "You moved into the house so
you could plant a garden?" he asked, sounding conversational
and not accusatory. Niki shot him an irritated look and said
nothing. Jack spoke again. "I was just wondering. I thought you
had a great apartment in Roswell. Close to everything. Good
shopping. You still work from home?"

"Yes, I still work from the house—the advantage of being a
technical writer. Of course, it's easier now that I have a new
computer. Word processor. Whole new world over the old
electric typewriter."

Jack nodded knowingly, said that, yes, he was sure the
computer helped. They stood in silence again, drinking coffee
and listening to the birds making morning sounds. When Niki
didn't offer anything else, Jack asked, "What exactly do you do
as a technical writer?"

She frowned. "I'm sure you aren't really interested."

"No, I am interested," he said, though he really wasn't interested in what Niki did for a living, only in finding some
common ground he could stand upon to convince her she
would be happier if she moved out of his house.

Niki was suspicious. Nobody cared about technical writing, unless you were the client. Okay. She'd play along. See where he was going. "Well, let's say you were John Deere and made a new mower. I would write the instruction manual so your customer knows how to operate it without chopping off a foot or hand in the process. Or, sometimes I do technical presentations for someone like a pharmaceutical company. Explain a new drug. Whatever the product is, I figure out how it works and then explain whatever the client needs to know in laymen's terms."

Jack managed a wan smile. He was sure he'd rather be jumping from a low-flying helicopter into the war of the week. My God, he thought, no wonder this woman is so uptight. She spends her life dissecting some lousy piece of equipment, or drug molecule, and explaining it to dullards like me who don't really give a rat's ass how it works. All we want is the thing to do what it is supposed to do.

Niki handed Jack her empty cup and replaced her hat. She knew by the glazed over look in his eyes that the discussion of technical writing was over and done. "But the garden wasn't the only reason I wanted to move into the house. I also thought I might get a dog. Nothing big and slobbery, just a normal city-sized little guy."

Jack's eyes opened saucer-wide. A dog? That certainly came out of left field. I don't like dogs. They always want something. He cleared his throat and told himself to be calm. "Why do you need a dog? You kept Mavis' canary as a pet."

The edge to his question let Niki know she'd succeeded in annoying him. Too bad. She didn't care what Jack thought; she really did want a dog. She decided to ignore his reaction to the dog issue. It wasn't his decision anyway. "Abelard has a lovely song, but you can't exactly take him out and scratch him behind the ears. And you know he's fifteen years old, ancient for a canary. Besides, haven't you heard, dogs, unlike humans, offer unconditional love?"

Jack replied smugly, "Yeah, I think I read that somewhere."

Mavis had heard Niki's comment and came down from the tree to stand beside her. *Did you say a dog? You can't have a dirty-dog-thing running around my house. We have white carpet in the bedroom, for goodness sakes. What if he pees on the leg of my antique Chinese table in the foyer? That is a two hundred year old lacquer finish, you know.*

Enjoying the dismayed look on Jack's face, Niki rubbed the salt in a little deeper. "I mean I know I'll have to take up the carpet in the bedroom and refinish the wood underneath. But I'm willing to pay for it. I explained all of this to you in the letter. The letter you say you didn't get."

"I really didn't get the letter. It'll probably arrive forwarded from London sometimes in the next century."

Mavis narrowed her eyes and leaned into Niki's face. *Did you say rip up my white carpet? I love that carpet. I'm sorry, no dogs. Definitely no dogs.*

"Sure, London mail is probably pretty slow. Anyway, that's the story, letter or no letter. I'm moved in and settled, so we really do need to work out something."

"Work out something? That's for sure. Both of us can't live here. I'm used to my privacy. I've lived alone since I left college. Maybe we should just draw straws. Short straw gets the house."

"Draw straws? That's ridiculous. You're being childish. I'm going in to shower."

Niki stalked into the house leaving Jack standing beside the spinach. He decided to stay outside, drink the remainder of his coffee, and allow his anger at being called childish to dissipate.

He walked the length of the yard, thinking. How was he going to get her out of his house? He doubted there was enough cash in his working account to buy her half, and a new mortgage was out of the question. Who'd make him a loan now that he was a retired, or rather unemployed, photographer?

Mavis put an arm around his shoulder and leaned in to kiss him lightly on the cheek. *Poor Jack. The women in your life have always been trouble, haven't they?*

Without wanting to, Jack smiled and said under his breath, "I can't believe that crazy woman is thinking of getting a dog. Aunt Mavis will spin in her grave if Niki brings home a dog." As he wandered around the yard drinking his coffee, and seemingly studying Niki's gardening efforts, he concentrated on formulating a plan that would net him the loss of a roommate. When no workable solution came to mind, Jack was no longer amused about Niki and the dog. He had to think of something to get rid of her.

Mavis sat on a concrete bench under a white dogwood tree and watched him. *Whatever is the boy doing? He's never been interested in gardening. Looks like he's struggling to tell the kale from the spinach. No, I raised that boy. I know him. He's plotting something.* Then it occurred to her that maybe her nephew was simply feigning outside interest in the garden to avoid Niki. *I hope I didn't make a mistake with those two. Oh well, spilled milk, I always say. Spilled milk.*

With a decisive flick of the wrist, Jack chucked the remaining swallow of cold coffee from his cup onto the vegetables. For the moment he would set aside the idea of getting Niki out of his house and concentrate on himself—post retirement. He asked himself: What the hell do retired men do all day? I hate golf, don't paint prissy little pictures, and my leg is too crapped up to play tennis. Jack studied the neat rows of vegetables again and knew he would have to work at something other than gardening, or there was a real danger he would go bat-shit crazy, like Niki.

Mavis decided not to follow Jack when he ambled back to the house. The warm sun was too delicious to leave. A phoebe sailed down from the dogwood tree above with a sharp cry. She sat for a moment beside Mavis, switched her long tail, and then picked a stray thread from the hem of the sun-lit woman's silk dress. Mavis dismissed the bird with a wave of her hand and it flew away with the prize.

Mavis settled in to enjoy the sunshine. *They are too preoccupied with their own lives to even hear me.* Her slim hand went up to worry one naked earlobe, sending a ripple of sadness through her chest. The absence of the matching pearl brought back a longing to have what was meant to be hers alone. She wanted the missing earring returned. After all, it was hers. Mavis touched the one earring she wore with tenderness. The smoothness of the pearl and its teardrop shape was always comforting.

*Ah well, where was I? Oh yes…Marie and I thought the best part of Moody Street was its proximity to downtown Atlanta and the Grant Park Zoo.*

We spent many Sunday afternoons at Grant Park, picnicking under its young oak trees and listening to the elephants and big cats calling across the acres and acres of wonderment. Daddy, sitting crossed legged on a bedspread brought from home, would play his fiddle and more often than not draw a group of admirers. Marie and I threw our bread scraps to honking ducks paddling atop the dark waters of the park pond and pestered Daddy endlessly, I'm sure, to stop his music and row us out in one of the flat-bottom boats closer to the swimming, begging ducks. No doubt, Marie and I got our way sooner or later.

I can't recall Brother Frank as part of those happy afternoons. Being ten years older than Marie and me, he probably had other interests besides picnics with us. What those interests were, I can only speculate. Frank was my only brother; but he was a man of secrets. I know more about what lives in the heart of my yellow canary than I did my brother's. I think of his heart as beryl, a hint of blue hiding inside a Newfoundland iceberg, unreachable, unknowable.

I don't know where his hardness came from, certainly not from Daddy. Frank was different. He was… well, he was a man who needed to control things, and people. He would weave in and out of our lives, leaving his own particular shadow until he died. But I never really knew him. None of us did.

# *Six*

During that lovely April of 1996, Atlanta ripened with spring. By Easter weekend armies of red and yellow tulips marched in front yards all over Mavis' neighborhood. Pollen drifted down from bursting dogwood blooms, settling on the sidewalks like expensive face power, and the sound of sneezing was heard everywhere in the city. All the while, Mavis watched Jack and Niki alternately try to coexist, and then slay each other with equally sharp tongues. It was not a pretty sight.

There was the day Niki arrived home from an errand to find Jack and a young man on hands and knees studying the baseboard under one of the bookcases in the small corner room, once Dr. Book's study and now primarily Niki's reading nook. After she stood in the study doorway for a reasonable length of time, waiting in vain for one of them to acknowledge her, she asked, "What are you doing?"

Jack continued to poke around at the baseboard and didn't look up. The young man stood. Niki noticed the name, Phil, stitched across his blue uniform shirt pocket. "Cable TV, ma'am. I'll have you hooked up in no time. No more fuzzy reception from that old antenna on your roof."

"I don't want cable TV in this room," Niki announced emphatically. "This is my quiet room. This is where I read."

Now Jack looked up, wobbled to his feet favoring his bad leg, and faced her with his hands on his hips. "Where else would the cable go? You want it in the living room where the noise will echo off the tile floors and reverberate all over the house?"

"I personally don't see why cable is necessary at all. There's nothing worth watching except the PBS station, and that comes in just fine on the little TV in the kitchen."

Jack tried to compress the temper he seldom flared. He failed. "What's wrong with you, woman. There's a whole world out there beyond Cherokee Place and your all-important garden. Atlanta gets the Olympics *once, just once,* in my lifetime and you want me to huddle in the kitchen watching history being made on a fifteen-inch screen?"

Mavis watched while a compromise between the warring factions was reached. One cable outlet in the study, one in Jack's bedroom–to be used when Niki requested a quiet night of reading. Each felt they had won the argument.

On another day, Niki retrieved her laundry from the dryer and found that Jack had removed her *almost* dry clothes and piled them on top of the dryer. Apparently this had happened several hours earlier, because her wash and wear pants and shirts were hopelessly wrinkled, damp, and smelled of early stages of mildew. Her scream and subsequent tirade could be heard out on Ponce de Leon Avenue.

Jack said he was sorry. Said he didn't realize her things weren't dry, and how come they weren't dry? He'd been waiting to use the dryer for two damn hours already.

Niki re-washed her clothes and stood watch over the dryer until her things were properly done. After hanging her clothes in the closet, she left the house without saying goodbye, and drove to the mall on LaVista Road. There, she window shopped and treated herself to a Southern styled, fresh vegetable sup-per accompanied by homemade cornbread and lemon ice box pie. She felt smug knowing that Jack was probably eating two hotdogs cooked to rubber in the microwave.

Then there was the disagreement about Jack's Irish flute, a lovely little wooden instrument he'd bought in Dublin some years ago. Jack found the flute relaxing and was in the habit of playing before he went to bed. Mavis had to agree with Niki that repeating the same tune over and over each night was a bit annoying. Niki felt compelled to knock on his bedroom door and complain. "Can't you read a book or have a glass of wine to relax? 'Danny Boy' over and over again is driving me up the wall." Jack ignored her, but did give some thought to learning a different tune, as soon as he had this one down pat.

All in all, Mavis was left wondering if the Cherokee Place house wasn't too small for Jack and Niki, after all. She sat be-side Niki's chair one night, on Dr. Book's old, green velvet has-sock and tried to bridge the gap between them. Niki was lost in a Sue Grafton mystery novel, her mind somewhere on the Northern California coast where Kinsey Millhone was about to trap the killer.

*Niki dear, I know your life hasn't been all fig jam and fresh bis-cuits. But honestly, sometimes it really is a good thing to learn to be a little more flexible—make lemonade from the lemons you are given. Mind you, there are never any guarantees.*

Niki looked up from her book and scrunched her face into a frown. For a second, Mavis considered Niki's frown meant she'd at least heard her. But no, her hopes died as Jack's flute tune intruded into the study and reverberated off the plaster walls. *What in the world is he trying to play? Surely not "Danny Boy" again? I hate to say this, but some people just aren't musically inclined.*

Niki got up, closed the study door, and returned to her chair and book.

Mavis decided being the lecturing aunt was not her forte. Who was she to tell another person to be more flexible? She'd try another, more subtle approach. *Niki,*

*I want to tell you more about my daddy, and about your grandfather Frank. Just read your book and maybe some of my story will sink in. I hope so.*

*I have a clear recollection of the last time Brother Frank and Daddy spoke to each other. It was one of those still summer nights when Mama put Marie and me to bed on a pallet in the living room because it was cooler out there than in our tiny back bedroom. Marie slept soundly, but I was awakened by Mama's presence in the room. At first I thought she came to check on us. Then I heard my daddy's voice drifting through the screen door from the front porch, and realized she was there in the dark to listen.*

"Frank," Daddy said, "I give this a lot of thought." Mama took a step closer to the screen door but stayed hidden in shadow. "I know some boys from up home always made corn liquor. Sure enough, you can haul a load of liquor for a lot more money than a load of corn. And I hear the talk at the mill. What with the whole country going dry, liquor is a bigger business than it ever was. They say there's plenty from up in Rabun County, and over into North Carolina, that's stilling a lot of whiskey to sell here in Atlanta.

"Course you know you'll do a year and a day at the federal prison here in Atlanta if the revenue boys get you. But, son, even if you don't get caught, selling shine ain't no way for a man to make a living. A man needs to make his living by work that amounts to something, not by running county roads in the middle of the night carrying shine."

Daddy knocked his pipe against the porch rail to spill spent tobacco into the yard. Time passed in silence and then Daddy's stout wooden match scratched against wood. Blue flame quickly fired into the darkness of the porch, then died. The sweet smell of fresh pipe tobacco meandered from the porch to my pallet on the floor. Frank said nothing. Daddy spoke. "Well son, what I'm telling you is you need to get an honest job. Stop toting shine for whoever is paying you to run that Ford sitting out there in the yard. What do you say?"

Mama was stone still in the darkness of the room. I couldn't hear her breathe or see her face, though I sensed her body tensing when she folded her arms tightly across her chest and leaned her head against the screened door, listening for Frank's response.

Another match fired blue. More silence. Then Frank answered flatly, making no effort to convince or excuse, "The money is damn-good, Daddy. Another month and I'll own me a Ford. Three more and I'll have boys driving for me."

More silence. Daddy knocked his pipe against the porch again. He was through smoking. "Well, all right, Frank," he said. "That being the case, I reckon you need to drive that Ford on off somewhere else then. It ain't in me to be proud to have a bootlegger for a son."

No more conversation drifted into the living room. The next sound was Frank's Ford engine cranking over and then the laboring thump of tires navigating potholes on Moody Street. Mama stood silently in the darkness of the living room for some time, and then she turned and went back to her bedroom. The last sound I remember before I surrendered to sleep was Daddy's fiddle. I don't know the tune he played that night, alone in the darkness of the porch, but I do remember it was slow and sad.

We didn't see Frank again until the funeral, July 12, 1924. Daddy had been building a brick chimney for a grand new house out in Druid Hills when the scaffold gave way and he fell three stories to the ground. Mama nursed him as best she could at Moody Street and the doctor came every few days. But Daddy didn't get better. Remembering those weeks now, as he lay in the bed swaying in and out of our world, I suppose he had suffered some sort of brain damage from the fall, and the doctor, as well as Mama, knew he wouldn't recover. But, as a child, I was only aware that Daddy was very sick, did not recognize me, and that my own pain was nearly unbearable.

When Daddy died, Mama, following the custom of mountain folk, covered all the mirrors in our house with black cloth and arranged his body in the living room so friends and relatives could say goodbye and mourn his passing. Daddy was so tall he had to be laid out on long boards stretched across both of Mama's parlor tables rather than on our dining table. I remember Mama fretting about what the neighbors would think to have Daddy laid out across common boards, then she quickly got to the business of making do and draped a clean white spread over the boards. I wondered at the time if the spread was the same one we sat on for picnics at Grant Park.

All around Daddy's black-suited body Mama tucked small nosegays of wild flowers from the neighborhood–meadow rue, yarrows, daises, and Queen Anne's lace–making it look as though the flowers had grown beneath him as he slept. In the bend of Daddy's left arm, Mama rested his beloved fiddle and its well-used bow. Then she drew the green window shades against the summer heat so no one would see how sad he looked in death and stationed herself in a straight-backed kitchen chair at his head. I did not see Mama shed a single tear in front of the company that passed through our house that day and night. She would mourn her loss later in private. On that day and night she sat silently, one hand in her lap and the other clutching the loose sleeve of Daddy's suit coat, as though by refusing to release this small piece of fabric she could refuse his leaving our world.

I was not like Mama. When Daddy died, I cried shamelessly in front of relatives and alone. Never have I felt such loss as I did that morning standing in the filtered light of the living room and knowing my daddy was dead. I watched his still face for a long time looking for the life that was my daddy. Then when my child's mind had to be satisfied, I went to him and touched the cold skin of his cheek. Then I knew my daddy was gone forever. No more songs, no more hugs, no more anything. I remember standing beside him for a time with my hand on his face, and then feeling a cold stillness inside my chest. I wondered if this cold was what Daddy felt, being dead. Then the crying stopped as suddenly as it had begun, and I left the room to help Mama with what had to be done.

By mid afternoon a thunderstorm was building in the southern sky. Four men Daddy worked with at the mill and his two younger brothers from Tennessee lifted him into a rough pine casket. One of the brothers nailed the casket top down and the men hoisted Daddy into the back of someone's pickup truck. Soon our little band of mourners was crowded into cars and wagons to follow the truck that carried Daddy.

We all gathered around the open grave while the men lowered Daddy into its darkness. A preacher prayed, read from the Bible, and made some kind of short sermon to the family. I have no recollection of what he said. I do remember vividly the redolent smell of fresh-turned earth and the feel of the rain as it fell, first in wisps of moisture more like dew than drops, then in sideways sheets stinging our faces and threatening to fill Daddy's grave with summer water. I remember close-rolling thunder, and jagged lightning breaking across the sky, and I remember Brother Frank. He arrived late, like an actor with perfect timing, emerged from a black Ford sedan wearing an elegant white linen suit, white felt hat, and white and brown wing-tipped shoes. With a single flick of his wrist, he opened his black silk umbrella. Then without so much as a look at Daddy's coffin, he marched over to Mama like a man with deadlines and commitments to keep.

I saw him hug Mama and watched his mouth move, but the noise of the rain muffled his words. She returned his hug but said nothing. Frank took a white handkerchief from his coat pocket and wiped the rain from Mama's face. Afterwards, he swiftly wrapped a roll of bills into the wet handkerchief and stuffed it into Mama's dress pocket. I am sure she was too occupied with her grief to feel the money in her pocket. Then, as quickly as he arrived, Frank was gone without so much as a word to Marie or me, and without even a glance at the open grave of our daddy.

Two days after Daddy's funeral, Tennessee relatives and Atlanta neighbors left our house to pick up the patterns of their own lives. I stood half-hidden by the doorframe and watched Mama as she sat at the kitchen table piled high with fried chicken, biscuits, green beans, sweet potato pie, and yellow cakes with boiled icing; food brought to us by considerate neighbors we either knew well, or only in passing. A tired summer breeze from the window over the sink was little enough to stir the oppressive heat in the room. Sweat collected on Mama's upper lip and moistened the thin light hairs at her temples.

She drummed the fingers of her right hand on the green checked oilcloth covering the wood table. In front of her, several short stacks of coins and a few loose bills were lined up in a row. A red and black Luzianne coffee can, always the depository for Mama's cash, sat beside the coins. In her left hand she slowly turned a roll of bills bound by a rubber band–probably the money from Frank's handkerchief hidden in her pocket at the funeral.

She seemed to be deciding where the roll of bills belonged. Whether she sensed me behind her or quickly made the decision on her own, I don't know, but she gathered up the coins with the loose bills and dropped them into the can. After that, Mama added Frank's money, and then the can was hidden on top of the sideboard behind the wide trim skirting its edge. In another four days Mama was working nights on a machine in the carding room at the Fulton Cotton Mill, where from six until six her small hands made endless passes, back and forth, back and forth, to comb and separate fibers. After work she walked home by the rising sun, and sat on the swaybacked pine steps of the porch on Moody Street to brush out her thick brown hair and send cotton lint out into the morning like dandelion heads setting sail.

Mavis was exhausted by the grief contained in her memories. When she felt herself slipping away she looked to Niki, now sitting with her eyes closed and her book on her lap. *Did she hear me? Can she hear me?* Then wanting so much to feel the warmth of another human, Mavis reached over and covered one of Niki's hands with her own. *Niki dear, do you understand now about Mama and Daddy? About how hard life was when I was a child? So much sadness.*

As soon as they touched, Niki's eyes opened with a start. She looked around, saw only the worn comfortable room and yawned, deciding she'd drifted off into a dream of Aunt Mavis' hand on hers. Presently, Niki closed her eyes again.

Mavis had no power to stop her leaving. The pull of slipping away was like being caught in an eddy, down and down, at the mercy of watery currents. Momentarily she was stretching lazily under the warm blue waters, lulled by a distant whale's siren. Above her, hundreds of pumpkin-sized, illuminated glass orbs rocked atop a calm sea, watching, welcoming. *Hello, hello again*, she murmured, and followed her words rising in tiny bubbles to the surface. Then, Mavis slept.

# *Seven*

It was late at night when she woke and found she was standing in her own bedroom, looking down at the sleeping Niki. She did not know how long she'd been away. She could not know that Jack had found several excuses to be gone from the house most of that day—had to get the oil changed in his car, needed to check on some camera equipment he'd ordered from Wolfe's Camera, wanted to get a haircut, and on and on—his manufactured errands were numerous.

In fact, Jack had spent the last five days flitting around Atlanta telling himself he was getting reacquainted with his hometown and familiar with his gently used BMW—bought sight unseen over the telephone from London from the dealership in Buckhead. He was glad he'd coughed up the cash for the steel gray beauty and felt the investment of a substantial automobile meant his retirement would stick, and he'd be happy and content being back in Atlanta.

Niki knew he was avoiding her, and that was fine. She had the garden to think about and suspected that Jack would be on the first plane out of town when the opportunity presented itself. And, considering the daily news, she was sure there would be opportunities for a seasoned photojournalist like Jack who could stomach wars, wars, and more wars.

Niki also had her own professional work to do. For the past two days she'd worked on an instruction booklet for a new Melita coffeemaker. On this particular day, when she needed a break from the work, she'd enjoyed a brief afternoon nap and gone for a walk around the neighborhood, meeting a Mr. Terry Spiegel—rhymes with legal he'd said—who was walking his white Highland terrier. They talked about dog breeds, the new Kroger market on Briarcliff, and that he was a friend of Aunt Mavis' for many years. His first name was Alistair and insisted Niki call him Terry. Nice older gentleman.

When Jack hadn't returned by seven, Niki made cheese eggs, washed the dishes, and went to bed with her book, *H Is For Homicide*, staring Kinsey Millhone. She wondered if Sue Grafton could indeed write an entire series of murder mysteries titled from each letter of the alphabet. Just before she fell asleep, Niki also wondered what would it be like to create stories about strong women and wrongs being righted against a backdrop of balmy California nights. Probably more fun than coffeemaker manuals, she decided.

For Mavis the past few days were but a breath taken between the lines of a song. Time turned on itself, her memory of the days only a sense of rocking peacefully in the arms of sleep. Now, standing in the dark coolness of her bedroom, she said goodnight to her restless canary and covered his cage. *Niki dear*, Mavis whispered to the sleeping woman, *you must remember to cover Abelard at night. He gets anxious if you don't*. Niki turned in her sleep and answered, "Okay."

Mavis whispered again. *Niki, there is more to the story I was telling you the other night. During those first couple of years after Daddy died, Marie and I were busy being self-absorbed schoolgirls. Mama was working herself into an early grave and we were so selfish we didn't even notice. After all, everyone we knew worked in the mill.*

Mavis listened for a few seconds to Niki's even breathing and then sighed with a soft whimper. It was useless to try and talk to the girl if she insisted on sleeping. She tiptoed around Niki's bed and quietly opened one of the French doors out to the back patio. If her niece wouldn't listen, she'd just tell it to the night birds. Mavis eased the door closed and reclined on a newly painted wrought iron chaise Niki had recently bought at a yard sale and refurbished. But in two seconds Mavis was standing again, worried that the fresh paint would rub off on her silk dress. She removed her leather pumps and walked barefoot out to the bench under the dogwood tree.

A large, mottled brown rabbit, who was accustomed to dining alone on Niki's spinach, considered hopping away when she saw Mavis' feet tramping through the damp grass then changed her mind, held her own, and did not move from the vegetable plant she munched. After all, she had babies to feed and spinach doesn't last forever. Mavis waggled a reproachful finger at the rabbit, but did not speak to her.

Once comfortable on the bench, and her shoes replaced, Mavis took in the beauty of the cool night and began her story again. And Marie and I didn't care what Frank did for a living or who drank illegal liquor. Whiskey was whiskey to us, and it seemed everyone we knew, except Mama, liked to take a drink. We were more concerned about whether rinsing our hair in lemon juice would bring out the red highlights and about the cost of a new pair of shoes.

The worst tragedy we endured during those mid-teenage years was the death of Rudolph Valentino in 1926, a full year before our innocence left us. It was in late August I believe, and it seems poor Valentino died of a perforated ulcer. I wonder if his death was related to all the bootleg whiskey Hollywood consumed? When Valentino died, Marie walked around the house for three days wearing Mama's black funeral hat and veil–in mourning for the "Son of a Sheik" who had aroused her and about a million other girls to romantic fantasy with his films. My personal favorite was Blood and Sand. Ah, the lure of the desert night. God help us. We thought real life would be a remake of a Valentino movie. It seems to me now that Marie and I, as ne'er-do-well mill girls, were remarkably naive for a short time after Daddy died. We didn't realize Mama worked terribly hard at the mill to preserve our childhood. And to his credit, Brother Frank sweetened our lives with occasional help.

In retrospect, our lives were soft in comparison to many other families we knew back then. We didn't go to bed hungry and Mama managed to keep the house on Moody Street. Things went along fine for us, or so we thought, until the change. Life always does that–change that is. Usually change is as gradual as the shifting tide. You must watch closely and mark a line of foam along the beach to reckon its intention. Who has time for that? The water moves on and so do we.

Mavis yawned, leaned back against the bark of the dogwood tree, and closed her eyes. She wanted to tell Niki the story, but since Niki slept snuggled in her bed Mavis was left alone to replay the events in her mind, like black and white pictures jerking in slow motion on an old time movie reel.

Yes, there we are. Mama was working in the cotton mill. Marie and I were teenagers. It was 1926. Women had been able to vote for six years by then, a nineteen-year-old named Gertrude Ederle became the first woman to swim the English channel, and sound had come to motion pictures when Al Jolson spoke in The Jazz Singer.

We thought we were so grown-up prissy-potting around in our midi-blouses and pleated skirts. We were so determined to be real twenties girls that we went to Rich's and had our hair bobbed on the sides and shingled up the back, just like Alice Terry in The Four Horseman. We chewed Juicy Fruit gum until our jaws ached, and on Saturdays Mama, Marie, and I would ride the electric trolley downtown and window shop at Rich's or Butler Shoes where I daydreamed of boxes and boxes of slim heeled pumps. We even shaved our legs.

Our biggest treat was a stop at Nunnally's Candy and Ice Cream Shop at Peachtree and Broad Streets, where we got ambrosia egg flips for twenty cents, probably bought with some of Frank's money. In fact, Brother Frank met us at Nunnally's on occasion. His favorite was the sherry wine flavored ice cream topped with toasted coconut and served in a tall frosted glass. Mine was the caramel pecan.

It was at Nunnally's that we learned Frank had a wife and baby. We were sitting in Nunnally's one Saturday, Mama all starched and prim with her Sunday purse clutched in her lap, and Marie chattering to Frank about seeing Douglas Fairbanks in *The Three Musketeers*. He eased a picture out of his coat pocket, as casual as can be, and rested it on the marble-top table. Peering up at us was a fat, smiling, little baby dressed in a white gown. He waved a toy horse at the camera. Mama leaned over the table to get a good look at the picture. No one said anything at first, and then Mama picked the photograph up for a closer look. Marie apparently could not stand the tension in the air and blurted out, "That baby looks just like Fatty Arbuckle, doesn't he Mavis?"

Needless to say, Marie was obsessed with the moving picture shows. I kept my mouth shut. Mama shot Marie a look that could have boiled grits and Marie hung her head. Mama then turned to Frank, giving him a somewhat softer but obviously hurt look. "No, Marie, I'd say he has Theron's eyes,"

Mama said. Frank managed a thin smile and told us the baby was Frank Junior. "Does he have a mother?" inquired Mama.

"Her name is Sophie," Frank volunteered. "She's the nervous type, doesn't get out much. I'll bring the boy into town sometime to meet you, Mama, if you want. He's almost three now so he's some bigger than this baby picture."

Mama's eyes clouded over and I thought she was going to cry. But of course she would never do that in public. She sniffed and got a hanky from her purse. I wanted to ask why he would keep his son a secret from Mama for three years, but I said nothing for fear Mama would cry in earnest. "We'd like that, son," she said, "we'd like that very much, wouldn't we girls?" Frank gave Mama the photograph to keep. And he did bring Frank Junior to meet us in town on occasion.

Frank Junior was a handsome child, fair skinned, freckle-faced, strawberry colored hair. A serious child though; even then he always seemed to be watching Brother Frank to gauge his daddy's reaction to everything. Once Frank treated us to lunch at Harry's Restaurant over on Luckie Street where all the waiters seem to know him. Brother Frank was a generous tipper, usually leaving more money for the waiter than Mama made in a week. We were not invited to Brother Frank's home and never met the mysterious Sophie. Though Frank did finally offer that she'd left him and Frank Junior. Went home to her people in Florida, he said.

As I remember, once he left home and Daddy died, Frank didn't come to the house on Moody Street until that December 24th when Mama married Henry York. It had been terribly cold in Atlanta. The ice that had crippled the city had finally begun to melt, liberating oak, poplar, and pine arms of their frozen shackles. Sun and rising temperatures changed icy roads to muddy slush. Children, held prisoners for days in either too hot or too cold houses depending on the economic conditions of their parents, descended on the city streets and lawns, playing rough and wild like chained up dogs finally set free.

"Mavis," Marie called to me in the kitchen, "Come out here and look at these kids. They're gonna kill each other."

I stuck my head around the corner. Marie was watching a group of children through the sweating living room windows as they attacked each other in a game of stickball. She peeled a thin shard of ice about the size of her thumb from the corner of the glass and watched it melt between her fingers. "Marie, I can't come and see anything right now. In case you forgot, we are having a wedding here in about three hours."

Marie turned on her heels and joined me in the kitchen. "How could I forget Mama's stupid wedding. I swear I'm about as embarrassed as I can be. I bet everybody at school is laughing at us. Mama is too old to get married again. Bootsy Turpin at school says Mr. York's a whole lot younger than Mama, and besides, this house is too small for another person to be living here. What good is the new indoor bathroom if we'll never get to use it because some strange man is in there sitting on the pot, or shaving, or something?"

"Marie," I pleaded, "please don't start that again. Mama is not too old, and you have no idea how old Mr. York is. Mama is lonely. She deserves to be happy, doesn't she? The four of us lived in this house when Daddy was alive, so what is the difference?"

"Well, that's just the point. The difference is that Mr. York is not Daddy, and I don't want some strange man in our new bathroom." Marie flipped her brown curls away from her face and perched atop the kitchen stool, arms crossed tightly in front and jaw set like a bulldog. "You just wait. When I get out of beauty school, I'm going to get my own place. I'll have my own bathroom."

"That's real good, Marie," I said. "You do that, okay. But right now how about getting some clothes on cause your tits are hanging out of that bathrobe in front, and I need some help in here with making sandwiches."

Marie stood up and tightened her robe. "You better be quiet, Miss Perfect, or I'll tell Mama you said tits. Besides you are just jealous cause I've got big ones and yours look like little bitty fried eggs." Marie headed for the bedroom. Mama met her in the hall. "Hi, Sweetie," she said to Marie, "I can't wait to see you in your new dress."

"Mavis said tits," Marie mumbled under her breath.

Mama joined me in the kitchen and leaned over the sink to pull back the curtains. "I hope Mr. York gets here. You can't have a wedding without the groom. I suspect only God and a crackerjack engineer could get a Southern Railway train back in one piece from Birmingham on a day like today, what with all the ice and everything."

"Don't worry, Mama, it's melting. He'll be here. Why don't you go and lie down for a little while? You look pale."

"I believe I will, Honey. The smell of those boiled eggs is making me a little woozy."

I remember thinking: Mr. Henry York, employee of the great Southern Railroad, and a foot shorter than Daddy, who never says any more than good day. And Mama, who is sick to her stomach from smelling eggs on her wedding day…uh-huh…for a quiet man Mr. York sure does work fast.

Because it was the day before Christmas, and because of the weather, none of Mama's family from Tennessee came down for the wedding. Marie and I were decked out in our new lavender chiffon drop-waist dresses. In the wedding pictures I'm the tall scarecrow on the left, Marie is the cute one on the right who looks like a shapely tap dancer from down at the Roxy Theater. Mama is one standing between us with the single red rose and baby's breath bouquet who is looking at the camera as though smiling and the wedding are both a heavy burden. Mr. York isn't even in the wedding picture. I think he insisted on being the photographer, or was it that Frank had shown up by then and Mr. York had ceased to think of himself as a bridegroom? I'm not sure. But oh well, at least our dresses were beautiful.

Mama's friend, Peggy Turpin, from the mill, mother of the infamous Bootsy, came to the wedding. She brought a three-layered lemon cake. Peggy, not Bootsy. The only thing Bootsy brought was her big mouth to blabber all over town what happened after the ceremony. I was really angry at the time. But that's okay because years later, after Bootsy became Mrs. Randy Holiday, her husband spent a lot of time at Baker Street talking a great deal more trash about Bootsy than she ever did about us Banks women.

Mr. and Mrs. Fellers from the Holiness Church, where Mama dragged us every Sunday, were also there. I guess they were friends of Mama's. The only other person who came was our neighbor to the left, the old widow Pease, who was deaf as a post and said about a thousand times, "Thank you so much for asking me, it was a lovely wedding," even after Frank rolled in and ruined the day.

I don't recall exactly what happened. I just have this mental picture of the preacher saying: I now pronounce you man and wife, and Mama feeling faint and sitting down on the sofa. I went to the kitchen to get her a glass of water and Peggy Turpin fanned her with a magazine. Mr. York was standing beside Mama looking useless. Marie was doing I don't know what, probably sneaking a taste of the cake icing; she had a terrible sweet tooth.

As I came through the swinging door from the kitchen, I saw that Frank was in the living room. He grabbed Mr. York's coat lapels and backed him past me into the kitchen. I heard Brother Frank say, "The weather kept me from getting here before you said I do. But I do, or no I do, I'm telling you to take a long trip on your railroad. Otherwise, you can take a short ride with some of my boys. I don't much care which one you do."

Mama recovered and stepped around me in the doorway on her way to separate Frank from her new husband. By now, everyone in the living room was looking our way. I guess Mr. York felt he had to do something to show Mama he wasn't to be bullied, so he took a swing at Brother. Missed him of course. Frank stepped aside. Mr. York lost his footing and fell against the door casing into the living room. That is probably how he got the black eye. I don't think Frank actually punched him. Mama went into the new bathroom to throw up. Frank did not stay for lemon cake and punch.

Later when we were clearing up the party, I asked Mama why Frank was against her marrying Mr. York. She told me that she didn't know for sure, but suspected that it had something to do with him missing Daddy, and feeling guilty about leaving home the way he did and not ever being able to tell Daddy he was sorry. I told her I thought hell would freeze over before Frank said he was sorry to anybody. Then I think I complained I was sick and tired of everyone being scared of Frank. That's when Mama said, "I just don't know what I done wrong by that boy. I raised him like my own. Loved him the same." Poor Mama. She sounded so sad.

That's when I found out that my Mama was not Brother Frank's mama. She told me that Daddy's first wife—Frank's mama—died when Frank was two years old and she had married

Theron Banks, son and all. She never spoke about Frank's mama again, and I think Jack is the only person I've ever told about Brother Frank—except Ellis of course. He and I shared everything. I don't know why I never told Marie that Frank was our half-brother, maybe because Mama tried so hard with Frank I felt she wouldn't want to separate him out from the family by saying he had a different mother. I don't know. Of course, Frank was an expert in separating himself out from the family, so I need not have worried.

Less than two weeks after the wedding, Mr. York left—took a transfer to the Memphis-Little Rock run, or so he wrote in a short note left on the kitchen table one morning. And Mama? Well, Mama stayed sick for a while because she was pregnant. Bootsy gossiped so much at school about Mr. York leaving Mama that Marie punched her out cold in the girl's bathroom and then refused to go back to classes—not that the school would let her back in after that. Instead, Marie announced, she would graduate herself early and go on to beauty school. Mama went back to work at the mill for a few months until her baby was due. We didn't hear from Mr. York again.

So, Brother Frank got his way. There was no other man to take Daddy's place at Moody Street. It was always hard to keep Frank from having his way. One way or another, he usually won.

# Eight

Jack spent part of yesterday checking out rental houses in the area, thinking he could show Niki some charming little bungalow, maybe in Decatur or Druid Hills, and offer to pay her more than her half of what the Cherokee house would rent for to sweeten the pot. She'd fall in love with the house because it would have ample room for a garden and dog. He'd volunteer to help her move and all would be well. He'd have Cherokee Place to himself. Jack smiled. Great plan. However, with the Summer Olympics coming to Atlanta in August, rental properties were already getting booked–at exorbitant prices–and the pickings were slim. After a half-day of searching, he found one house located near Agnes Scott College that might work, so now the idea was to drive Niki by the property and hope its charm would do the rest.

Thus, Jack suggested they go by the cemetery after he took her for a lunch treat to an interesting little restaurant called Doc Cheys, just a few miles from Cherokee Place. She'd cooked for him many times since he'd been back, he told her. Time he treated her. He did not mention the restaurant was very near the cute little Arts and Crafts bungalow he saw as a carrot to dangle in front of his unwelcome housemate.

"Why go out for lunch?" Niki wanted to know. "People usually go out for dinner." Niki suspected he was being nice to her because he was up to something, but in the end she changed her clothes and they drove the few miles to the trendy Asian restaurant located on the first floor of a renovated office building on Memorial Drive.

They both ordered a Thai soup made with chicken and coconut milk and a side of noodles, then sat at one of the booths away from the sun-filled storefront windows facing the street. Jack racked his brain for a clever entrée into why another house would be better for Niki than the one on Cherokee Place. In the end all he could think to say was, "I wonder how much it would cost to pull up the carpet and refinish the wood floors? Seems like a lot of expense just to own a dog."

"Not to me," was her short answer.

They ate in silence until Jack asked, "So why did you think getting married again was a good idea?"

"What? Don't you think that's kind of a personal question?"

"Oh yeah, I guess you're right. I was just wondering."

Niki looked across the table at Jack. This guy, she was thinking, hasn't a clue how to carry on a conversation with a woman. She rested her spoon on the plate under her soup bowl and thought for a few seconds. "Not that it's any of your business, but I think I mentioned before that I hadn't laughed in a long time. He made me laugh. Silly me."

Even though Jack had asked her the question, Niki noticed a faraway look on his face. Was he tuning her out, or reaching way out there to the edge of his experiences to try and understand her comment? She couldn't decide what he was thinking, so she rattled his cage to get his attention. "What about you? Haven't you ever even thought about getting married?"

Jack munched on a cluster of rice noodles then wiped his hands with his napkin before he answered. "Well you know how it is. I've been traveling for a long time. Work was…well, probably more important to me than a relationship."

"So you never thought about marriage?"

He squirmed under the weight of Niki's question. She waited. He finally answered. "Yeah, I guess I've thought about it, once or twice. But seems like by the time I got back around from wherever I was working for the magazine, the lady in question had moved on. Just as well. I'm more content with myself than anyone else."

Niki thought of all the petty arguments they'd had over issues like the washer and dryer, and the cable TV, and laughed. "I know what you mean."

Jack searched around for a change of subject, wondering how they had gotten on the subject of marriage in the first place. "You know, now that I'm retired. I'm thinking of doing commercial photography, maybe for businesses. You ever think of changing gears and writing something other than technical stuff?"

Niki sipped more of her soup before volunteering, "Sure. I've tried writing fiction, but rejection slips from agents were all I got. Guess I'm a fact and not fiction kind of person. Rejection slips in the mail can sting the ego, big time."

He nodded as though he understood. Niki couldn't imagine Jack ever being rejected at anything. "I'm going for more tea. You want a refill?"

Niki shook her head no, and watched him saunter in the direction of the beverage station at the front of the restaurant. His slow walk gave her mind time to wander.

Jackson Ellis Rainwater. Mavis always said he was the best photojournalist in the business. She was proud of him. Hmm. The looks don't hurt. Reminds me of the Paul Simon song, except instead of crazy, the line is still handsome after all these years.

The memory of her adolescent crush, extinguished after she accepted the bottomless chasm between her fourteen years and Jack's nineteen years, smarted in her chest. She chalked up the feeling to indigestion; rubbed the tender spot, and continued to watch Jack.

He must take his blue jeans to the cleaners to get them knife pressed like that. He's favoring his right leg again. He was doing that last night. Pain? Hmm. Wonder if the leg has anything to do with his early retirement. I bet he paid forty dollars to a fancy Buckhead salon to layer his thick black hair away from his face like that. The new style is a ton better than the shaggy-dog look he used to wear though–even if it costs more than I spend on haircuts in six months. I wonder if leaving the back longer at the collar is a London fashion. He's so tan. Outside a lot, I guess. Or used to be. God, look at my pale arms. Working in the garden just makes more freckles. No tan. I need a trip to the beach and a new hairstyle. Maybe when the garden is finished…

I have to admit we've talked more in the last thirty minutes than we ever have, at least about personal stuff. Aside from phone calls about Mavis' house, I don't think we've had ten conversations over the years, four if you don't count the awkward attempts when we were teenagers. Who is that man Jack's talking to? He looks familiar. Jack certainly doesn't look pleased to see him. Jeez, what is that all about? The man put his hand on Jack's shoulder and Jack jerked away like he wanted to slug him.

As Jack walked back to the table, their eyes met for a second before he looked past her into the distance. She sensed he would hold the same disinterested stare if he were leaving the scene of a car bombing in Beirut, or a war in Africa. When he slid into the booth he slammed his glass down with a clunk and sloshed tea onto the table. Niki handed him several paper napkins to mop it up. He took them, saying nothing, and she felt the need to say something soothing. But what? She knew he was angry, but hadn't a clue why. She finally commented that the lunch was delicious and thanked him for bringing her.

When she spoke, Jack looked at her as though he'd just noticed she was sitting across the table from him. After a long pause, he asked tightly, "You ready to go?"

Once they were in the car, Niki reached around to the back seat to gather the red azalea blooms she'd wrapped in wet paper towels after Jack cut them from the front bushes at Cherokee Place. "Don't forget we're going to the cemetery."

"I've not forgotten. It was my idea, remember?"

"Well, I know that. You don't have to be so short with me. I'm sorry that man upset you, but it isn't my fault."

"I don't know what you're talking about. What man?"

"Oh God, Jack. Don't be obtuse. The man who tried to talk to you in Doc Cheys. Who was he, anyway?"

"Nobody."

"Didn't look like nobody. He was dressed like some yuppie salesman trying to look casual. I mean really, who wears a black linen sport coat, jeans, and Gucci loafers–without socks–on a Saturday? He looked familiar."

No response. Jack turned left across the intersection and then right at the next block into the entrance to Oakland Cemetery. He pulled the car into the tree-lined avenue and stopped against a long expanse of granite curbing. They got out, Niki carrying the flowers, and walked the short distance to Mavis' grave. Jack removed the vase from its brass holder beside the gravestone and walked off to the nearest water spigot to fill it with fresh water for the azaleas. Once the flowers were in place, Niki searched around on the ground for a small pebble and placed it on top of the gravestone.

Jack looked as though he was having one of those ah-ha moments. She was relieved that his anger had disappeared. "What's the purpose of leaving a stone?" he asked her. "I've seen people all over the world do that, but never known why."

Remembering only that she'd learned the gesture as a child when she held her mother's hand and stood beside the graves of her mother's parents, Niki had to think about the why of leaving a stone. She couldn't recall if she had ever asked her mother. The gesture just seemed right. "I guess the stone is a symbol that someone visited and mourns her passing. I still think of Aunt Mavis. It was hard when Mama died. I was twenty years old, angry, and alone. Mavis was kind to me, and accepting."

Jack found his sunglasses in his jacket pocket and shaded his eyes. He wished he'd taken a couple of ibuprofen for the pain in his leg at the restaurant. "She was usually like that. Accepting, I mean. And kind. Unless you crossed her, that is." Jack smiled. "Then you had better sleep with one eye open."

Niki read the inscription on the stone aloud, "I will lay you beneath a sigh of newborn grass with water tumbling lazy at your feet. Sunshine to kiss your closed eyes, and rosemary to whisper goodbye." She looked to Jack, trying to see what emotion hid behind the dark glasses. "Where did you find that poem?"

He reached down and righted one of the azaleas that had fallen to the side of the vase before he replied. "It was marked with a blue satin ribbon in a volume of poems on her desk. The book probably belonged to Dr. Book. Mavis wasn't the sentimental type. I thought he would have wanted the inscription on her stone."

"It's a lovely thought." Niki paused while an emergency vehicle whooped its way along Memorial Drive and receded into the distance, then looked across the forty-plus acres of oaks, magnolias, elaborately carved stone memorials, and well-tended gravesites. "I read somewhere that all the burial plots in Oakland Cemetery were sold by the late 1880s. Only the rich and famous get to rest here for eternity. How is it that Mavis and Dr. Book are buried alongside the likes of Margaret Mitchell and Bobby Jones?"

Jack nodded, acknowledging her question. "I think the Banks' family plot was purchased from the Fulton Bag and Cotton Mill when Mavis' daddy died in the early 1920s. The way I understand it, the cotton mill bought a section of the cemetery and then sold plots to employees. You probably know that Mavis, her mother, and her dad, all worked at the mill at some point. The old Fulton Cotton Mill building is near here." Jack motioned to the low, oak lined hill to his left. "Over there. Not far. Except the mill building was converted to condos, I think.

"Much later, when Mavis married Martin Book, I suspect they bought burial plots for themselves from descendants of owners who'd decided they didn't care about being buried at Oakland. Knowing Mavis, being buried in the posh part of Oakland may have been a thumb-your-nose-at-Atlanta-society kind of thing. As you remember, Aunt Mavis could have a wicked sense of humor."

Niki nodded and looked down again at the inscription on Mavis' stone. She conjured Dr. Martin Book in her mind. Wild, silver gray hair, freshly pressed seersucker suit, navy blue tie, reading glasses hanging from a gold chain around his neck. "Mavis, my dear," would be his usual preface to any conversation. Yes, Dr. Book would have indulged Mavis' whim to be buried among the Atlanta elite. From what Niki remembered, he would have indulged any of Aunt Mavis' whims.

Jack chatted on. "When the Banks family came down here from Tennessee, they lived in a house on Moody Street–just across the railroad tracks from the cotton mill and about five blocks from Oakland Cemetery. Moody Street was where Mavis met my dad. Later, she and Dad bought a house together nearer downtown, on Baker Street, as an investment. Course, the Baker Street house is gone now. New hotel, wider interstate…"

Moody Street, near the railroad tracks, the Fulton Cotton Mill? All of that was a Mavis Niki didn't know; one she could not conjure. "I can't imagine Aunt Mavis ever being a mill girl."

Jack shrugged. "It was rock hard times in the South, *Miss Scarlet*. Being poor was the norm. Mavis told me more than once that a mill job was just about the only job."

"Hmm. We are fortunate." Niki's mind skipped to a question. So long as Jack was making light conversation she thought she'd ask it. "Jack, can you help me get something straight? I had a weird dream last night and woke up going through a mental family tree in my mind. Mavis was your aunt and my aunt, but I'm confused about how it all plays out. Were you and my father first cousins?"

Jack turned away from the grave and walked a short distance to a poplar tree where he leaned against the trunk. Niki followed. He raised his glasses on top of his head. "It's confusing. Here's the way I understand it: your grandfather Frank was Mavis and Marie's half-brother. Frank, Marie and Mavis had the same father, Theron Banks, but not the same mother."

Niki concentrated on what Jack was saying. He continued. "And my mother–who was a lot younger than Mavis–had a different father because Grandmother Banks, Marie and Mavis' mom, married again after Theron Banks died. I think the second husband was a fellow named Henry York, who worked for the railroad. So York was my mother's daddy, *my* grandfather on my mother's side. Your great-grandfather was Theron Banks. I'm not really blood related to him. And oh yes, I almost forgot, Henry York stayed around only about fifteen minutes after the marriage. Mavis made the comment more than once that her Brother Frank ran him off. I can't say why, or even if that's true."

Niki held up a hand. "Wait. Can you go over that again? You lost me."

Jack gave her an indulgent smile, took a breath, and slowly repeated his account of the family relationships, omitting the part about Frank running off Henry York. Once her face registered understanding, he went on. "When Grandmother Banks died, Mavis raised my mother, or did the best she could. I think Mavis and Marie were about sixteen when my mother was born and Grandmother Banks died. Mavis and Marie were twins you know. Their brother Frank, your grandfather, was probably in his mid-twenties when my mother was born."

"Wow, you are right. It is very confusing. So, let me get this straight—my Grandfather Frank's mother was not Grandmother Banks. She was his stepmother, and she raised him after she married Theron Banks, Frank's dad. So Grandfather Frank wasn't related to your mother, at all. Their relationship was all through marriage. Your mother's name was Fern Banks though. Right?"

"Yes, that's right. Technically, I guess she was Fern York, but she went by Fern Banks. I don't know how the name thing worked, since she wasn't actually a Banks. The one thing I know for sure is that I'm a Rainwater, not a Banks. No doubt about that."

Niki noticed the name, Fern, had sounded stiff coming out of Jack's mouth. Rainwater was softer, like the rain itself.

"When I was growing up, Mavis referred to your grandfather as my Uncle Frank, and for years I thought your daddy was a cousin, but I suppose that's not technically true. I remember your grandfather at the Baker Street house when I was little. Sometimes your dad was with him. Seems they were always in the front parlor playing poker. After my mother died, and Mavis sold the Baker Street house, I rarely saw them. I was busy trying to survive boarding school in New Hampshire. I know both of them were killed in an car accident, but wasn't that later, after your mom divorced Frank Jr.?"

The accident was only the last chapter of the story. Yes, Niki's mother had divorced Frank Jr. and taken her only daughter north of Atlanta to the small town of Roswell. In Niki's heart though, where all things are clear, her father was the daddy who left–the man who didn't care enough about his daughter to stay sober. "Yes," Niki answered, "They died five or six years after the divorce. My father was driving, drunk as usual."

Jack frowned. "Ah, sorry. I don't recall ever being told who was driving. Your dad and grandfather were buried beside Marie and Fern in the Banks' family plot, next to Theron and Grandmother Banks. It's only a short walk from here. Do you want to go over there?" The way Niki tightened her lips and looked away answered his question. "Me either."

Niki changed the subject. "Wonder why Mavis didn't want to be buried in the Banks' family plot?"

Jack had never really questioned Mavis' decision of where she wanted to be buried. He turned the question over in his mind. "Well, Aunt Mavis is next to her husband. That's usually the custom, I believe." Then another thought intruded.

"Though, I think her decision to be buried with Dr. Book and not with the Banks' family had other roots."

"What other roots?"

"I'm not totally sure. It just seemed to me that Mavis and Brother Frank had unfinished business between them. The air around them always had the tension of a temporary truce. You always felt the shooting was about to start, you just didn't know when." Jack paused, listening to the memories forming conclusions in his mind.

"I remember thinking Mavis was angry with Frank, but then she wouldn't say so outright–just made side comments here and there. I did overhear once, when I was a kid, that Frank put a lot of pressure on Mavis to put Fern up for adoption after Grandmother Banks died." Jack hesitated and seemed to be deciding whether or not to continue.

Niki prodded him to go on. He looked off into the distance and finally said, "I was just remembering that I was here in Atlanta when your father and Frank died–home for summer break, I think. The night before the funeral I took Mavis to the family viewing. When we walked past her brother's casket, Mavis slipped something gold in the breast pocket of Frank's suit. I'm not sure what it was; I'm thinking maybe a pair of cuff links. Once we were outside, she said something like, 'I'll tell you one thing, Sugar, they better screw the bastard in the ground and pour concrete on top, or he'll be back.' I have no idea what she meant by that, but it struck me as a hard thing to say about your own brother."

Niki winced, though something about Mavis' remark didn't surprise her. "I don't remember much about Grandfather Frank, except that I was afraid of him. I don't know why. After the divorce I didn't see either of them again, and Mother wouldn't talk about them. Except for our contact with Aunt

Mavis, the Banks side of my family was wiped away the day Mother left. Mother was a tough lady. She was the type of person who, once she was through, was through. No looking back."

Jack nodded. Tough was not a bad thing, he decided, if you want to survive with minimal wounds. He wondered if he was tough or just numb. Too many wars maybe. They left the shade of the poplar tree and ambled toward the car, stopping to inspect a worn, granite tombstone carved with an 1887 epitaph–*Dutiful son. Faithful Husband*.

"What about your dad?" Niki asked. "I don't remember him."

If she had been looking at Jack's face, instead of wondering if a faithful husband had ever really existed, Niki would have noticed his relaxed smile, would have seen remnants of the little boy who once lived in this man's body.

"My daddy, Ellis Rainwater. Where to begin? He was a big, tall man. Loved to give hugs. Had a laugh like a baritone tuba. Fists like iron. I could go anywhere with him and feel safe."

Niki thought of the Jack she'd seen sitting cross-legged on his bed with his flute, playing "Danny Boy" over and over again. My Lord, how many times does he need to play that tune? Why the same tune, over and over? Now she wondered if the mournful song was because a little-boy-Jack still missed his dad. No, that couldn't be. Could it? Jack was fifty-one years old, after all. No, Jack was simply a slightly loony, obsessive sort of guy who *had* to get it right–even if it was the tune to "Danny Boy." That thought made Niki bite down on her lower lip to keep from smiling.

Jack went on, happy to chat about his dad. "Obviously, I didn't inherit his manly-sized body, or his wavy hair. Dad moved to Atlanta from New Orleans to go to college. Met

Aunt Mavis. They became close friends. Business partners. He and I had an apartment over the garage at the Baker Street house. Sunny windows all along one wall. I could see the trolley on Peachtree Street—if I stood on a chair."

Jack's smile vanished when his mind stepped onto the slippery path leading to the painful end of his daddy's story. "About a year after my mother died, he went out west to work in the oil fields. He was killed in a rig fire."

"Oh, I didn't know that. I'm so sorry."

"Me too. Come on. We better hustle. Looks like we are about to get rained on."

They reached Jack's BMW just as the gray sky opened up and threw dime-sized balls of hail at them. And then as quickly as the shower of icy pellets began, it stopped and rain poured like an open faucet. Once inside the car, they sat silently to wait out the storm, neither of them wanting to finish the conversation they'd started.

# *Nine*

It was three in the morning and Jack was up again with insomnia, resuming his position in a damp wicker chair on the screened porch. He was still angry with Hamilton Rabonette for approaching him at Doc Cheys. And more than that, he couldn't block out the look on Niki's face when, after visiting the cemetery, he'd driven her by the attractive rental house and talked up how perfect the backyard was for a dog. He sipped the two fingers of scotch over ice he'd brought out from the kitchen and searched his mind for a word to match her look. After two healthy swallows, the word came to him. *Betrayed.* Niki had looked betrayed. Jack drained the last of the whiskey and slowly rattled the ice cubes around in his glass.

Mavis reclined on a wicker chaise opposite Jack. Her ivory colored pumps leaned casually against one another on the sisal rug beside her. She studied her slim right foot as she flexed her toes inside sheer pantyhose. *You know, Jack, there are advantages to being back here in Atlanta. I feel as good as I did at forty, prime of my life. Of course, those were the best of years, and the worst of years.*

*I was thinking about downtown Atlanta in the late 1940s just today. There was so much more open space back then. Dappled sunlight falling on sidewalks, window shopping at Davison's, a movie at the Roxy, stylish women in tailored suits, brown and white pumps, doe-hued felt hats with those saucy little brims over one side of the face—and the Planters Peanut Man. Do you remember the Planters Peanut Man, Jack? I wonder who he really was underneath that bumpy, peanut costume and bowler hat. Remember, he'd walk along the street near the Planters shop giving away roasted peanuts. Enticing folks to go in and buy a pound or two. Oh, I can just smell those roasted peanuts.*

Mavis took a moment to savor the taste and smell of fresh roasted Georgia peanuts. *My-o-my, they were delicious. And in those days the Fulton National Bank was the tallest building downtown. It had a fancy brass decorated elevator. You could ride to the top floor, climb the last flight by stairs to the roof, and look down on Atlanta below. Magnificent. You were a little boy then, but I remember Marie and I took you up there. And, at least one night during Christmas season we would take you over to Rich's to ride the Pink Pig up on the roof. Under a twinkling Atlanta sky, the Pink Pig pulled the little train of animal cars round and round above the busy shoppers below. Just think of it, before there was a Disneyland, we all thought riding the Pink Pig Christmas train at Rich's department store was the most fantastical thing imaginable.*

*Speaking of riding animals. Do you remember the pony your daddy bought you? Bingo, you named him. My Lord, I could not keep you from riding that animal up and down the back steps at the Baker Street house. It is a wonder that poor pony didn't buck you right into Bibb County. And your daddy got such a joy out of you and that pony…I never found out how he came by a Shetland pony in downtown Atlanta. I miss your daddy. He's really the only person from the old days that I'd like to see again. Oh, I loved Martin, don't misunderstand me, but our life was…well, it was completed…everything that it was supposed to be. You know what I mean?*

Mavis sat up and leaned closer to Jack in the darkness. *I have to tell you, Jack, you're not doing as well with Niki as I'd hoped. Not that I'm disappointed with you. I could never be that. It's just that you are a little slow on the uptake, Old Son. I don't know what you did to upset her today, but she went to bed crying. Try a little harder, please.*

When Jack thought a breeze played over his arm, making the hairs rise, he smelled Mavis' gardenia scented perfume and tried to remember the name. Maybe White something? He wasn't sure. As his mind continued to wander, he thought of the story Mavis had once told him about meeting his daddy.

She'd shared the story the first Christmas after his daddy was killed in the oil rig fire out in Oklahoma. Marie had announced she was spending Christmas with her new boyfriend, so Mavis decided she and Jack would rent a cabin up near Cashiers, North Carolina, and have themselves an adventure over the holidays. As Jack remembered, the trip did become an adventure–snow up over the wood steps of the little log cabin by the creek, no electricity for two days, and no possibility for Mavis' Cadillac getting them off the mountainside until the snow melted. All in all, they had a grand time. One evening he ate an entire package of toasted marshmallows. That was the night they sat by the fire and Mavis told him about his daddy. Now that he looked back on it, he wondered if Mavis was missing his daddy that night as much as he was.

Mavis walked over and pinched off several spent blossoms from Niki's red geraniums, letting the dried brown crusts fall on the porch floor. *My perfume is White Shoulders, Jack. That's the name of it. And yes, I remember that Christmas in the mountains. You were nine, I think, but such a grownup young man. Do you remember insisting on being in charge of going out in the snow to bring in firewood from the woodpile? We made popcorn in the fireplace and then strung necklaces with it to decorate a little scrawny pine we chopped down for a Christmas tree. We both were missing your daddy terribly. It was hard enough Fern dying the way she did. But to lose Ellis? That was almost unbearable. Now I wonder if perhaps it wasn't a good story to tell a nine-year-old. I was being selfish. Hopefully I tempered the facts that night. But this is what really happened.*

It was the May after Mr. York left Mama. I woke up, heard Mama in the kitchen, and went in there to check on her. She was sitting upright in her rocking chair, her gown pulled up above her knees, pressing a washcloth into her face with both hands.

"Is it time, Mama?"

"Time and then some, Mavis. I didn't want to wake you before daylight. Didn't want you going to colored alley in the dark, but you better get on over to Mae's. This baby's not gonna wait for breakfast. And wake Marie. She needs to be of some use."

I shook Marie awake and shoved her into the kitchen with Mama. With my nightgown tucked into a pair of Daddy's old overalls and my hair hidden with his worn, felt work hat, I headed out the back door. I would walk the distance across the railroad tracks, back behind the cotton mill, and into colored alley looking like a tough boy, and not a scared sixteen year-old girl. But believe me, I was scared and fast walked the distance to Mae Rainwater's down in colored town. A tall, solidly built, handsome young man opened the door before I climbed the three steps to her tilting, shotgun house, and motioned for me to come inside. Mae was already up, dressed, and closing the latch on her black leather midwife's bag. "How'd you know I was coming?" I asked.

"Full moon," she answered, "white babies like to get born at full moon. Course, men drunk on shine like to howl and cut folks on the full moons too. That's why I been waiting for you to fetch me and not stepping around in the dark. These is dangerous times, child. Mean times. More bootleggers and evil in

Atlanta these days than I wants to know about." Mae nodded to the young man who'd opened the door for me. "This here is my nephew, Ellis Rainwater. He'll go with us. He from New Orleans. Used to taking care of hisself. Don't no fools mess with him. Unlessen they wants to be sorry that is."

Ellis said good morning to me and met my stare with a guarded, serious face. No smile. Mae's words, *my nephew*, played back in my mind. With his confident gray-green eyes, and angular face, Ellis did not look like any colored man I had ever seen. Even in the dim kerosene lamplight of the house, his skin was the same shade as the Italian women working at the mill with Mama, and his hair was combed off his forehead in the same deep finger waves as their Italian husbands. As comfortably as I would swallow, he eased a pistol from under a stack of towels on the kitchen table, tucked it into his belt at his back, and put on a black suit jacket to cover the gun's bulge.

The three of us were back at Moody Street before Marie had the coffee made. Mae told us to heat water in the canning pot and stay in the kitchen until she called us. Then she took Mama into the bedroom and closed the door.

Marie and I sat at the kitchen table, and when the boredom took over we played poker for matchsticks. Ellis refused to sit and stood by the back door. I remember asking him several questions. He answered two: he was nineteen and he was in Atlanta because he'd won a school contest in New Orleans. The contest, sponsored by Atlanta businessman Alonzo Herndon, awarded him a scholarship to Atlanta University. When Marie asked who Alonzo Herndon was, Ellis told us that Mr. Herndon, born a slave in Social Circle, Georgia, and the son of his white owner, had become wealthy by working hard and being smart in business. Later, I learned a great deal more about the Herndon family and their Atlanta Life Insurance

Company, when no white bank in Atlanta would finance the Baker Street house and Atlanta Life happily made the loan. But on that morning in 1927, I was impressed simply because Ellis Rainwater was the only person I knew who attended college. Soon after that Marie would be keeping steady company with Bucky Mitchell and his Georgia Tech crowd, but that's another story.

Speaking of Marie. With her usual lack of tact, I think she asked Ellis that early morning if all colored men in New Orleans looked like him. I'm sure I kicked her under the table and told her to shut up. Your daddy laughed at her question, but I noticed the laughter was somehow kind, not mean spirited. Truthfully, for all the years we knew each other, I never pieced together Ellis' heritage. All he ever said was that he was a Creole from New Orleans and his mother had died. No mention of his father, though I guess he was somehow kin to Mae Rainwater, since they shared the same last name. As you know, Jack, your daddy spoke Creole French and Spanish, so he could have come from a myriad of places. It didn't matter. We became friends. We would be friends for the rest of his life, and I like to think we are friends still.

Back to my story. Mae Rainwater delivered Mama's baby girl just before noon on that May morning in 1927. She tried to come butt first, but Mae skillfully turned her around, and finally her blond head crowned and she was born screaming a blue streak, kicking wildly, and grasping at the air with her little pink hands.

"Lord, Lord," Mae called to us in the kitchen, "no need to spank this girl, she know how to cry. I seen babies born crying and grabbing everything like this before. All I can say is: Jesus help us all." Mae laughed, then said more seriously, "This pretty baby be trouble to somebody all her life." Mae shook her head back and forth several times and mumbled something I couldn't hear, then she carefully wrote the birth time, weight, and length of the baby in her black book, and told us that the last thing she needed was trouble with some fool, white man down at the Fulton County Court House telling her how to record numbers in her midwife's book.

When the baby and Mama were clean and comfortable in Mama's bed, Mae wrapped the afterbirth in newspaper and brought it to the kitchen. "Son," she told Ellis, "go bury this way out back there, good and deep, so them chickens don't scratch it up." When Ellis was out the kitchen door, Mae fixed a solemn stare on Marie and me. "Ellis don't respect the old time ways," she said, "thinks his fancy college education protects him from the evils in this sad life. Uh-huh. Truth is I worry about that boy. But you girls don't fret none. I went ahead and put the words and some powerful conjure root in that paper he's burying. That old root will help your little sister with her natural born, wicked ways."

At the time, I had no idea what Mae Rainwater was talking about. Years later, I wondered if she shouldn't have added more root.

Mae changed the subject as Ellis came back in from the yard. "Your Mama told me she want the baby named Fern. That right?"

"Yes Ma'am," Marie and I answered together.

"Well all right then, that's what I put in my black book here so you can get her registered at the court house. Your mama also say she want the baby named Banks, and not after that other man what left. And if that's what your mama want, that's what's going in my book. Any white man tell me different I'll say show me she ain't a Banks. You girls want to look in at your mama and Baby Fern?"

So that's how Baby Fern became Fern Banks. Mae Rainwater wrote what Mama wanted in her midwife's ledger. I remembered what Mae had done about eighteen years later when you were born at Baker Street, and Dr. Martin Book—my Martin—recorded you as Jackson Ellis Rainwater: white male, weight 7 pounds, 11 ounces, length 21 inches. Father: Ellis Rainwater, age: 37, white male, born in New Orleans, Louisiana.

*As I remember our cook weighed you on the flour scale from the kitchen. I didn't blame your daddy for Fern getting pregnant. It was a vulnerable time for your daddy. I'm sure she seduced him for a morning's entertainment, and nothing more. I'm sorry to say that about your mother, Jack, but Fern was like that. Sadly, I think your daddy loved her, though I can't imagine why. She treated him as shabbily as she did everyone else. As you know well, Jack honey, loving Fern was not profitable.*

With a brush of her hand across Jack's shoulder, Mavis walked over and sat back down on the wicker chaise. She looked beyond the darkness of her yard to the park across the street. Were the shadows crows perching in the pecan trees? She watched the birds take turns stretching their wings and contemplated ending her story with Fern's birth. Not telling the rest of it. No, she knew she had to finish it, needed to finish it. Maybe if she played it out one more time, she could be done with it. Mavis looked over at Jack. She hurt with him as he rubbed his injured leg. *Poor child. You don't need to hear this part again.* Mavis crossed her arms tightly across her breasts, closed her eyes, and let the rest of the story play only in her mind, like a television set with the sound turned off.

When Fern was just a few days old, I'd worked my after school job at the grocery store and gotten home about eight o'clock. I don't know where Marie was. Off with her friends after beauty school, I supposed. I heard the baby before I got my key in the back door. Then I followed the crying to Mama's bedroom doorway. I remembered Daddy, so I knew as soon as I saw her lying face up on the bed, staring up at the ceiling, eyes fixed on the sky beyond her room, that she was dead. I remember gagging on the coppery smell of blood and urine, and covering my mouth with my shirt sleeve to keep from throwing up. Drying blood covered the bed, irregular rings of rusted brown soaking up through the sheets and rimming down over the edge of the mattress, reaching for the floor like creatures searching for darkness. Even Fern, cradled and kicking in Mama's arms, her tiny fists clenching and unclenching as she cried, was crusty with blood.

Poor Mama, she must have held the baby to her at the last, knowing she was bleeding to death and hoping, praying, one of us would come home to save her. I'm sure I stood in the doorway for a time, not able to move. Not knowing what to do. I remember leaning against the doorjamb, hearing water rushing in my ears, and thinking I was going pass out. But I didn't pass out, or throw up. I went to the bed and listened for Mama's heartbeat. There was none. She was as cold as Daddy had been on the day I touched his cheek and they buried him in Oakland Cemetery. Fern kept on screaming. I didn't know what else to do other than wrap her in a clean bath towel and run for Mae Rainwater's house. It was dark by then, too early for a moon and no streetlights. I was frightened to be walking the streets headed for colored town, and was terrified by the screaming baby in my arms. What if Mama's baby was dying, too? I didn't know anything about babies. I had not even held Fern before that night. All I could do was keep walking and hope Mae would be home.

When I stood on the bottom step of Mae's porch, I could see only part of the front room through the open window.

A yellowing, paper window shade blocked the other half of the glass. Outlined against the shade, I saw Ellis' shadow as he hunched over a small table reading by the kerosene lamp. His head shot up at the sound of the crying and he met me on the porch before I could knock. "Come on," he said and turned me around away from the house. "Auntie's down at Yozell's. It'll be faster if we go down there."

That night was the first of many times over the years that Ellis' cool thinking was my guide. He led me down the narrow dirt street past a row of shabby look-alike wood houses, all perched on cinder blocks and decked with tilting front stoops, to another house just as shabby. It looked identical to Mae's outside, but inside, unlike Mae's clean- smelling, scrubbed wood floor and tidy kitchen, the two rooms of this house smelled of coal soot, pork grease, and unwashed bodies. We stepped around four, maybe five, young children squatting on the faded linoleum floor playing Jacks, to a double bed by the fireplace where a large black woman, Yozell I assumed, was propped against several pillows. She looked tired, and happy, as she clutched a quilted bundle of newly born tiny brown hands and wrinkled face.

Mae slowly rose from the slat-backed kitchen chair beside the bed when Ellis and I came in, looking at me as though a white girl with a screaming baby was the most normal thing in her life. She took Fern from me and quieted her with soft words and a gentle rocking in her arms. I told her about Mama, and not knowing where else to go. She didn't ask any questions. She hugged me, my teeth chattering with fear against her shoulder, and said, "Blessed Jesus. I am sorry about your Mama, I really am. I reckon she was sick and worn out from so many trials and sorrows. And you, poor child, your trials done just begun. You here now though. Mae ain't gonna let you tote this burden by yourself. We'll think it out. There is always a way to do what you got to do." That's what Mae said to me, and she was right. There is always a way to do what you have to do.

Mae gave Fern to Yozell, who lovingly nursed her into a full belly and quiet sleep. Then Mae washed Mama's blood off Fern as she dozed and snuggled her beside Yozell's newborn. By that time, I was calm enough to realize I had to call someone about Mama. Yozell didn't have a telephone and her house was closer to Moody Street than Mae's, so it was decided Ellis would accompany me back home. From there I would phone the Atlanta police about Mama.

Mae's instructions to Ellis were curt. "Keep to the shadows. They's white men would kill you for walking up town beside a white girl. Only stay till you know things is right, then you get your tail out of there. Don't let no white man find you alone up there with a white girl and a dead woman. You understand me, son?"

We walked in silence and followed Mae's orders to stay in the shadows. I believe even Ellis was frightened that night. Three nights before that, the Klan had beaten a black man nearly to death for supposedly "sassing" a white clerk on the sidewalk in front of a grocery store on Grant Avenue. That was less than five blocks from our house on Moody Street. After the Grant Avenue beating, it was rumored the wild dog Klan was on the move again, hunting for any excuse to "teach those nigras respect." Even though Atlanta was like a cluster of small towns back then, and we knew who rode with the Klan–and I'm sure they knew us–we also knew better than to trust some bigoted white-trash Klansman jacked up on whiskey and self-righteousness. Better not to cross paths with them.

It seemed like a long, very dark five blocks that night, and I remember dreading going back into the house with every block that brought us closer to Moody Street. When we reached the house, Ellis and I stood on the back porch, still silent, neither of us wanting to open the door. Finally, I steeled my backbone and swung the kitchen door into the lighted room. Mama's death filled up the house like water trapped inside a glass box. I telephoned the police on the phone in the kitchen and didn't go back into the bedroom. I also tried to phone Brother Frank, but a colored lady answered, said she was the housekeeper, and that Frank was in Florida on business.

Ellis and I waited in the dark in the living room until we saw a car drive up in front of the house. Through the window, I could make out the Atlanta City Police emblem on the car's door. Ellis was out the back door and beyond the abandoned outhouse headed back to Mae's before the officer dragged his slow moving butt up the porch stairs. Marie came home soon after the officer arrived. I remember she pitched such a crying fit that he had me go out to his car and get his half-pint bottle of bourbon from under the front seat. It seemed to me that Marie had been drinking already, so I didn't see that one more drink would calm her down, but I wouldn't argue with an Atlanta policeman. I don't know why, but I didn't cry about Mama that night. It wasn't that I didn't love Mama. I did. It was just that things had to be done. Things always have to be done.

Poor Mama. I don't think I ever had a chance to cry for her. That awful night ended with Marie passed out on the sofa and me dragging Mama's bloody mattress out back and burning it. Mae Rainwater was right; my trials were just beginning. Brother Frank returned from Florida two days later and paid for Mama's funeral. I was grateful that he did, because I had already counted the money in Mama's Luzianne coffee can and there wasn't enough for us to make it through the month, much less pay funeral expenses.

Marie stayed drunk until it was all over–a sign of the times to come. And baby Fern? I can't recall any of the relatives even asking about her. Maybe they didn't know Mama had a baby. When the funeral was over and all the Tennessee relatives left, I went over to Yozell's, paid her a dollar, and brought Fern back home to Moody Street. I didn't have a clue how to mother a baby and really didn't want to learn, but it seemed like the right thing to do. The only thing to do. She was our sister and as much as Brother Frank argued we should take her over to the Methodist Children's Home to be adopted out, I couldn't do that. After Mama's funeral Marie and I grew up in a hurry. I did what I had to do, with help from Mae Rainwater. I suppose doing what I have to do has always been my long suit.

It wasn't that I brought Fern home without a plan, mind you. Mama had worked at the Fulton Cotton Mill, close to our house, really just three streets over and across the railroad tracks. I could walk the distance, just as Mama had, in about ten minutes. My plan was to get a job at the mill, maybe even Mama's old job in the carding room, and work nights until Marie finished beauty school. Then she would have a day job and I'd switch to working days, and we could hire someone to come in and take care of Fern. But until this grand plan for the future materialized, Marie would be responsible for Fern at night while I worked, and I'd care for her days. I was confident I could handle it.

And I did handle it, I guess, for the most part. Though, as I remember, Marie fought me every step of the way with her complaining and poormouthing. Fortunately, I had no trouble being hired for the night shift with Fulton, starting at twenty-two cents an hour, two cents an hour more than my old job at the grocery store.

In late May when I started, it was warm and stuffy in the mill, even at night. The job was backbreaking from the bending and stooping, though not mentally challenging by any means. By mid-summer I'd lost eleven pounds. My feet stayed so swollen I resorted to taking the laces out of my saddle shoes at work to give them more room. Muscles I didn't know I had ached as though pounded by wooden meat mallets. I got used to the work, though it didn't get any easier. About a year later I made other choices. I quit the mill for good and never looked back.

Mavis left the chaise to stand beside Jack again. *Do you ever look back, Jack? Wish you'd done something different with your life.* She kissed the top of his head.

*Your choices seem to have made you happy. Or maybe we've all just been lucky. Your daddy would say that life is always a crapshoot. Lucky, or not, no one is safe from the snake eyes' roll.* Mavis laughed as she remembered Ellis' easy way of putting everything in perspective.

# Ten

Jack noticed Niki working away in the back garden when he finally dragged himself awake and went to the kitchen to brew a cup of coffee. He watched from the windows as she pulled a pot of daylilies from a tray of ten, and began planting them along the wood privacy fence on the left property line. Since he'd returned to Atlanta, he'd watched her tend her vegetables, plant strawberries in a whiskey barrel on the patio, dig a hole for a peach tree big enough to sink a '57 Chevy in, and shovel up a half-moon of grass under an oak to house a family of low growing, green striped plants. What did she call those things? Hosta? Yes, hosta. She'd explained hosta thrived in shade, thus she needed to plant them under the oak tree.

Whoopee-do. Who cares about hosta? Jack certainly was not interested. What was this with the garden anyway? The woman was obsessed with growing things. Now it was daylilies. She probably wouldn't stop until every inch of the back yard was covered. At least she would be occupied for a while. That was good. The backfire of his wow-her-with-another-house plan still smarted with guilty residue, and Jack had a peace offering that needed a little time to organize.

After gulping down a half-cup of coffee, he found a screwdriver in the everything, kitchen drawer and headed for Mavis', now Niki's, bedroom, and the walk-in closet. Abelard hopped about in his cage and trilled out a song when he entered the room. Jack spoke to Mavis' canary and checked his water and food. Both were full and clean. He grudgingly gave Niki credit for taking good care of the aging bird. When Jack turned away from the cage a sweet fragrance settled on him and he thought for a second that he was back in time when his aunt occupied the sunny, ivory painted room. With a second sniff, Jack realized the scent wasn't Mavis' at all; it was slightly lemony and a little like the red geraniums on the screened porch. He liked the fragrance. It was fresh, yet ripe.

It took him only a couple of minutes to slide back a section of Niki's clothes, locate the small wood panel, remove the screws he'd put in after Mavis died, and drag out the cardboard accountant's box. All he had to do then was replace the panel, tidy Niki's clothes back to their original location, and he was done.

Back in the kitchen, Jack placed the box on the kitchen table beside several stacks of papers that hadn't moved since he arrived. Hadn't Niki said the papers were from Mavis' old desk? That she was sorting them, deciding what to keep and what to discard? How long could it take to figure out twenty-year-old Georgia Power bills were worthless? This woman was truly weird.

Jack was pleased with himself for remembering the box. He rubbed his palms together and allowed himself a conspiratorial smile. All would be forgiven. Niki was interested in family history; she would probably ooh and ah over what she found in the box. After all, he knew women were like that; they love all the sentimental crap. Jack hesitated, just for a single moment. He'd not read the papers rescued from Mavis' fireplace on the night she died. But then, he didn't need to. Did he? He'd lived it, heard all the family stories, and was so certain that Mavis would never write down the one story with the power to cut him like a razor across fingertips, that he didn't think twice about offering the box to Niki.

As for the brown envelope of old photographs lying on top of the papers, he couldn't be sure when he'd last looked at it. Maybe before he'd moved to London? As a last minute gesture, to sweeten the pot, Jack leaned the envelope against the box.

His hands were dirty so he washed them at the sink and tore an extra paper towel from the roll to wipe ten years of accumulated dust from the top of the box. It was when he was cleaning the box that he noticed a small white business card sitting atop one of Niki's stack of papers–a card he would swear was not there ten seconds ago. He picked it up. It was a literary agent's card. Why would Niki have a card from a literary agent? Under the card was a white, letter sized envelope.

Must be the rejection letter she was talking about at Doc Cheys, he decided. How bad could it be? Without considering the gravity of snooping, Jack opened Niki's letter. He quickly scanned the usual greeting and went on to the excuses for why the agent was rejecting her story. The last paragraph hit him like a punch to the gut. "Though your work is well written, perhaps you lack sufficient distance between your personal experience and your fictional story to offer a unique perspective on the experience of losing a baby." Jack read the sentence twice to make sure he'd understood.

He turned the envelope over to the front. The postmark date was February 27, 1990. Then he hurriedly slid the letter and agent's card back into the envelope, put it under the stack of papers and walked to the window again. Niki was sitting on the bench under the dogwood tree with her face to the morning sun and her eyes closed. He wanted to dig back into the papers and find the letter again. Read it a third time. Just to make sure.

No. I can't do that. I shouldn't have read her mail. What did the agent say? Losing a baby? A polite way to say your baby died. I can't believe the agent was talking about Niki. That would mean between Mavis' death in April 1986 and the next time I saw her, Niki had a baby? And the baby died? Then some time later Niki wrote about what happened? No, that can't be right. How could she do that? And how could she be pregnant, have a baby, and the baby die, without my knowing? How could I not know about her having a baby? It isn't like we haven't talked over the years.

Jack busied himself at the counter with pouring another coffee and continued to watch Niki. His mind bounced against the missing years between Mavis' death in 1986 and when he remembered actually seeing Niki again.

Where was I working during those years? She wasn't pregnant at the funeral in 1986. How could I have talked to her after that and not known? Wait. I remember I talked to her around Christmas in 1988. I was here in Atlanta. We'd rented the house to an Emory professor. He's the guy who stayed only one semester. Forfeited his deposit to move on to a position in California. I remember I asked about her husband. What was his name? Larry, or something like that. No, Lynton. Lyn. She said they were getting a divorce. Just as well. Seemed like a controlling prick to me. So, if she had a baby, the baby must have been born between the end of 1986 and the end of 1988.

Crap. I remember the Emory professor wanting out of his lease and all that, but where was I after Aunt Mavis' funeral to the time I talked to Niki at Christmas in 1988? Maybe I didn't see Niki during that time, but surely we talked. At least I think we talked. Oh crap, I don't know. It all runs together.

The point is she probably did have a baby. And she didn't mention it to me. Still, where was I during those years?

With an urgency he didn't stop to question, Jack found a note pad and pencil in a kitchen drawer and leaned over the counter. He began with Mavis' death on April 11, 1986 and wrote Uganda in bold letters beside that date. He was sure he'd been there just before Mavis died. Below Uganda he wrote Haiti and underlined it. No way he could forget Haiti. Then he navigated his mind forward, writing down assignments after Haiti–Libya, Lebanon, Honduras, Panama, Iraq, back to Libya–and with a few gaps, he worked his way to December 1988.

*I've got it.* I'd covered the earthquakes in Armenia and then the Pam Am flight exploding over Lockerbie. Then they sent me to New York in December for some UN thing and I flew home for a few days. Where did I stay? Oh yeah, that new hotel across from Lenox Square. I could see the shopping mall from my window–Christmas decorations and all that good stuff. I'd had dinner with someone–can't remember who–and I decided to call Niki on the hotel phone in the lobby after I'd said goodbye. There was a big Christmas party going on in the ballroom. It was noisy…oh yeah, it was old Terry Spiegel I'd had dinner with that night. The Emory professor was a friend of his and he was concerned there would be hard feelings with him about the guy wanting out of the lease. Jack wrote down Terry's name on the pad and drew Christmas holly–complete with berries—around the letters.

Impressed with his recollections of Terry and the hotel, Jack drew more holly leaves and berries at the margin of the paper, expecting additional revelations. None dawned. He asked himself: And then what? I called Niki, and? There wasn't much after the *and*. Jack recalled talking to Niki but didn't recall if she was cheerful or seemed depressed. Maybe she had asked about Lockerbie. He probably didn't want to talk about it. Never wanted to recount the details. They probably wished each other Merry Christmas, discussed the Emory professor and renting the house to someone else, and maybe he asked about the husband as an afterthought. There certainly wasn't any conversation about a baby. Looking at his list again, Jack filled in a few more lines from 1988 forward to Bosnia in 1993. Bosnia was the worst, he decided, even worse than Haiti.

Jack was thinking he'd probably logged more air miles than Henry Kissinger–slept more in planes than in beds. He tapped the pencil head a few times on the tile counter top, making a rat-tat-tat sound with the eraser. And I've been pretty lucky really. Except for the usual intestinal stuff, this leg thing is my first major injury. Damn lucky. Probably a good idea to get out while the luck still holds.

But Niki? A baby dying? Not lucky. That's snake eyes in a crapshoot for sure. I still can't believe I didn't know she was pregnant. I wonder what happened. Was the baby stillborn? Or got some horrible baby sickness? I remember taking photos of mothers in Haiti holding their dead babies. Their eyes looked…how did they look? Beyond sad. What lies beyond sad? I don't know. Is it helplessness? Hope ground into sand?

Jack stayed at the window for another minute or so, thinking about death. He'd had to face his father's death as a child. It hurt, but that was a long time ago. His dad was writing letters to him about working on the oil rigs one day, and then gone the next–like yesterdays math problems on the chalkboard–erased. And Mavis? She was ill with emphysema for several years. The grief when she died was real and painful, but her death was not a surprise. It was almost a relief when she passed away peacefully.

Hadn't Mavis told him that Marie died of cancer? Liver cancer maybe? He'd never been totally sure. He was a sophomore at the University of Florida at the time and full of youthful delusions of immortality—at least for himself. Now, at fifty-two, Jack suspected it was the booze that really killed Marie. He had lived long enough to know that you couldn't drink like Marie did and see a gentle old age.

Then there was a guy in the newsroom at the magazine who'd had colon cancer. Jack watched him deteriorate, begin to look sickly. But then he went to Haiti, where he took photographs of so much slaughter that when he returned, and learned the guy had died, his death seemed almost anticlimactic. Jack recalled how the guy looked as his body failed—the sunken eyes, grayish skin. Cancer was slow and humiliating. Better to step on a road bomb in Libya. What was the guy's name, anyway? Jack couldn't remember—just that he'd not known him well, but thought he had a wife and a kid.

Watching Niki sitting so still on the bench, her blond hair laced with gray in the sunlight, Jack was struck with the realization that he didn't know Niki well either. Didn't know how she would deal with the death of a child. How would anyone deal with the death of a child? People die every day. Sure. Old people. People caught in the insanity of wars. But your child dying? He couldn't imagine how that would feel.

So, who was this Niki person living in his house? How had she gotten from being the shy, bookish teenager he remembered to this middle aged woman obsessed with gardening? Admittedly, she was attractive, quick-witted, and obviously resilient since she'd weathered the death of a child and two divorces, and was still standing upright. And, he had to admit she was pretty good company when they weren't arguing about who should move out. But no, he probably didn't really know her any better than he'd known the guy in the newsroom.

Jack shook his head to clear the bombardment of disjointed thoughts. So what? Who wants to know all the details of anyone's life? For that matter, who needs to know? That's way too sticky. For a fleeting moment, he was sorry he'd read the letter, sorry he knew about the dead child. Then the knowing crept slowly from his mind into his chest like a puppy sneaking under the bedcovers, and he wasn't sorry that he knew this one intimate thing about Niki. Not sorry at all. Though he had no earthly idea why.

Jack's mind took a different path. On the other hand, Mavis must have known Niki well to leave her half of the Cherokee Place house. Or at least she thought she did. But why would Aunt Mavis leave her half of the house? Not that he was jealous of Mavis' gift. He wasn't. After all, a house was just a house. He'd camped in so many apartments and hotels over the years, one seemed pretty much like the other. It was just that he wondered why? Niki was family only by marriage, really. What was Mavis thinking? When the coffee maker on the kitchen counter beeped to tell the world it was shutting off for the day, Jack remembered he had an appointment and needed to shower, dress, and hit the road.

# *Eleven*

Niki was pleased and exhausted from her morning's work of planting daylilies. Soon burnished red petals with school bus yellow throats would stand at attention along the fence line. What would she plant in front of the lilies for more summer color? Maybe bronze and yellow coreopsis, foxglove nesting beside, and a generous helping of bright pink cosmos rising in between. Her next project would be a raised bed for herbs. She knew if she wanted to have fresh basil, rosemary, and lemon mint any time soon she had to get the plants in the ground. Later today, she told herself, definitely later today.

It felt good to sit on the warm concrete bench and feel the sun on her face, even though the calm feeling was interrupted periodically by her anger with Jack. Such a sneaky bastard, she carped silently, taking me to lunch and then driving me over to that rental house. I guess he thinks I'm simple-minded. Such a male thing to do. And they say women are manipulative. Men are so much more manipulative, especially the handsome ones. Well, I can be stubborn. If Mr. Jack Rainwater likes that cute little rental house so much, let him move into it. I'm not leaving.

Besides, I don't buy his retirement story for a minute. Just wait. He'll be off to some war before the month is out, so what does it matter where his pile of worn out leather suitcases live while he's gone? I need to keep my cool–not give him the satisfaction of knowing he's upset me. I'm staying put and watching my garden grow, and I'm starting my dog search tomorrow. I am *so* over men and their selfish ways.

Niki's warm beam of late morning sunlight was blocked when Mavis appeared beside her. She shaded her eyes with the soil caked garden gloves and looked up; expecting to see a cloud passing over, but the sky was Georgia clear, and April blue. As Niki watched, the sun found its way through Mavis' shadow, illuminating her outline with a pulsating aura. How odd, Niki thought, a mirage. An optical illusion of a heart beating.

Mavis bent over, removed one of her shoes and knocked a small shiny pebble out onto the ground. Niki, thinking she'd seen a pebble mysteriously fall from above, bent to pick it up and turned the pale, worn shard over in her hand. She recalled seeing similar white stones as a child, on the beach at Saint Simon's Island. Her mind traveled to hot sand, seagulls wheeling overhead, and the dependability of ocean waves. We went there: Mother, Aunt Mavis, and I. A few days at the beach would be lovely.

Mavis, now sitting beside Niki on the bench, leaned into the warm sunlight as though it was a favorite sweater she could wrap around her shoulders. She stretched out her arms to feel the heat through the sleeves of her silk shirtwaist dress, and closed her eyes for a moment before she spoke to Niki.

*I know what you mean about men. Just when you think you know the rules of the game, they change them to suit themselves. I like making the rules myself. I don't even like a surprise birthday party. That's why it took me eleven years to agree to marry Dr. Book. I wanted to know what I was getting.*

*Now your mother, there was another lady who liked making the rules. Of course, your dad was so charming and handsome I think he had her* marching down the aisle before she stopped to calculate what that trip was likely to cost her. Every time he fell off the wagon he recited another litany of promises. Finally she'd had enough of him not following three simple rules: stay sober; support your family; come home at night.

I remember the end came when you were about five years old. She brought you over to Baker Street because she was looking for him. Came in the kitchen door, or so I was told. I was in town shopping when it all happened. Our cook, Little Flora—who weighed about three hundred pounds, and was the best cook in Atlanta—snitched on your dad and told your mama he was upstairs.

While you were in Flora's kitchen eating chicken and dumplings, your mama went upstairs and found him asleep—not alone, I'm sorry to say. She tiptoed into the room, took his clothes, brought them down to the kitchen, and burned them in the wood stove Flora used for baking those yummy cinnamon rolls we all loved. They only thing left of his suit was the metal zipper from the fly of his pants. You know what they say: justice can be a bitch.

That's when your mama packed y'all up and moved to Roswell. She didn't bring you back to Baker Street after that terrible day. I didn't blame her. Yes, your mama was a tough lady. When she'd had enough, she was gone, gone, long gone.

By the way, Niki, I was out here in the garden last night. It was glorious in the moonlight. I am amazed to see so many stars this close to downtown. Looking up at them reminds me of those unusual glass spheres I see on the water's surface when I sleep. Or no, I'm not sure I'm sleeping. It's more like a deep, quiet rest. I'm floating, lying under the water. Can that be? Floating under water? And the spheres…there're even bigger than the red and gold glass balls on the Christmas tree at Rich's department store. They seem to float above me like…well I don't know like what…they are just there. Lights pulsating from within like the twinkling of thousands of fireflies. Comforting…very comforting.

*Anyway, as I was saying, I was out here last night. Those pesky rabbits came again to eat your spinach plants. I shooed them away, but I have to tell you, I don't think it's going to work for long. They are out for the easy pickings, and your tender little spinach is definitely easy. Maybe a small dog wouldn't be such a bad idea after all. Nothing intent on killing the rabbits, you understand, or tearing up the yard or the house, just a little guy to bark and chase away the rabbits when I'm not here.*

*You know, dear, I don't have any idea how long I'll stay. And even when I am here, I find myself in the garden one minute and then in the kitchen the next. Last night, just as I was enjoying the stars, I found myself on the screened porch with Jack. Sweet Jack. He isn't sleeping well. I think his injured leg is bothering him more than he will admit. I understand it took the doctors hours to pick out all that flying metal from the bomb. Lucky he didn't step right on top of the thing, or we'd be busy burying him over at Oakland Cemetery.*

Mavis drew in a deep breath and squinted through the glare of the sun to look at the house. She was sure she saw Jack standing in front of the kitchen windows watching them. *Now what is that boy up to? I know a guilty look on Jack Rainwater's face when I see one. Maybe I should go inside and see what he's doing.*

However, when Niki drew a handkerchief from her shirt pocket and wiped beads of perspiration from her face, Mavis forgot about Jack. She reached over, attempted to take the small square of cloth from Niki, and caused it to flutter to the grass at her feet.

*My word. That's Mama's handkerchief. I'd know that lace border anywhere. I'm glad you didn't toss it away in the Goodwill bag. Yes, it is getting hot out here. Maybe you should go inside. You really are working like a farm hand on this garden. I'd rather phone up a gardener to swoop over the grass with a lawnmower and prune the shrubs in a couple of hours, and be done. Sweating is fine if you're dancing or making love. But it isn't fine in the yard. Sweating, that is…or rather…well, you know what I mean.*

Niki retrieved the fallen handkerchief, settled back on the bench, and closed her eyes.

Pleased that her niece wasn't moving to go inside, Mavis began chatting again. *All right, if you're not going in the house just yet, and since we were talking about men, I'll tell you a story. It's about the old days. But more importantly to you, it's about a man I used to know. A handsome man who flew airplanes. The story begins in August 1927.*

Niki yawned and Mavis began her story.

I remember summer heat expanded over the city, a suffocating rubber sheet smothering any stray breezes trying to sneak south from the mountains. For seventeen days straight anybody in Atlanta with a thermometer nailed up beside their back door knew the red line hovered in the high nineties. Then for two days the temperature climbed to over a hundred degrees, only dropping to the eighties at night.

Fretting with heat rashes, diarrhea from the questionable summer water, and mosquitoes, families tugged bedding to the cooler screened porches for nights of less fitful sleep. Mothers cooked what was necessary before daylight and served the fried chicken, green beans, and buttermilk biscuits cold at noon. Downtown shoppers along Peachtree Street moved only in the first and last hours Rich's and Davison's were open, and even then bodies dragged in slow motion from the weight of the heat. When noise escaped from the few automobiles chugging up and down the street, the drowsy sound seemed to float in the air as though it came from under water. Finally rain fell on the seventeenth day of the heat wave and steam arched off the concrete sidewalks, rising and moving like a living thing, and clinging to pants legs and cotton dresses like warm syrup.

As was the habit before house air conditioning, families of well-to-do Atlanta businessmen and doctors escaped the city, by train or chauffeured car to mountain homes in Highlands or Cashiers, North Carolina. There, giant white pines and hemlocks held cool air like Christmas gifts, and the fortunate could wait out the dog days of August on breezy porches. Not so fortunate city children gravitated to the cool waters of Peachtree Creek and the Chattahoochee River, or to the shade of a pecan tree, to suck on a prize of shaved ice flavored with vanilla extract.

At Moody Street, Marie and I didn't have the money or the time for escape during that first summer of Fern's life. There was one day I remember well. Marie banged the screen door to the kitchen closed and stripped down to her slip. Her damp cotton dress went across a chair and she stood there for a few seconds, fanning herself with a dishtowel. That didn't seem to cool her enough so she came out of her open toe white pumps, as well as her under pants, and tossed them in the bedroom.

"Good God Almighty, Mavis. It's so hot I can feel the sweat running down my crack. How can you just stand there and wash those baby bottles in all this heat?"

I turned from the sink to frown at her, too tired and hot to make conversation. I had five bottles washed and sterilized and had five more to go. After that, I had to boil the nipples, make formula from evaporated milk and water, mixed with Karo syrup, and then assemble at least three bottles for Marie to give Fern while I was working that night.

Seeing Marie standing there in the kitchen, home from a day at beauty school, brought my mouth into high gear. "Marie, how come you are not wearing a bra? Those big tits of yours are going to be hanging down to your knees before you are twenty if you don't support them with something better than a thin cotton slip."

"Mavis, what's eating you? It's too damn hot for a bra. And besides," Marie cooed in a low playful voice as she cupped a breast in each hand and glided her palms across the roundness and down to her flat stomach, "Bucky likes me where he can get to me. I swear Mavis one of these times, real soon, when that boy wets his fingertips and slides them ever so lightly around my nipples, I'm gonna give up and do it with him. And don't look at me like that. You just don't understand what it feels like to get hot around a man, and Sister, Bucky makes me hotter than this here August."

I turned back around and scrubbed baby bottles even harder. Marie was really getting to me as only Marie could. Jealousy, as I look back on it. "Sister," I remember saying, "The only thing I feel is tried. Tired of working till I ache, tired of trying to be a mama, which I don't know shit about, and don't get any help from you WITH. And I'm tired of your bull crap about Bucky Mitchell. He's nothing but a college boy looking to fuck anything that will stand still long enough for him to get his dick out of his high priced, just pressed, gabardine pants. Which I'll bet fifty-cents he has already done to you. Anyway, he doesn't care an ambrosia flip about you, Marie."

Well, that set Marie off like a firecracker. She practically flew across the kitchen, drew back, and slapped me across the face. I probably deserved it, but I was still shocked. Marie and I argued like all sisters, but she had never hit me. Mama probably turned over in her grave. "You better take that back, Mavis," she hollered, "or I'll slap you again. Bucky does too care about me. He already said he's going to take me to the Georgia Tech get acquainted dance in September. So there."

Of Course, Marie's moods changed quicker than you could flick a light switch. As soon as the words were out of her mouth, her lower lip began to quiver and tears ran from her eyes like water squeezed from a wet rag. I don't know if the tears were because she realized she had hit me, or that she'd realized as soon as the words were out of her mouth that Bucky had no intention of allowing her to mix with his rich friends.

I was the one with the red burn across my cheek from her hand, but I was sad for her. "I'm sorry," I said. "You're right. Bucky is crazy about you. Don't cry. It's too hot to cry and you'll give yourself a headache."

She did cry, of course, great body shaking wails that took her breath away and frightened Baby Fern into sympathetic tears. I held them both while Marie sobbed on my shoulder whining she missed Mama and how everything had gone crazy since she died. Nothing made sense anymore, she said. She couldn't sleep while I was working nights at the mill. She felt the house was watching her. And sometimes she could hear Mama calling to her from the kitchen. 'Get up Marie,' Mama would say. 'Do something useful and make coffee.'

"Oh Mama," my poor sister wailed. "I'm trying, I really am trying. But it's too hard, too hard." She pounded her fists on the table, sending the sugar bowl dancing, and dusting sugar all across Mama's flowered tablecloth. Fern thought Marie's fisting pounding was funny. She stopped her fretting and laughed her high baby laugh. I couldn't help but smile, and took Fern on my hip and paced the floor while Marie played the drama queen. Marie, being Marie, cried and flailed around for about a minute, and then her fit was over. All done.

After she wiped her face with the dishtowel, she righted herself in the chair, smoothed her slip down over her damp body, and smiled her best I'm-sorry-but-you-know- I-just-can't-help-it smile. "I have a super idea," she bubbled from a new world. "Bucky has a friend you can go out with. We can double date. Mavis, look at you, all you do is work. You need to have fun once in a while, and stop being such an old stick-in-the-mud."

I was speechless. The last thing I wanted was a date with Bucky Mitchell's friend.

"It'll be terrific. Lord have mercy, I'm beat. I'm gonna take a cool bath." Before she waltzed out of the kitchen, Marie chirped at me, "Oh, guess what? Guess what? At school today I did a permanent wave–all by myself–for an old broad with more hair than both of us put together. I rolled hair in little bitsy wave papers till I thought my arm would fall off. I was wet with sweat, that's for sure. But that old lady–who I'm sure, was at least forty-five–didn't have one drop of sweat on her upper lip. Isn't that something, Mavis? Do you suppose when you get old, you don't sweat?"

*I could have killed Marie. How could she change gears so fast? I tell you, Niki, my twin sister was always like that: spectacular highs and dreadful lows. Of course, she had her good points. For one, Marie didn't hold a grudge. Unlike me, who would nurse a wrong for so long that the pain it brought scabbed over, leaving a permanent knot of bitterness. Your Grandfather Frank could attest to that. I never forgave him for what happened with Fern. I'm sorry, but the man had the morals of a rat.*

# Twelve

Mavis paused her story to study the cluster of nearly perfect diamonds on her left hand–a platinum filigree setting of square cut stones on either side of a two-carat center. She loved the way the diamonds played with the sunlight. A wedding set from the Victorian era, she remembered. Martin Book bought them at auction and tried to tempt her with the jewels several times in exchange for her promise to marry him. She finally said yes, but not for the diamonds. Certainly not.

*Silly Martin.* Mavis smiled. *He should have known better than to think he could bribe me with diamonds.* She thought of Martin– of his loyalty, his devotion, and his respect for her independence–and realized that he probably did know better. It was just Martin's way of reminding her that the offer of marriage was still there.

Mavis' mind drifted from the goodness of her husband, back to the tawdry actions of her brother Frank. *Perhaps I shouldn't have said what I did about Brother Frank. Niki really doesn't need to be reminded of her grandfather's sins. It must have been hard enough for her to separate herself from the Banks men and their various character flaws. Her mother did a good job with her. I'm proud of them both. Well, I can't take back the spoken word, or the written word either. Spilled milk, I always say, spilled milk.* Mavis cleared her throat and turned back to Niki on the bench.

*I drifted off the subject, didn't I? Forgive me. Let me get back to the kitchen at Moody Street and what happened.*

I believe I mentioned it was a sweltering August afternoon. When Marie finally left me alone and went for her cool bath, I put Baby Fern down on her pallet on the linoleum floor. I had just mopped that floor, by the way. Then I folded up the sugary tablecloth and sat down at the table. I wasn't old, but I felt older than the lady Marie had given the perm to that day, and I was certainly wet with sweat.

I tried fanning myself with the tail of my apron. All that did was move the hot air around. I lifted the electric fan from the top of the icebox and put it on the table, adjusting the black metal rotating blades to blow directly on me. I wanted to say something to Marie, something that would impress upon her how much I needed her to be sane and sober, help me with the baby, and spend less time in the back seat of Bucky's car. In the end I kept quiet, knowing anything I said would be useless.

In about five seconds, Marie came back from the bathroom making a face and holding her nose. "Mavis, there are about a dozen nasty diapers soaking in the tub. How can I take my bath? I hate that smell. It makes me want to puke." She sat down opposite me, tilting her damp face into the breeze of the fan, and reached down for Fern's tiny hand. "Hey Cutie-Pie, you been a good girl today?" Fern smiled with all the gratitude her baby heart would hold. "You're so pretty, just like a little angel. Mavis, look at her sweet face, she really does look like an angel."

Before I could agree, Marie moaned dramatically and lowered her forehead to the kitchen table. Then rolling her face in my direction, she whined, "Oh Sister, how can we raise Baby Fern? We don't know two things about raising a baby. Don't you think we ought to consider what Frank said? We can hardly feed ourselves, and Fern needs things all the time—diapers, milk, and bottles. What if she gets sick? Frank says the Methodist Children's Home is really nice. Fern would be taken care of real good out there. And you heard what he said; if we keep Fern he won't help us with a nickel. Not like he did when Mama was alive. If we don't do what Frank says, how are we gonna make it, Mavis?"

A series of moans, louder than the first one, followed Marie's speech. I should have had sufficient experience with Marie's moods by then to know she wasn't serious about giving Fern up for adoption. She was just having one of her mile deep lows, which always followed one of her cloud nine highs. But I was tired and frustrated, so her talk about giving Fern up really ticked me off.

"Shut up your damn whining," I barked. "What kind of brother would want us to give Fern away to strangers? You think Mama would want that?" I grabbed Marie's arm and probably pinched it harder than I should have. Then I asked her again, "Well, do you?" The pinch must have gotten her attention because she looked too shocked for tears. That was a good thing, because as angry as I was, if she had started a crying fit again, I would have really lost it.

As it was, I ranted on. "You think you hear Mama calling you from the grave now? You just wait. Mama's ghost will be doing more than talking if we dump her baby in some orphanage like a sack of week-old garbage. Fern stays with us. And that is final. We are family. Daddy always said, 'Family abides.' And, by God, abide is what we are going to do."

Seriously prissy speech, huh? It's a living wonder I didn't choke on my own self-righteousness. But oh well, I had the precarious vantage point of youth fueled by inexperience. Believe me, I paid for it later.

Fortunately, Marie straightened up and dropped the subject of giving Fern up for adoption, at least for the moment. Her mind, and her conversation, flipped to another subject with the speed of a trout's tail. "Oh. Oh. I almost forgot. You won't believe what is going to happen. It is just too, too exciting. Tomorrow night, seven o'clock, at the Paramount, they're going to show *Blood and Sand*, and *Son of The Sheik*, back to back, as a tribute to Valentino. I can't wait. Everybody in Atlanta is going to be there, Mavis. We just have to go. Even WSB radio was talking about it today. All of us girls from school are going to do it–bring candles I mean. At just the right moment in the movie, we'll all stand up and light the candles in honor of the Great Valentino. Imagine hundreds of flickering candles, all for him. Won't it be just too, too dramatic?"

Weeping Mary and Joseph, Marie, I think I said. All the candles in Georgia can't bring a dead man back. Rudolph Valentino? What has he got to do with us? I'm bone tired from working all night with only a thirty-minute break and sleeping only when Fern naps in the day. My head feels like it is stuffed with cotton lint from the mill. And this heat–will it ever break? If it's a hundred outside, it must be a hundred and fifty in that damn cotton mill. The mill. Shit fire. I have to get to work.

I grabbed my purse and headed out the door with Marie hollering after me, "But Mavis, what about the dirty diapers?"

*I tell you Niki, we would never have survived without Mae Rainwater sending food and hand-me-down baby things given to her by white women whose babies she'd birthed. I kept moving, one foot in front of the other for a year, and tried not to think about how much I hated working at the mill. Then it was spring again and Mae sent Ellis over with a birthday cake. Fern's first birthday cake. He must have been waiting for me behind the shed because when I cut through the backyard from work in the early morning coolness, he stepped out in front of me holding the iced cake out like an offering.*

"Holy cow, Ellis," I squealed at him, "you just about gave me a heart attack. Can't you make a little more noise, give me a little warning? Where'd you learn to creep around like that? You must be part New Orleans Indian and not all Creole."

Ellis gave me his best half smile. All you ever got from him was a half smile. If he won a million dollars all you'd see was that determined tight set mouth. He could laugh though. I heard him laugh many times over the years; but even then his mouth never went as far as a grin. You'd hear his baritone laughter rolling deep in his chest and then spilling out into the air like a tympani being played in a cave, but his mouth never opened all the way with the pure joy of the feeling. Ellis always held back, leaving a private part of himself protected. I admired that in him. After he handed me the cake, we sat on the back porch steps.

"How you liking your job at the mill?" he asked.

I pulled the waxed paper covering the cake up just enough to run my finger around the side. "Yum. Butter cream frosting. My favorite. Be sure to thank Mae for us. The job's all right I guess. It pays the bills. You still in school?"

"Yes, ma'am. In another two months I'll be a certified, for real, accountant. A man these days needs all the education he can learn, if he wants to get ahead. And me, I want to get ahead. Besides, I'll be twenty next week. I need to be moving along. Get a full-time job. Decide if I'm going back to New Orleans, or stay here in Atlanta."

I teased him, "Birthday boy? Maybe we should put some candles on this cake for you. Have a party for you and Fern."

"Oh hush. Don't be talking nonsense. Grown men don't have birthday parties. I'm serious about making something of myself."

I don't think I'd thought of Ellis as a grown man before that moment–a big bear of a boy, yes, but not a man. He chatted on. "You know I've been working after school for Mr. Herndon down at Atlanta Life Insurance Company. The job is part of my scholarship from Mr. Herndon. He says any man shows initiative and works hard for him can count on a job. I work harder than any man down there. I'm hoping that'll get me on with Mr. Herndon fulltime when I graduate."

"Mr. Herndon must be making good money selling life and burial insurance."

"Oh yeah, he makes good selling burial policies to colored folks. That's his main business. Who else in Atlanta is gonna see the folks get a proper funeral? I hear he has other businesses, too. Just like his daddy. You remember him, Mr. Alonzo Herndon, died last year. I think Mr. Herndon loans money to folks wanting to start businesses–like Fulton National Bank does for whites. Him being colored and knowing all the colored businessmen in Atlanta, he knows who can make a go of a business, and who can't."

Pausing to stretch his long legs out into the lower step, Ellis narrowed his eyes and gave me his grown-up assessment of good business as he saw it. "Yes, ma'am. Far as I can see, it's important to always know your customers personally. You got to know the good about them, and the bad.

"The other thing is: if you can find out what a man is wanting and is willing to pay money for, then you can make a good business outta that wanting. Colored folks want to see loved ones laid to rest with dignity. Yes ma'am, dignity is important and they will lay down their last nickel to see their mama or daddy buried with dignity. Your brother Frank understands the business principal I'm taking about. He knows some men will always pay well for a drink of whiskey, no matter what the law says. Whether it's a burying, or a drink, it's all in what a man will pay to satisfy the wanting. I can't say I like Frank, but he understands that. Frank's smart like that."

I refused to admit there was anything smart about Frank, but Ellis was making a good point. Several years later Ellis and I applied his ideas and went to Atlanta Life Insurance Company for a loan to buy the Baker Street house. They made the loan when no other bank in Atlanta would touch us with a ten-foot pole. Baker Street turned out to be a good business deal for Atlanta Life, and for Ellis and me.

After Ellis' little speech about business, neither of us said anything much for a while. We were content to sit on the wood plank steps and watch the yard fill with morning. Finally Ellis said, "Speaking of Frank, I saw your brother last night down in the neighborhood. He's down there a lot. He ever help you out with the bills?"

"Hell no," I answered but did not say Frank would help if Marie and I put Fern up for adoption. "Why do you ask?"

"Oh well, you know, he was hanging out throwing down some sizable money. I just wondered if you ever get any of it."

I was puzzled. "What's Frank throwing down money on?"

Ellis looked at me as though I had just dropped from the moon. "Why The Bug, of course. You know, he's playing The Bug."

I had no idea what he was talking about. "The Bug? What the hell is The Bug?"

Ellis looked amused. "You really don't know what The Bug is? It's betting, Miss Mavis, betting on the numbers. I'm not for sure how it works, but the winning numbers get printed somewhere in the want ads of the Atlanta Journal newspaper. If you pick the right numbers for that day, you win money."

"And just how do you know about this bug thing?"

117

Ellis gave me one of his playful looks. "I tell you how. Being a light skinned Creole man has a bright side. I can hold my head high, look confident, dress to the nines, and talk white with the whites before they start asking who I am. Likewise, I can jive step down with the coloreds in the neighborhood and get the skinny on everything going on down there—just like any Auburn Avenue man can do. You might say I'm a man for all places. Shoot, most folks think I'm Cuban anyhow."

Imaging Ellis sashaying down on Auburn Avenue made me smile, but I was still furious with Frank. We were living on greens and cornbread to buy milk for Fern, and he was driving his well-dressed skinny ass around in colored-town throwing money away on gambling. The Bug. Who ever heard of such a thing? I wanted to stomp Brother Frank.

# Thirteen

*Niki? Are you asleep?* Mavis reached out her hand and lightly touched her niece's cheek. Niki brushed the spot as though a butterfly had kissed her, and then opened her eyes. *Oh good. Pay attention, dear. I know it took me awhile to get here. But, this is where the story about the sexy man starts. You might find it useful.*

Now, it was a few weeks later–after Fern's first birthday cake–late spring of 1928. It had been a good day. Fern took a late morning nap and for a couple of hours I slept to the spring rain drumming on our tin roof. Sleep–heaven after working all night at the mill. And this was my night off, so I was about as happy as I could get. I took a long bath while Fern played with some tin spoons and cups on the bathroom rug beside the tub. We had just gone out to the front porch, partly for me to towel dry my hair, and partly to enjoy the last of the raindrops as the shower pushed eastward, bound for the coast. Fern reached one of her cups out into the air, caught a stream of water overflowing the gutter of the porch and screamed with delight as the splash wet her face.

About that time, Frank's black Ford rolled up to the curb and stopped. He trotted gingerly from the driver's side of the car to the porch, being careful not to splatter rainwater on his white linen suit. I watched his spit-shined, brown and white wingtip shoes climb the steps two at a time, and planned how I would start an argument with him to vent my anger about him playing The Bug. He was a selfish, poor excuse for family, and I wanted to tell him so.

A second car door slammed. A slim man, about Frank's age, in no hurry at all, sauntered through the rain to the porch. When he stood beside me, he removed his tan cowboy hat. Trapped rain from the curled brim poured onto my bare feet.

"Well, hell-fire," he drawled and showed a sexy, sleepy smile. "Ain't I a monkey's uncle? I'm truly sorry, ma'am." He bent down to dry my feet with a handkerchief from his khaki pants pocket. Nice thought, but the handkerchief was saturated with snuff colored machine oil. Now my right foot was not only wet, but greasy brown.

I closed my eyes and bit down on my lower lip to keep from pushing him off the porch with my greasy foot as he knelt. I'm sure I was wondering where in the world Frank came up with this foolish cowboy. He made Marie's boyfriend, Bucky Mitchell, look like a mental whiz. And believe me, Bucky was too dumb to direct a one-car funeral. My mind went back to Brother Frank. Whatever Frank did was to profit Frank, so I knew this cowboy, this tall, lanky, drink of water must figure into Frank's profit plans. But more importantly, what was Frank doing here at Moody Street?

"Meet my buddy, Slydell Ritter," Frank said pleasantly. "He flies airplanes–carries the mail from Atlanta to Miami, Florida, then back to Atlanta. Pretty dandy, eh?"

*Pretty dandy, indeed, I was thinking. A hick cowboy who is also an airplane pilot. Another reason to never, ever, get up in one of those dangerous flying machines…*

Mavis reluctantly paused her story, lifted her face into the high noonday sun, and watched Jack approach. He walked slowly up to Niki and Mavis as they sat on the bench. Mavis thought he looked like a man with a mission, and wondered what he was up to now. She smiled at Jack, was pleased, as always, to see him. *You're the son I didn't have.* Mavis wiped a tear with her little finger before it had an opportunity to ruin her mascara, and assured herself that the tear was a result of bright sunlight.

Niki opened her eyes, thinking she had drifted off to sleep and dreamed of Mavis. Her aunt's mellow, slightly theatrical, voice echoed in her mind, but Mavis' words from the dream were lost as soon as she realized Jack was standing next to her. She shaded her eyes with her hands to put him in focus.

He was dressed in newly creased jeans and a Polo tee shirt. My Lord, she mused, does this man never wear a pair of jeans twice? Even in the glaring sunlight, the red of his shirt deepened the brown of his eyes. Pity, Niki thought. To look at him you wouldn't think him mean and conniving. He looks positively trustworthy and entirely too handsome. She blinked and concentrated on projecting a neutral facial expression. She couldn't know that her left eyebrow raised as the other eye squinted from the sun, alerting Jack that she was still angry.

He took a step back. "I'm leaving now," he said. "Going to Athens to see about some equipment a guy is interested in selling." He paused, and then added, "Thought I might try commercial photography." When Niki gave no response, he said, "I'll be back tomorrow afternoon."

"Fine," she said. "This isn't the Ritz Carlton. You don't have to make reservations. I may or may not be here. I think I have an appointment."

The space between them grew within a long pause. Jack put on his aviator sunglasses and pretended to study a chickadee bouncing from limb to limb above them in the dogwood tree. Niki told herself she didn't care if he went, or came. At least she wouldn't be annoyed with his nightly flute playing. I mean really, how many times *do* you need to play "Danny Boy"?

Mavis stood up and blew as hard as she could on the back of Jack's neck. His perfectly coiffed hair ruffled and he reached around to smooth it back into place. She laughed and the chickadee took flight. "Look Niki," he offered so quietly that she, and Mavis, had to strain to hear what he was saying. "Yesterday was a mistake. My mistake. I'm talking about the driving by the rental house thing. I'm sorry. Can we sit down and talk when I get back?"

"About what?"

"I don't know. Just talk. What we've both been doing for the past ten years…what kind of ice cream we like. I don't know. Just talk like sane adults."

"I thought we were talking yesterday at Doc Cheys. Course now I know you had a hidden agenda. Got another plan to get rid of me?"

Jack's brow pinched as his lips narrowed into a tight bow. Niki was sure the hidden look behind the sunglasses was a mean one. "I said I was sorry. What more do you want?"

"Nothing. Just forget it."

"I'd like to forget it, if you would let me. Again, I'm sorry. This is why I don't do well with women. I can't predict the crazy side attacks."

"What? I'm not attacking you," Niki shot back and got to her feet. "Look, I know you don't want me here. I hadn't exactly planned on a roommate either. And I'll tell you right now I don't have the cash to buy you out of the house, if that's what you have in mind. I'm self-employed like you, but I don't make the big bucks. Also, the move down here from Roswell was expensive. So frankly, I'm tapped out of extra cash right now."

Jack felt his face flush. He was reminded again that women were too confrontational for him, no sense of fair play, or subtle negotiations. " I wasn't going to suggest you buy me out. And I don't have the cash to offer you either. We agree we have to do something, but I don't have a plan. I was just thinking perhaps we could talk about it like civil human beings. Preferably, without backbiting or sarcasm."

Niki puffed up, her eyes wide open. She didn't consider herself a person who resorted to backbiting, or sarcasm. I am a civil person, she was thinking. I don't even complain if a person breaks in line in front of me at the grocery. Aunt Mavis always complimented me on my good manners. Aunt Mavis. What was she thinking to leave us the house together? Surely she would have known how untenable the situation would be?

In the past ten years, Niki had thought very little about the why of Mavis' gift–of her intentions. She had assumed Mavis left them the house because she wanted to pass along her inheritance to family members, and she and Jack *were* the only family members. Now she wasn't so sure.

Why wouldn't she leave me the antiques and Jack the house? After all, he'd at least called the house home base since he moved here with Mavis when she married Dr. Book. Maybe because he's not here very much–always running off to some war? Mavis probably thought he wouldn't take care of the house, and she knew I would. Yes, that's me. Niki, the responsible, and dependable, and boring...

She put on her gardening gloves and slapped them together a couple of times, knocking off the loose soil. "Okay, we'll talk. Tomorrow. Right now my project is an herb garden–fresh basil, rosemary, that sort of thing. And to start clearing out those honeysuckle vines covering the greenhouse, or potting shed, whatever it is. I noticed it has a couple of broken windows."

The greenhouse. It'd been so long since Jack had thought about the glass enclosed shed, he'd nearly forgotten it existed. He automatically looked to the rear of the garden at the tangle of vines humping up from the grassy lawn. Mombassa, Kenya, on the way to Uganda, washed across his mind, bringing with it an involuntary shudder.

'Watch for Black Mamba snakes in the bush,' the guide had said. 'They bite you, you dead thirty minutes. But no worry. Plenty time call home, say goodbye to girlfriends.' Jack still didn't understand why the others had laughed. He shook free of the memory.

"It'll take a machete to hack down those vines," he commented.

"No doubt."

"Wait until I get back from Athens. I'll help you."

"I thought you hated yard work."

"I do." He checked his watch. "I have to leave now. Ciao"

Jack turned to walk back to the house. Niki headed for the greenhouse and waved over her shoulder. "And ciao to you, too," she called after him. Then she wondered: Was that sarcastic?

Jack turned around, remembering there was something else he wanted to tell Niki, but forgot what it was when he saw where she was going. Damnation, that is the most bull-headed woman ever born. Just had to go on back to that stupid greenhouse. Couldn't wait on me, like I told her. Hope she gets poison ivy. And what is it with this nonstop gardening? Now it's herbs. How much stuff does the woman need to grow?

Cutting back through the kitchen, Jack realized it was the box he'd meant to tell Niki about. Considering the information he'd discovered in the literary agent's letter, and Niki's stubborn attitude, he excused his forgetfulness and wrote her a note.

*Niki:*

*I pulled these papers from the fireplace the night Mavis died, but I haven't read them yet. I don't know why I didn't let them burn—probably because she'd worked on them for weeks. I think maybe she changed her mind and wanted you to read what she wrote. The photographs in the envelope are mine. Thought you might want to see them.*

*See you tomorrow. Jack.*

He anchored his note on top of the box with a red and black, ceramic rooster saltshaker and was out the door as fast as one good leg and one damaged leg could carry him. He was on highway 316, about ten miles from Athens, cruising along at sixty-five in his beloved steel gray BMW, when it occurred to him why Niki might feel compelled to grow a garden, to nurture small tender plants.

Maybe that's something women do? They need to grow things. And she wants a dog to keep her company. Trying to replace the baby with a dog and a bunch of plants? That's pitiful. Oh shit, I hate pitiful. I cannot deal with pitiful.

Should I tell her I know about the child? No, I can't do that. She'll know I was snooping. Besides, I really don't want to talk about it. Maybe I should take an apartment in town, or buy a condo near the art galleries and restaurants. Yeah, near restaurants. I mean it's been kind of nice to cook at home with Niki, but I won't cook for myself when I'm alone again.

Alone again. The words sounded alien. Jack questioned if he'd ever felt alone before. No, not that he could remember. He wondered if Niki felt alone sometimes. She didn't seem lonely, even considering the obsessive gardening thing. Maybe he was wrong about the gardening thing. Maybe she just liked to grow stuff. After all, it had been seven, maybe eight, years since she'd lost the baby. Yes, Jack decided, Niki was probably over the baby by now. She'd had plenty of time to get over the baby. Hadn't she?

With his BMW purring along the highway, Jack rolled the driver's side window down to feel the air rushing against his face, and whistled a *Moody Blues* tune. But when Niki's betrayed face from the rental house episode came out of nowhere to stop his song, Jack rolled up the window, turned on the air conditioner, and pushed the accelerator pedal down.

# *Fourteen*

Hunger and the realization that Jack was correct about needing a machete to cut away vines from the greenhouse drove Niki inside. Mavis found herself drawn into the house along with Niki on the tail of a warm, early afternoon breeze. She immediately turned up the volume on the radio sitting atop the refrigerator. Another of her favorites from the 1940s, "September Song," filled the kitchen.

While Niki made herself a tuna salad sandwich, Mavis sang along with the radio. *Oh it's a long, long time from May to December. But the days grow short when you reach September.* When she reached the last lines of the song, her voice trailed away soft and sad. *...and these precious days I'll spend with you.* When it ended her sigh was so extended, Niki thought the air conditioner had cycled on.

She looked up from her lunch, wondering if Jack had switched the unit over to ac from heat. When the breath of air suddenly disappeared, Niki looked around the room, puzzled. That's when she noticed Jack's box on the table. With half of her sandwich in one hand, she munched along the edges of the crust and read the note. Then she opened the box. The acrid smell of burned paper assaulted her nose. "Yuck," she said aloud and replaced the top.

Mavis swished over to stand beside Niki, causing several stacks of papers on the table to rustle with the breeze. *No, don't put it away. Take the top off and read what's inside. You may as well go ahead and read what I wrote.*

Biting into the heart of the fragrant tuna, mayonnaise, and pickle sandwich, Niki reconsidered and pulled the box closer. With her free hand she put the top aside on the table and rifled through charred pages, pulling out a small hand full. The first few pages were a mystery of lost words. Too burned to read. She put those into the open box top and turned the first readable page to the light from the kitchen window.

Mavis looked over her shoulder. *Yes, yes, read that part. It's about the sexy cowboy Brother Frank brought to the house.*

Niki hesitated, having second thoughts about reading Mavis' papers. *I wonder if Jack is right and Mavis changed her mind about burning her papers. Though, I have a hard time seeing Mavis changing her mind about anything. If she decided to keep her thoughts to herself and burn the papers, perhaps that was her last wish. If so, it would be disrespectful to read what she decided to burn.*

Mavis groaned and stomped her feet on the tiled kitchen floor. Niki thought the thumping noise must be air trapped in the kitchen faucet and went to the sink to flush out the tap. Mavis followed and reached around Niki to turn off the water. *Sometimes, Niki dear, you are much too rigid. You think an issue to death. Just read the damn papers. Believe me, it's important to both of us.*

Niki turned the water back on for a few seconds and then, satisfied she'd solved the problem, sat down at the kitchen table to finish her lunch. She rested Mavis' papers beside her plate, finished her sandwich, and licked several smudges of mayonnaise from her fingers. Now, satisfied from a full stomach, she rationalized that Jack knew Aunt Mavis better than anyone. His intuition that Mavis had changed her mind seemed pretty strong in his note. When Niki rose to take her plate to the sink, Mavis worried she wasn't going to read the papers. In a fit of temper, she jerked the kitchen door open, and then slammed it as hard as she could. It shut and then opened again. Niki reached over and clicked the door closed. Old houses, she thought–doors uneven, drafts out of nowhere, water pipes rattling. In the time it took to wash her plate and refill her tea glass, Niki decided to read the papers in the box.

When she finally sat down to read, Mavis flew over and stood behind her, reading over her shoulder. The first undamaged page began: *Slydell Ritter smoothed his tousled dark hair back with one hand and offered the other to me, palm nearly up. I had a silly feeling that we were about to dance rather than shake hands.*

"My friends call me Two-Step, Ma'am," he said. "On account of Slydell is too much a mouth full for most folks. I'm real sorry about your wet foot. I wouldn't never do that on purpose." His pale green eyes looked sorry enough and promised he was harmless, though if he was a friend of Brother Franks, I had to wonder about the harmless part.

Niki looked up, smiling. Why Mavis, I believe you were smitten with this Slydell person. I wonder how your foot got wet? She went on with her reading: *I took Mr. Ritter's hand, nodding hello. It was a man's hand–lean, hard, and callused, but not much bigger than my own. He seemed to pull me to him as we touched and I shifted my weight to keep balance. He smiled a wide gracious grin full of experience I did not have. The smile made me uncomfortable and immediately conscious I was standing on my front porch, right out in the open on Moody Street, bare feet and damp hair, wearing nothing but a thin robe. I made an attempt to close the robe a little tighter around my body.*

"Pretty little baby," Ritter said enthusiastically, looking down at Fern, who had climbed out of my arms and wrapped herself around the tail of my robe. "Looks a-might like a Kewpie doll. She yours?"

"Mine more than anybody else's, I suppose," I answered and turned my attention back to Frank. "What do you want, Brother? Isn't like you to drop in out of the blue. Fact is, isn't like you to drop in at all."

"Why sister. You act like you aren't glad to see me, and here I brought you and Marie presents and everything. Can't we go on in the house and get out of this rain? It's making the starch in my shirt go limp."

Frank opened the screen door. I picked up Fern and stepped between the two men into the house, brushing as I did against Mr. Ritter. I realized he was about my height or a little shorter, if I had on my dress shoes. But that didn't bother me. I was used to being taller than a lot of the men I met. I've always been proud to have my daddy's height—makes me feel I carry something of him around with me wherever I go.

Inside the small living room, cherry pipe tobacco and saddle soaped leather from Mr. Ritter filled my nose with sweet scents. Don't be impressed, I told myself. He's still nothing you want, just another one of Frank's shady friends. Didn't Frank say he flies the mail back and forth in his airplane from Atlanta to Miami? Oh yes, and I bet he takes along a little extra liquid weight for Frank, going and coming.

We went through the front room to the kitchen, where I started coffee on the stove and excused myself to dress. When I came back, Slydell Ritter had taken Fern onto his lap and was rolling her fat little hands around and around chanting, "Patty-cake, patty- cake." His eyes danced from Fern to me. "I'm the oldest of nine," he said. "Five girls and four boys, so I know all about playing with babies." I nodded, not sure what to say to a grown man singing a baby's song. Mr. Ritter nodded in the direction of the front door. "Frank went out to the Ford to get a bottle and your presents."

I think I crossed my arms at that point and tried to look disgusted. "I certainly don't care about any whiskey, Mr. Ritter, it's hardly two o'clock."

"Me either, ma'am. I ain't much of a whiskey drinker. Coffee will do me just fine. To tell you the truth, whiskey makes me stupid, and besides I need to be flying out later to-day, if the weather clears. That's how come we had the time to come on over here today–the weather I mean. Been raining like a son of a bitch all day. Can't fly in that soup. Well, I guess I could. But I'd be a fool to, and my Mama didn't raise no fools."

I poured us coffee, sat down across from him, and almost said: Well I don't know about that, you're hanging around with Frank. That might make you a fool. "Where are you from, Mr. Ritter?" is what I said to him.

He heaped sugar into his cup and stirred before he answered, "San Antonio, Texas, ma'am. Can't you call me Two-Step?"

I sipped my hot coffee. "No, I certainly can't. Sounds like something one man says to another in a poker game, just after they have a big laugh about some poor girl he's been cheating on."

Ritter laughed. "No, not poker, ma'am, and I don't never talk about my women. Two-step is a dance. You know, Texas two-step–holding your partner, gliding across the dance floor to the music. You dance Miss Mavis?"

"Maybe," I answered. "I'll tell you what. You stop saying Miss before Mavis and I'll call you Dell instead of Slydell. That suit you, Mr. Ritter?"

"Mighty fine," he answered and smiled that wide smile I'd seen out on the porch. "My mama always called me Dell. That would please me right fine. It sure would."

Frank joined us in the kitchen, dripping water from his umbrella all over my clean floor and complaining that the rain was coming down harder. "Looks like it's settling in for the rest of the damn day," he barked, "if that package isn't in Miami by tomorrow night, Two-Step, I'm gonna be in deep shit."

"Easy does it, Big Man. We'll make it," Dell soothed. "No rain can last forever. I talked to the man out at Candler Field early this morning. He says this here rain will pass before the night is over. When it does, I'll fly your package with the Miami mail run. Don't worry." Frank grunted and poured himself a healthy shot of whiskey in his coffee. Dell winked at me and asked Frank if he had brought the presents from the car.

Holding his coffee cup with both hands, Frank slid a bag with his foot from the front room into the kitchen and beside my chair. "Of course I did, that's why I'm soaking wet."

Sure, I thought. I know you, Frank Banks. You went out in the rain for the whiskey.

Dell looked as happy as a kid with a full bag of jellybeans. I couldn't imagine why. "Open yours Mavis. Your brother had me bring them the last trip I made for him. They come all the way from Cuba. I did the picking out myself. There's one for you and one for your sister."

What was this? A man I'd not even met until today chooses a gift for me? I reached into the bag. Two bundles wrapped in white butcher paper. I lifted up the one with my name printed across the top and unwrapped it. Folded inside was an exquisite, coral pink, silk kimono style robe with intricate turquoise, yellow, and deep blue birds of paradise embroidered across the back. I was speechless. To be sure, it was a useless garment. Wouldn't help one minute to keep you warm in January. Certainly out of place for a mill girl who didn't know a kimono from a bed sheet, but I tell you, it was positively, electrically beautiful. I still have it. By the grin on Dell's face, I knew there had to be more to the story of how he came to bring us gifts.

Dell leaned to me and carefully stroked the kimono's silk sash, then threaded its length through his fingers as though weighing it by the touch. His voice was low and familiar when he spoke to me. "Frank told me you were a redhead. I've seen a picture of you at his house. I thought that pink color would set off your hair like a desert sunset, and I was right. It suits you, Mavis. Try it on for us."

I stood up, probably self-consciously, and wrapped the kimono around my drab housedress. By then I knew the present idea was all Mr. Ritter's. Brother Frank hadn't brought us a gift since before Mama died. All we got from him was a hard time about us refusing to put Fern up for adoption. Looking at Dell, I said to Frank, "Why thank you, Brother. I've never seen anything so beautiful."

Frank nodded and yawned. "I'm beat. I drove in this morning from up Towns County way. Took me most of the night on those damn, twisting mountain roads. I believe I'll catch forty winks on the sofa. Wake me when it stops raining."

And that is how I came to spend the afternoon sitting in the kitchen on Moody Street with Dell Ritter. We drank coffee, Dell adding two spoons of sugar to every cup like he hadn't known hard times when sugar was rationed like tolerance from a stiff-necked preacher. I tuned on WSB radio. Dell seemed to know every song they played. "I spend a lot of time alone," he told me. "Gives a man plenty of opportunity to memorize pretty words."

I thought about my daddy and his clear tenor voice. "And the circle will be unbroken, by and by Lord, by and by..." I think it was the rain, and missing Daddy, and maybe the music. But as I sat there in the kitchen watching Fern play on the floor, and listening to Dell talk about his home in San Antonio, I forgot to be angry with Frank. Maybe I'd been holding the anger too long, and lost the why of it. Whatever the reason, at least for that afternoon, my anger retreated like the rain draining down Moody Street.

I recall Dell saying his mama and daddy were dead, like my own. His parents died with the Spanish flu, within three weeks of each other, while he was in France during the Great War. Later that same year, flash floods washed away his family's Texas home place. When Dell got back to the States, and made it to San Antonio, the only thing left of the house was the front steps–sitting in the dirt–stepping up to nowhere.

In the fading afternoon, as Dell's sad voice filled the kitchen, I realized how alone and frightened I felt. I was a kid living in my mama's house on Moody Street trying to masquerade as an adult, but I couldn't talk to this stranger about my feelings. I think I believed if I spoke about what I felt, some secret dam would break inside me and I would be swept away forever like Dell's Texas home. So I just listened to him.

After a while, Dell told tales of flying his airplane so low over the Florida swamps he could count the gators sunbathing on cypress logs and I laughed with him. He'd fought a world war in France, survived the ruin of his home, and the loss of his family, and learned to master flight, when many days it was hard for me to get out of bed and drag myself to work at the mill. Fear didn't seem to be part of this man's makeup. Dell gave me something to think about.

Just before dark, Frank woke up from his nap and announced he was going to town to see a man about a dog—whatever that meant—and he would bring us barbecue for supper from Sugar Ray's Restaurant down on Auburn Avenue. Marie came home—well on her way to being three sheets to the wind—soon after Frank left. She stayed for about five minutes to announce Bucky was waiting for her in his car. It was her turn to babysit, but Marie had a plan that would keep her in the fast lane for fun. She would take Fern over to Ellis' Aunt Mae Rainwater's for the night. Seems like after Mae delivered Fern, and Mama died, Mae was regularly to the rescue with our little sister.

This particular night, Mae was willing to take Fern so Marie and Bucky Mitchell could see Al Jolson in the "The Jazz Singer" at Lowe's movie theater, and then whoop it up at a party with some of Bucky's Georgia Tech friends.

Marie barely noticed Dell Ritter sitting in our kitchen, so I decided to save her present until later—when she was sober. And oh yes, Frank showed up at 8:00 the next morning, without the barbecue.

Niki lowered the papers to the table. Aunt Mavis' recollections of her life as a young woman were not what she would have imagined, and Mavis feeling frightened and alone was something Niki couldn't begin to picture in her mind. Aunt Mavis' was always so…so in charge, so self-sufficient…so… so Mavis.

Mavis sighed and raised her eyes from reading over Niki's shoulder. She didn't want Dell's memory to fade. For the moment it was fresh and lingered as a lightness singing through her body. She remembered his smell, the way he tapped a matchbook on the table sometimes when he told one of his long, funny stories. She remembered that night after Frank left for town. Mavis tried to tell Niki to keep reading, not to stop, but her niece had gotten up from the table and was looking out the windows, transfixed on something outside, something in the yard.

Mavis went to the windows, curious at what was so interesting. To her the back yard was a patchwork quilt since Niki moved in. Here a plant, there a plant. Vegetables growing where her goldfish pond once occupied the sunniest spot in the yard. And that silly peach tree was standing at the edge of the garden, looking like a ragged, skinny, stepchild at a family reunion.

Mavis decided Niki was determined to fill every inch of the yard. She shook her head, dismayed. What was wrong with a clean expanse of mowed grass–tidy perimeter camellias and azaleas? Call the gardener. Let him worry about it. Mavis turned from the windows and studied Niki's face, drawn tight with some serious thought or other. Is she thinking about her garden, or about Dell Ritter? Does she know why our story is important to her?

Niki wasn't thinking about her garden or Dell Ritter. Her mind was skipping rocks of information across her memories. The way Mavis talked about her grandfather Frank it seemed he had a hidden motive for whatever he did. She guessed the only reason he stopped by Moody Street that day was because of the rain, and maybe he wanted to take a nap. And he obviously lied about the gifts being his idea. But why? What did he want?

Niki washed her hands in the kitchen sink, dried them on a paper towel, and tried to recapture her grandfather Frank in her mind. The only credit Mavis gives him is for being clean and well dressed. I do remember him being a fashionable dresser, always decked out in a suit and starched dress shirt.

But I can't remember exactly what his face looked like, only that he was tall, reddish hair and freckles. Or was that my father? I'm not sure.

Niki returned to the table and reached for the brown envelope of old photographs Jack had left with the box. Maybe there was a photograph of Grandfather Frank. She slid the stack of photos out of the envelope and held up the one on the top of the pile. It was a black and white of Mavis sitting in an overstuffed armchair, facing the camera, looking elegant and thoughtful, as though the photographer had distracted her from an important discussion. To Mavis' left, a big man in a double-breasted suit leaned against the arched doorframe. His arms were crossed casually over his chest; one foot was cocked over the other. His smile was pleased, guarded.

Niki saw the resemblance to Jack in the forehead, the deep-set eyes, and dark hair. Though this man's hair was wavy and combed straight back. He looked Latino, maybe Cuban, or New Orleans French-Creole. Must be Jack's dad, Ellis, Niki decided. She turned the photo over. On the back was printed: *Dad and Aunt Mavis. My first camera.*

Mavis looked over Niki's shoulder. One hand rested on the table and the other gripped the back of Niki's chair. Her lips were close enough to Niki's ear to tickle the fine hairs of her cheek.

*I remember that photograph. Ellis was talking about leaving Atlanta for a while. The Atlanta police were asking questions about Fern's death, though I don't know why. They didn't seem to care on the night it happened. I think that murdering bastard put them up to it—couldn't look Ellis in the face without feeling guilty. Get rid of Ellis, get rid of the guilt. Anyway, Brother Frank said that someone downtown was hinting Ellis had something to do with Fern's death. Who knows if Frank was telling the truth? I doubt it.*

*Whatever the case, Ellis believed Frank would protect his bootleg partner and to hell with the rest of us. Ellis was right, of course. Even though we had friends ourselves downtown, it seemed safer for Ellis to leave town for a while. Except, leaving turned out not to be safe at all. I remember Jack came in the room while we were talking—with his new camera—a present from his dad.*

*I'm sure Ellis went out west soon after the picture was taken—and then there was the oil rig accident and he was lost to us forever. Oh, Niki, look at that face. My stars, Ellis was a handsome man. I wish he had loved someone other than Fern, anyone other than Fern. Someone who would return his love. Ah well, as Daddy always said: if wishes were horses then beggars would ride.*

Mavis straightened her shoulders and ran her left hand to her French twist to tidy any stray curls that might have escaped. When she was satisfied, she spoke to Niki again.

*Go ahead, dear. Finish reading my story about Dell Ritter. I want to hear it again myself. Like all great love stories, there is passion, surrender, and sadness.*

# *Fifteen*

Niki discarded the idea of searching for a photograph of her grandfather in Jack's envelope, and replaced the black and white snapshot of Ellis and Mavis back inside the envelope. She didn't want to look at any more photographs. Mavis' writings had already opened the door for memories to sneak uneasily into her heart, and she decided against dwelling on the memory of the Banks men—had never found that exercise made for a happy day. But Grandfather Frank Banks wouldn't stay out of her mind.

Niki looked off into the past. What was it about Grandfather Frank that was so frightening? I'm sure he never laid a hand on me; still, the possibility always seemed to be looking out at me from his eyes. My father must have felt that too. I suppose it's like Mavis said in her letter to me: With a father like Grandfather Frank, and his mother leaving him to be raised by a series of housekeepers, my dad had little chance of being anything other than a drunk.

Niki considered that statement. Little chance? Actually that wasn't true. It's the last thing Aunt Mavis said in her letter that was true. She said we all make choices. My father wasn't strong enough. Tough enough. Many people don't get the parents they deserve, and are decent human beings.

After standing up and stretching the kinks out of her back, Niki thought about the remainder of the afternoon. She needed to start on her new writing assignment. After all, only work paid the bills, but she felt too restless to sit still. Just enough time to get to the nursery and check out the herbs. The memory of fresh rosemary sprinkled on little red potatoes smothered in butter made her mouth water. Yes, she definitely needed herbs.

Mavis reached out to Niki and brushed her arm to get her attention. She wanted Niki to read the rest of her story about Dell Ritter, but when Niki ducked back to the bedroom to find her purse and keys, Mavis knew she'd lost her audience. She followed her niece, scurried about the bedroom moving Niki's purse from one location to another behind her back, while Abelard jumped from perch to perch, chirping, being a tattletale. Niki found her purse anyway and left the house by the front door, leaving Mavis alone with the aged bird singing happily for the company of his favorite person.

Mavis went to the cage and opened the door. *Come out here you silly old bird. I guess we can both stretch our wings while Niki is gone. Let's go through her closet and separate out the frumpy clothes that need to go to the thrift store. We can make a pile of the do-not-wears on the top shelf. If she doesn't find the pile, then all the better. That girl really does need serious wardrobe assistance.*

Exactly two hours later, Mavis heard Niki's car in the drive. She collected Abelard and put him back in his cage where he quickly settled down for a nap, and then strolled out to the kitchen where she drew back the organdy curtains on the windows. From there, Mavis watched her niece pull a child's wooden wagon around the corner of the house. Peeling green paint flaked to the ground on all four sides as its rusted metal wheels squeaked to a stop on the patio. Mavis surmised the wagon was probably made around the year Jack was born. Thank goodness, she mused, Jack had weathered better than the tatty wagon. *What is that girl up to?*

Next, Niki came into the house to find her battery-powered drill. She made a series of holes in the already leaky bottom of the wagon with her drill, and filled the cavity with moss, and then with potting soil from bags she retrieved from her car. One more trip to her car netted five small pots. While she hummed an off key version of "The Impossible Dream," Niki lifted young herbs out of the pots and planted them in the wagon. When she was finished, she sprinkled them with water from the hose, and stood back to admire her handiwork.

Parsley, sage, rosemary, and thyme, she mused. Just like the folk ballad. On my Lord, I'm starting to sing all the old songs just like Aunt Mavis used to do. She shook her head to stop the music playing in her mind, and went about sweeping loose dirt off the patio.

When Niki came back into the kitchen and poured herself a glass of iced tea, Mavis quizzed her: *Niki dear, why do you have a ragged old wagon on my patio? I'm sorry but that pealing paint thing looks just plain tacky.* When Niki made no reply, Mavis added: *By the way, I tidied up your clothes closet a bit. And dear, beige is really not a fashion color, you know. Too indecisive.*

Niki took her tea and sat at the kitchen table. She mentally measured the stacks of old bills and receipts she'd vowed to reduce to only what was needed, and had to admit the pile was not smaller. Have I not thrown away anything? Jack's cardboard box with Mavis' memories sat beside the offending piles. A faint voice of guilt told her to deal with the old bills. Curiosity drove her to open the box. She spread the papers out on the table, and turned on the overhead light to brighten the smudged typing. Even though she told herself that she should be feeling like a voyeur, she hoped that Mavis' story about Dell Ritter would continue. A tiny wave of excitement rolled over her when she read Dell Ritter's name on the first page.

*Dell left for Candler Field around 4:00 in the morning–in a taxicab. He knew better than to plan life around Brother Frank and his black Ford.* But what happened between dark and 4:00? To this day I am still a softie for a rainy night and music on the radio. Here is how I remember that night.

The house was dark except for the kitchen where we sat at Mama's table. We'd talked through the afternoon. He taught me to play solitaire with a deck of cards he usually kept in his jacket pocket. And I believe we danced a little to the music on the radio. In fact, I believe we danced more than a little to the radio–slow dancing and swaying, learning each others' moves around the tiny kitchen. I cooked eggs, fried ham, and made biscuits for supper. Dell washed the dishes.

I'd never seen a man wash dishes before and haven't seen many do it since. I was drying and putting them away and I guess he was talked out because he had been quiet for a while. Bessie Smith's throaty voice crooned from the radio, "When I see two sweethearts spoon…underneath the silvery moon …it makes my love come down." Bessie knew how to tell a story with a song.

I'd only kissed one boy before, a kiss not worth writing home about and an experience I didn't think I cared to repeat. But by the time Bessie brought up the idea with her song, I wanted to kiss that slim man who could wash dishes, smelled of saddle-soaped leather, and made me laugh at his tall tales.

Whether it was the dancing, Dell, the rain, or my own loneliness, listening to Bessie I knew exactly how she felt and was just as hungry as she must have been for a kiss and what came next. I know Dell wanted to kiss me, too, because he did kiss me. Kissed me with such tenderness and longing that it took my breath away. With my back pressed against the kitchen cupboard, I leaned into his kiss, feeling his mouth and body coax against me like the pull of an ocean wave.

Sounds sappy maybe, but it's true. I know he was ten years older and probably ran illegal whiskey for my brother. I didn't care. No doubt he seduced me with his Texas talk and sweet dancing, probably planned it the whole time we were sitting there drinking coffee, probably planned it before he even met me, when he was buying that silky kimono. None of that mattered then, and it doesn't matter now.

It was my time. Something about Del got right up against the closed door of my loneliness, and that big empty room had less of an echo when we were together. We made slow love on a quilt spread down on the living room floor, Dell covering my body with baby oil and pleasing me like a man whose pleasure grows from giving.

"Honey," I remember him saying, "why didn't you tell me you were a virgin? I hope I didn't hurt you none. I wouldn't hurt you for the world. I took Fern to be your baby."

I put a finger to his mouth, "Shh. It's all right. Fern's my baby sister. I thought Frank would have told you. You didn't hurt me, Dell. I'm glad it was you, my first time and all." And I was glad. After all these years and what I know now about sex and men, I'm still glad Dell showed up that rainy afternoon. We drifted off to sleep that night under the glow of the street lamp on the living room window shades. When I woke a little after four, Dell was gone.

A note, written on the white butcher paper my Kimono came in was on the kitchen table. "Mavis Honey, I'm going on out to Candler Field to see about my plane. Maybe get on to Miami. I'll take you with me in my heart. Don't get mad at me because I'm leaving you some money. I know you got to be having a hard time. If you'll have me, I want to see you again. Love, Dell"

A twenty-dollar bill was showing from under the sugar bowl. In 1928, twenty dollars seemed like a lot of money. In fact it was a lot of money to me. At first I *was* angry he left the money. Then I read the note again and was touched by his understanding of how hard life was for us. I had to work almost two weeks at the mill to earn twenty dollars. In the end I told myself the money was a gift. I hadn't earned it. For a few seconds, I did question how Dell could make that kind of money flying airplanes, but my hope that he would come back blew those thoughts to the wind. Smuggling illegal whiskey or bringing in contraband Cuban cigars, it didn't matter to me so long as he found his way back to Moody Street.

The loving was always good with Dell. He was never in a hurry and careful to please. Always left a twenty-dollar bill under the sugar bowl, sometimes two. The unspoken agreement was he would leave what he could, and I wouldn't mention it. That first Christmas he gave me almond shaped pearl earrings, set off with lovely little diamonds. They are my favorite earrings and I still wear them, especially when I want to remember the good times with Dell. When Dell was there, my body sang with pleasure and my mind was at ease. I would have let Dell Ritter lead me anywhere.

A little over a year after Dell gave me the pearl earrings, he stopped coming to Moody Street—no notes, no letters, no nothing. I held on to hope as long as I could, but hope wouldn't bring Dell back. That spring, Frank casually mentioned Dell had crashed his Curtis CX-5 back during the winter. He had been crop dusting a farmer's cotton field somewhere in south Mississippi, or so Frank said. Except, I didn't think crop dusting was done in the winter. I'll never know for sure. It could have happened. Dell could have died. I just don't know.

I could never trust Frank to tell the truth about much of anything. Maybe Dell just got tired of me and moved on to another girl. I don't know. I just know I missed Del and when he didn't come back my heart felt about as sick as it did when my daddy died. Dell was kind to me. There was no meanness at all about him. Good company, and a good man. Loving him was easy. Nothing would be that easy again.

Niki stopped reading and took a deep breath to hold back her tears. "Oh no," she heard herself say aloud. She closed her eyes and pressed her fingers to her eyelids to compose herself, and after a few seconds, opened her eyes and counted the pages left unread. Satisfied the story was almost over, she decided she had to finish Mavis' story about Dell Ritter.

*When I stopped counting the days and accepted that Dell was gone, I felt alone again in a world of strangers. It was as though I heard and saw those around me from a great distance.* I went through the days and nights in a haze of sorrow for months, but I was too young to roll up and die from the pain. Life has a way of tugging you back with the tide and washing you up on the shore to deal with living. Fortunately, I had saved a little over nine hundred dollars. I say fortunate because by late 1929 the mill was laying off workers, and the whole American economy was crashing down around us.

When the mill went to half-days and the supervisor gave my job to a friend of his–because, my boss said, the man had a family to support and needed the job more than I did–I took Dell's money, and a case of Frank's best Canadian whiskey, and Ellis and I went into business proving what he'd said years before. Find out what folks want, what they're willing to pay good money for, and you have the makings of successful business.

Certainly, we weren't the only hard-up folks in Atlanta, or in the country, for that matter, who came to that conclusion. Since Prohibition became law, and even the beer breweries were shut down, it seemed Americans wanted to drink more than ever. I guess that's the way we are; tell us we can't have something and we'll move heaven and earth to get it. Prohibition had transformed Brother Frank from a small time bootlegger into a successful distributor with import sources for a variety of Canadian whiskeys and Bahamian rum. I think the rum, and the high priced branded whiskey, was smuggled in ships moored off Savannah harbor. I also heard that after Dell died, Frank had another pilot flying back and forth to Cuba for him. Back in those days, Cuba was a high-priced playground for partying and gambling. Most anything you wanted was for sale, at a price, in Cuba. Of course, Brother Frank never shared his business plan with me, and I knew better than to ask, so I'm just guessing about how the whiskey got to Atlanta.

The years between the enactment of Prohibition in the early twenties, and its repeal in 1935 were like a world upside down. How can something be okay one day, and illegal the next? I mean slapping high taxes on liquor was one thing, but to pass a law saying even drinking whiskey was wrong, and illegal, was a whole different matter. I think most folks were glad when the amendment was repealed. After that, being wet or dry was decided by a countywide vote—at least that's the way it was in Georgia.

Of course, any changes in the whiskey laws didn't seem to slow Frank's business down. So far as I know, he continued to make money on whiskey by either avoiding the taxes on the product, or bootlegging the product into dry counties until the early 1950s. And I admit Ellis and I bought our share from Brother Frank right up until the day I got word that Ellis had been killed out in Oklahoma. That was the day I closed the business.

Niki frowned and re-read the last paragraphs. What was Mavis saying? Did she mean they were selling whiskey from the Moody Street house? Aunt Mavis' house was a 1920s speakeasy? Mavis and Ellis ran a speakeasy? Surely not.

Niki knew the family story from her mother about Grandfather Frank being a bootlegger, but her mother didn't gossip about Mavis. She and Aunt Mavis were friends and Niki's mother depended on Mavis for some measure of stability in her daughter's life. As she recalled, her mother only talked about Mavis and her life after she married Dr. Martin Book. Niki wondered if perhaps her mother didn't know about the business at Moody Street. Didn't know what Mavis did before she purchased the large boarding house on Baker Street, and began to buy and sell antiques. Maybe her mother didn't know Mavis, or any of the Banks family, until they lived at Baker Street.

Niki tried to recall how her mother had met her father? Had her mother been a boarder in the Baker Street house? No, wait, that wasn't right. She thought her mother had lived at home with her parents until she met and married Frank Banks, Junior. Niki remembered the story now. They'd met by chance at the Woolworth's lunch counter in Atlanta when her mother worked at Rich's department store. At least Niki thought that was what her mother had said. Or did Aunt Mavis tell her that story? Yes, probably Aunt Mavis. Mother didn't talk about either of the Banks men.

Niki contemplated asking Jack about Mavis and Ellis' whiskey business on Moody Street. How much did he know about their illegal business? She was undecided. Bringing up that part of his dad's life might tarnish Jack's memory. She wouldn't want to do that to Jack. Turning back a page, she read the part again about Dell Ritter not coming back, and then tossed the pages on the table. Gone, gone, no word at all. Her face scrunched into a frown.

Oh Mavis, I'm so sorry for your pain. You say you were lonely, but there must have been more. Anger? Yes, I would have been angry. Weren't there nights of tears? Fists pounding against your pillow? Nausea that made eating impossible? Wanting to lash out at something? Or someone? To love a man so passionately, and for him to simply disappear? No calls, no letters? And for Frank to let you suffer for months before he told you Dell was dead–why would he do that? I would have wanted to kill Frank with my bare hands.

Mavis settled her hands on Niki's shoulders and rested her cheek on top of her niece's head. *There are no words for the despair I felt, Niki. No words. But we endure.*

Niki sat for a moment, listening to her own heartbeat, then wiped her eyes with the backs of her hands and went out to the garden. Mavis followed, watching her, as she paced off her vegetable rows, taking mental note of the progress, and turned on the hose at the spigot. Niki's mind stayed on Mavis, Dell Ritter, and the nature of passion and loss.

I've never loved a man like that. I don't think I'm capable of it. Where does so much passion come from? I've chosen badly, twice. Better not to choose again. I've learned to live with the loneliness. But the pain? That kind of pain never goes away, does it? Never a day that the memory doesn't wake, if only for an instant, to rise up and prick your heart. I do know about pain.

Niki dragged the garden hose from row to row, soaking each plant. Her wounded heart wandered, and she had no choice but to follow. I wanted to love Lyn like Mavis loved Dell Ritter. I do remember that. I craved the release of so much stored up longing and kept thinking, hoping, it was coming. But it was always later, after one thing or another happened, our lives could be different. Then the "thing" Lyn decided he wanted most was a baby. He was desperate for a child. A child would make us… make us complete. In the end it all went so wrong, so wrong.

Niki moved along the garden plants, salty tears swelling and then dropping to mingle with the water from the hose, falling on spinach, kale, purple lettuce, and tomatoes. She willed herself not to replay the gradual crumbling of her marriage after the baby died, not to remember the fights and accusations thrown like tight bundles of barbed wired. It's done and over. I do not want a man who could blame me. Where is the love in blame? She sniffed back the tears and watered her plants. Experience told her she wouldn't cry forever, that the pain would find a crack in her heart to hide for another day.

Niki's tears upended Mavis' uneasy peace with the way Dell's story had ended. In truth, pain from her lost love still replayed from time to time in her heart like one of her old songs: "kiss me once, kiss me twice, kiss me once again, it's been a long, long time." *Put it away*, Mavis told herself. The last thing she wanted on this fine spring day was to engage in a sympathy bawl with her niece. How could she stop Niki's crying?

In a desperate attempt at distraction, Mavis flew into the flowering Bradford pear tree and shook a limb. White blossoms rained down on Niki. At first she startled and looked up into the tree, then she opened her hands to the parachuting blossoms sailing down from the sky. Her tears stopped, and after she dried her eyes with the tail of her shirt, she announced to the garden, "And there you are. Another April, another spring."

*Exactly*, Mavis called out and stepped from the tree limb to the ground. *My point exactly. Another April.* Suddenly, a wide yawn, and then a second smaller yawn, both drawn from the warm afternoon sun, took Mavis' breath away. Her eyes closed for a moment, sunlight danced through prisms behind her eyelids.

*I'm sorry, Niki. I believe I'm leaving now. Blue tides and sleep are calling me. It's so lovely there. Swaying lights above …twinkling… globes…whales sing, you know, calling us all to sleep… and…*

Niki thought she heard a familiar tune drift from the kitchen radio out into the garden–kiss me once, kiss me twice– but by the time she'd cut off the hose to listen, the music had stopped. The only sound she heard was an excited squirrel fussing from a pine tree, and the ever-present hum of traffic along Ponce de Leon Avenue. Everyone's trying to get home, Niki was thinking, everyone.

# Sixteen

A little later in the day Niki picked through the cardboard box again. Following Dell's story, she found a handful of unreadable pages and then several that were smudged, but not charred. She began reading, not knowing what Mavis had written on the ruined pages that came before.

Yes, we were a success. There is no denying that. In the beginning, Bucky Mitchell, his Georgia Tech friends, and their extended friends were our clients. Those college boys liked partying at Moody Street and not having to haunt the west end of Atlanta for bootleg whiskey. Then, a short time after Bucky dumped Marie for a fresh debutante from Thomasville, we began to attract an older, more settled crowd.

I think it was Judge "Benny" Renfroe who stopped by one night to see where his son was spending his allowance, and then returned with his businessmen friends to play poker in the front room and drink Frank's Canadian import. It was also Benny Renfroe who later heard the Baker Street property was being sold by Fulton National Bank at a give-away-price because it needed repairs, and because the upfront cash to open a large boarding house wasn't something most folks had at that time. Fulton National Bank wouldn't make us the loan to buy the property, so we went to Ellis' old mentor, Mr. Herndon, who asked no questions about our ability to operate a boarding house. He knew the location near downtown was a gold mine, regardless. Smart man.

But back to Moody Street, and 1931. Having older businessmen and politicians call at Moody Street was a double blessing. They spent money generously, and we were assured the Atlanta police would leave us alone. Of course, there were the usual threats in the newspaper that local law enforcement was on the hunt for illegal whiskey suppliers, but we didn't worry too much about that. Every bootlegger in Atlanta, including Frank and his partner, knew where cash across the palm would insure a blind eye.

Of course, some years later The Atlanta Journal, and The Constitution, teased readers every day with hints of police raids on "known places of organized crime in Atlanta." I don't know about the organized part. The most organized crime I ever saw in Atlanta was between dirty politicians in the state legislature and lobbyists buying new road contracts. Now those guys were "organized." But were they part of some Yankee crime syndicate? I seriously doubt it. I don't think any of us would have trucked much Yankee interference from the Mafia types up North. We were, by and large, typical freelancing Scots-Irish Southerners who are not known for being team players—unless it involves football, or baseball. Anyway, from what I recall, Atlanta in the 1930s and 1940s belonged to those of us who called our beautiful city home, and not Yankee mobsters.

Niki stopped reading, put the papers on the stack in the box and replaced the top. This was not the Aunt Mavis she remembered. First Dell Ritter and now this….the Mavis she remembered lived with her husband, Dr. Martin Book, a respected physician, on Cherokee Place. Their profitable side business was buying and selling antiques and art, not whiskey. Niki had learned the difference between Queen Anne and

Sheridan furniture styles from Mavis, and how to tell period Chinese porcelain from English reproductions. Bootleg whiskey, or organized crime, had *never* come up in the conversation with Aunt Mavis when Niki was growing up.

She sat for a moment, frowning, and tapping Jack's envelope of old photographs on the table. Inside the envelope, smaller photos dropped between her fingers to the bottom, inviting her to open the envelope again and take a look. Who knows? The Moody Street crowd might stare from the black and white prints. She was curious, yet…Niki rejected the invitation and tossed the envelope aside. Her frown deepened.

Maybe I should not have read any of it. Why would Mavis feel the need to write about this after so many years? Why would she think I needed to know? Niki questioned if she was the only one ignorant about Mavis' life before Dr. Book. Did Jack know?

Niki searched the piles of old bills and receipts for Jack's note to re-read it. Ah, that's what I thought. He says he hasn't read any of the papers. So, he may also be in the dark about the Moody Street business. Though why would he bother to pull the papers out of the fire, if he didn't want to read them? And if he hasn't read Mavis' papers, how much did Mavis tell him, and how much does he remember? Mavis and Marie lived on Moody Street long before Jack was born. Jack's mother was a baby when they lived there. I know he remembers living at Baker Street because he talked about that house a bit at the cemetery. He said that he and his dad lived in an apartment over the garage. Niki tossed Jack's note on the table. I don't want to think about any of this right now.

She took her tea out on the screened porch and picked up the Sue Grafton novel. Better to replace her own shifting reality with Kinsey Millhone's life. The clever story line worked for a while, until the muffled tick-tock of the kitchen clock reminded her she was alone in the house, with only her unsettled thoughts for company. Jack's in Athens overnight. How long has he been back in Atlanta? Three weeks? Is it May already? What have we settled in the past three weeks? Nothing. We can't just rock along like this. Arguing one minute, trying to be civil the next. I need resolution to this house thing. One of us has to move out.

Abelard chirped from the bedroom and Niki left the porch, grateful to occupy her mind with the task of feeding and caring for him. After she visited with the aged canary, and assured him he was the "prettiest bird ever," she decided to carry a lawn chair to the front yard. Outside, she unfolded the green and white webbed chair and sat facing the front of the house where the fading afternoon sun played a glorious trick of the light, transforming the cream colored stucco to pearl pink.

This particular magic was revealed to her long ago, late on a hot summer's afternoon when she was visiting Cherokee Place. She and Aunt Mavis sat watching the color change often that summer, drinking lemonade sprigged with fresh mint and finding no need for words. Niki remembered Mavis could be like that, comfortable with the silence, making no demands, allowing an awkward sixteen year-old girl space to grow into herself. Remembering those lazy summers, Niki searched her memory for Jack. Was he already in college at the University of Florida? Yes, she recalled Jack was living in Tallahassee, taking summer classes to graduate early. Which summer was it that she'd suffered from a teenage crush on the handsome Jack Rainwater? Niki grimaced with embarrassment from the recollection of how foolish she must have seemed. Jack, of course, ostentatiously ignored her on his trips home that summer.

As she relaxed in the lawn chair and watched afternoon shadows lengthen, snippets of her past popped to mind like soap bubbles–bits and pieces of the collage that was her life. She saw Mama and Aunt Mavis reclining in chaise lounges around a pool, laughing, and sipping drinks from sweaty glasses while she played in the chlorine-laced water. Where was that? Oh yes, Jekyll Island. She didn't remember the name of the hotel, but knew it was on the beach and she was seven, or eight, and made a new friend named Kitty that summer. They fished for crab off the pier and Mama bought her pink sunglasses with huge, heart-shaped lenses.

Then there was school…Mama sitting at a teacher's conference, serious about the importance of a good education for her only daughter. All the valentines she and Mama made from construction paper, old ribbons, and glitter from Woolworth's for her to take to school, always careful not to leave out any classmates. Her first prom dress: shimmering purple taffeta with a sassy, white ruffle around the skirt. Mama made it for her. Niki thought it was the most beautiful dress at the prom. High school graduation: Aunt Mavis, Dr. Book, and Mama sitting together, second row, smiling.

Another summer at Aunt Mavis' house–Jack drove up from Florida in his yellow Volkswagen Karman Ghia, looking like a movie star in his aviator sunglasses. He was working for a Tallahassee newspaper. Niki was at Georgia State College by then. They grilled hotdogs outside, Dr. Book trying to look casual over the barbecue in his white dress shirt, red bowtie, and suspenders. By late fall of that year her mother was in the hospital. Dying. The person Niki called was Aunt Mavis.

A realization as clear as mountain spring water washed over Niki. Aside from the occasional freshly bruised feeling that her father was absent, and curiosity about a man she vaguely remembered, named Frank Banks, Junior, Niki didn't think of her father very often any more. The fact was that her daily life growing up was not altered to any great degree by his absence. His place in her life had been filled with all the everyday memories that make a child's life, and she was, at least most of the time, simply too busy growing up to realize she lacked anything major in her life.

And at those times when she did think of her father, she admitted that what shamed her was that he had failed. Failed her, failed her mother, and failed himself. He wasn't strong enough to stay sober, be a loving father, and support his family. From that realization it was a short step across a very deep abyss to remember that what she had worried most about growing up was if she would become like her father. Was she in danger of falling down the same rabbit hole as her drunken father?

But I haven't fallen she assured herself, as Mavis' cream-colored house glowed with afternoon magic and turned into a pearl pink. Niki felt a silly urge to jump out of the chair, up into the air, and raise her arms in a cheer. But, of course, she wouldn't do such an immature, spontaneous thing. She would affirm silently though that she was not like her father. She was like her mother. We endure. Mavis always said that, Niki remembered. And I have survived. I am tougher than my father. As Niki congratulated herself for beating the alcoholism gene and escaping failure, she thought she heard Aunt Mavis laughing and chide, "Thanks to your mama."

A friendly, "Hello, hello," brought Niki to her feet. She turned to see Mavis' neighbor, Terry Spiegel, standing on the sidewalk, Panama straw hat covering his thinning gray hair, and sunglasses shading his eyes. It was only the first day of May but Mr. Spiegel was already beach-frocked in madras plaid walking shorts and sandals.

His white Scottie dog, Winston, unhappy his walk was put on pause, jumped up and down like a windup toy. Terry reached down and patted the dog. "Take a break, Winston. I'll speak to the lady and we'll be on our way." The dog ignored him and continued to jump up and down. "Fine day," Terry said and tipped his hat to her. Niki replied that it was, and Terry smiled. "Watching the color go to pink, are you?"

Niki nodded yes, ready to ask how he knew about the color changing, but he tipped his hat again and walked on down the sidewalk. "If you're still out," Terry called over his shoulder, "I'll stop and visit after Winston has his walkie."

Niki smiled and waved, thinking every old man needs a little dog to tell him what to do. Before she could sit down again a white Mercedes convertible, top down, drove slowly past, turned around at the end of the street, and returned to park in the drive. She felt a flush of anxiety when she recognized the driver as the man who had approached Jack at the restaurant. She folded the chair and held it in front of her, hoping she looked like a person on her way inside, with no time to chat.

The blond haired man flashed an insincere smile of perfect white teeth. Too perfect. When he extended his hand, she held tight to the metal chair and pretended she'd not noticed the gesture. He said something she didn't catch. No matter. Niki disliked him on sight and wanted him off the property as soon as possible. "You've missed Jack. No idea when he'll return." She turned to make it to the front door before he could respond.

Too late–he stopped her with, "Actually I'd hoped to see you. Catherine Banks, right?"

She turned to face him again. "What was your name again? I didn't catch it."

His smug look showed he felt he had the advantage, though Niki couldn't imagine why. "Ham Rabonette. Rabonette and Rabonette Realty, in Decatur."

He offered a card. She took it and put it in her pocket without looking. "Why do you want to see me?"

"I understand you and Mr. Rainwater own the Martin Book property jointly. I have a proposition for you. Why don't we go inside and discuss it?" He took a couple of steps in the direction of the house.

Niki didn't move and resisted the urge to say the house had belonged to Aunt Mavis since Martin Book gave it to her as a wedding gift. Surely the man knew that. "You will need to call and make an appointment when Jack is here. I have other plans at the moment."

His smile contracted to a defiant look Niki had once seen on a rat cornered by the garbage can outside her old apartment. "Ah, I understand," he replied. Niki thought he probably did understand, but also determined not to be brushed off. "Unfortunately, I've been unsuccessful in getting Mr. Rainwater's attention. I thought you might be more reasonable." He extracted a folded paper from his jacket breast pocket and held it out to her.

She took it, unfolded it, and saw that it was a sales contract. The property being purchased was 24 Cherokee Place. The price was four hundred and fifty thousand dollars. Niki turned the paper over to the back. She couldn't read the would-be purchaser's name. "Why would you think this house is for sale?"

He extended his hands palms up. The smug smile returned. "Everything is for sale at the right price. Don't you agree?"

Niki didn't answer. She glanced quickly at his face again, being careful not to make eye contact, and folded the contract and slid it into her back pocket along with his card. Smarmy was the word that came to mind. Her thoughts bounced back to Jack. *He must know this man is out trying to sell our house. Why hasn't he told me about it? Though from what this Rabonette guy says, Jack isn't interested in selling. Wonder why? Maybe selling would be the answer. Both of us take our half and move elsewhere. Maybe that's what he wants to talk about when he gets back from Athens.* She realized Rabonette was saying something.

"So don't discount our offer too quickly, Ms. Banks. You could purchase a very nice home of your own with your part. Perhaps back in Roswell."

Niki wondered, *how does this Rabonette guy know I moved from Roswell?*

"And you'd be over having to deal with Mr. Rainwater. I'm sure the whole joint ownership arrangement has been difficult for you."

*How does he know what's been difficult for me?*

"Believe me, I understand a partnership between two such different people can be rocky, to be sure, especially since Mr. Rainwater isn't exactly, well…shall we say our kind of person."

Niki heard Rabonette's last remark loud and clear. She snapped back, before thinking. "What the hell do you mean by that?"

Rabonette did the hands-out- palms-up thing again. She wondered what real estate class taught him that annoying gesture. He went on, picking his words carefully, "No offense intended. It's just that he's more of a… vagabond, yes that's the word… not a Cherokee Place kind of person. I'm sure you've noticed we're pretty much established, old Atlanta people around here."

"We?"

He took a step closer to her. "Oh, we're practically neighbors, you see. The Rabonette family has owned a home on the street behind you for many years–since before there were any homes built on Cherokee Place. This whole street used to be our back yard. My daddy, and my granddaddy, played back here as children."

As she was thinking she cared less than nothing about where his good old granddaddy had played, Niki recalled that Rabonette had looked familiar to her when she saw him at Doc Cheys. Perhaps she'd only seem him around the neighborhood. It didn't matter. She didn't like the man and her focus returned to getting him out of the front yard and into his white Mercedes. "I'll discuss your offer with Jack. We'll call you if we're interested." She turned away from Rabonette and took a couple of steps.

"Ms. Banks," he called after her, "don't reject the contract outright. You could counter with a somewhat higher price. Not a lot, mind you, but a few thousand perhaps. Call me. I assure you the purchaser is highly motivated."

Niki turned back to Rabonette and tried to read the look on his face. She thought she sensed an emotion other than simple greed, but she couldn't name what it was. After a few seconds of playing the he-who-speaks-first-looses-mind-game, Ham Rabonette got in his convertible and drove up Cherokee Place to Ponce de Leon Avenue.

Winston's barking and Terry Spiegel being pulled down the sidewalk by the excited Scottie diverted Niki. Terry reined the dog in and stopped at the driveway. "What does Ham Rabonette want? A pound of flesh? Gallon of blood?"

Niki laughed. "So you know him. Come closer and tell me all."

Terry crossed the grass to Niki, dog in tow, and replied. "To tell all, I'll require a vodka martini with a twist, maybe two."

When he heard no objection from Niki, he smiled. "Winston and I will wait for you in the back garden. We are only allowed on the screened porch and in the yard. Mavis would haunt me for sure if I took Winston into her frou-frou house."

"Okay. Relax out back and I'll try to remember how to make a martini."

"Good Lord woman, were you raised in a barn? If you don't know how, just bring out the vodka, ice, and lemon. Forget the vermouth."

Pale gray morning doves cooed in the trees above as the two sat amicably in twilight on the slate-stone patio. Winston reclined at his owner's feet and eyed Niki's fledgling vegetables with interest. "I'll keep his lead tied to my chair. Wouldn't want your hard work to be wiped out by a digging little dog."

Niki reached down and rubbed Winston behind the ears, though he was more interested in watching the garden, especially when a young squirrel switched his tail and rooted among the kale plants for stray seeds. "I'm thinking of hanging a bird feeder to divert predators like that little squirrel away from the garden."

Terry drained his martini and poured himself another from the pitcher on the table between them. "Good idea. Unfortunately, the neighborhood is rampant with predators, which brings me to Hamilton Rabonette, IV. Or is he a III? I forget."

Niki toasted Terry with her iced tea and said, "Very clever. I'm listening. What do you know about him?"

"The question is: What do you know about him?"

"Other than he looks familiar, and he tried to talk to Jack at Doc Cheys restaurant a few days ago—Jack brushed him off, by the way—and he just handed me a sales contract for our house—which is not for sale, so far as I know—I'm clueless about the man. So tell me everything."

She thought Terry paused for a moment, as though weighing the word *everything* for thorns, before replying, "Then everything it is. I love good gossip. The story begins with one Navarro Rabon, a merchant—and I use the term loosely—of Spanish-French descent whose family settled in Savannah, probably coming from Florida, just after slavery was made legal in Georgia in 1751. Did you know that when James Oglethorpe settled Georgia, he vowed there would be no rum, lawyers, or slaves allowed in the new colony?"

Niki gave her storyteller an incredulous look. "Is that really true?"

"Oh yes, didn't you learn that in Georgia history? Oglethorpe brought over predominately poor English settlers, with a few Irish mixed in, many of them released from English debtors' prisons, or in danger of being sent there, in exchange for becoming settlers to the new world. Oglethorpe believed the colony's wellbeing was most probable without those three evils. Reckoning, I suppose, that it was the lawyers and rum that had ruined the poor folk's lives originally, and that depending on slaves would corrupt the economic system of small farming. Sadly, men being what we are, Oglethorpe's vow was soon broken and the three evils proliferated with wild abandon in our beloved Georgia.

"Anyway, after Abraham Lincoln deleted the Navarro family's mode of livelihood with the stroke of the Presidential pen, the patriarch Navarro waited out the Civil War with his Georgia slave trade earnings. Soon afterwards, he added the "ette" on his name—to become more French, and presumably more civilized—and hauled the family inland to middle Georgia for new opportunities.

"Old Navarro was a shrewd businessman and he had something most people didn't–federal currency. Sherman, you will remember, burned Atlanta to the ground and destroyed every cash crop from here to Savannah. Farms were sold for pennies on the dollar when the owners couldn't use Confederate money to pay loans, buy seeds, or replant crops. Navarro bought farm after farm from hard-pressed owners and became an absentee landowner, collecting rents from the sweat of sharecroppers.

"When his son, the first Hamilton Rabonette, came of age, he sold, traded, stole, or bartered the farms into properties closer to Atlanta. And by the time the grandfather of that little weasel who visited you today was born, the family was in what we used to call here in the South, *high cotton*. The Weasel's daddy came of age during the late forties and early fifties, just as I did, and was visible around Atlanta as the spoiled rich kid. He played a lot of tennis and enjoyed the fruits of the real estate fortune the previous Rabonette men had built. I've always wondered how Rabonette fared so well during the depression years. There was talk that the weasel's granddaddy was part of the illegal whiskey business, but who knows? That claim was made about just about everyone who prospered during those years."

"And what about now?" Niki asked, "How well does the weasel do?"

"Well, I'm mostly out of the gossip loop since I'm semi-retired, but as far as I know, the real estate business is good for the weasel. His daddy had several strokes and then died two or three years ago, so I guess he has all the marbles in the game now. The Rabonettes have owned that huge brick Georgian on Seminole Road, just behind our street, since the late eighteen hundreds."

"I think he mentioned Cherokee Place was his family's back yard at one time."

Terry helped himself to a third martini and made a disgusted *harrumph* sound. Niki wondered if perhaps she would need to carry her good-natured, and tipsy, neighbor home in her wheelbarrow. "Terry, how do you know so much about the Rabonettes?"

He wagged his finger at her and half-closed one eye, "Big secret, young lady."

"Oh come on. Tell me or no more martinis."

"Oh okay. You talked me into it. I'm fascinated with genealogy. Have all sorts of records and papers from early Atlanta families. It's sort of like legal spying. Probably a hold over from spending so many years as one of those evil lawyers Oglethorpe sought to keep out of Georgia. When Martin Book died and the weasel's daddy started hounding Mavis to sell out, I got interested in him and began a search. I'm sure I turned up a lot of juicy information. I've probably forgotten most of it. That was years ago."

"And you shared what you learned with Aunt Mavis?"

Waving his martini-free hand in the air, Terry groused, "No, actually I didn't. Mavis was a regular spoiled sport about the whole thing–said she knew more than she wanted to know about the Rabonettes already. Refused to listen to any of the good dirt I'd dug up. I was crushed. I had all this juicy gossip and no ear to listen to it."

"Why were the Rabonettes so intent on our house being sold?"

"Don't know. Mavis said she thought the bastard couldn't sleep nights knowing she was here. Whatever that meant. I've lived on Cherokee Place since 1950. Knew Martin Book before they married. Played bridge every other Thursday with him. We were great pals. Never heard any talk from him about Rabonette trying to get him to sell the place before he and Mavis married. You know, now that I think about it, old Rabonette and the weasel were at the funeral."

"Dr. Book's funeral?"

"No, Mavis' funeral. I can't remember who was at Martin's. Too long ago. Maybe that's why Rabonette looks familiar to you. His dad was the old man in the wheelchair. The weasel was pushing him around."

The scene came back. She was doing the polite greet the guests thing, speaking to everyone. She thanked the man in the wheelchair for coming and he said something strange to her. Repeated it two or three times. What had he said? "Ferns in the mud," Niki said, aloud. "He said it twice at the funeral. 'Ferns in the mud.' I'm sure."

When Terry leaned forward in the light metal chair, he nearly toppled over. "What? 'Ferns in the mud?' You mean old man Rabonette said that?"

It didn't make sense, but Niki was sure that was what he'd said. She nodded, yes.

Terry sat back in his chair, sloshing martini on his plaid shorts. "Well, that makes absolutely no god-damn sense at all, but what do you expect? His brain was probably scrambled from the stroke. I can't imagine why he even came to Mavis' funeral."

Niki agreed with Terry. Why were the Rabonettes at the funeral? It isn't as though they were friends with Aunt Mavis. Terry stumbled to his feet and untied Winston from the leg of his lawn chair. "It has been fun gossiping with you, but I have to tell you, I'm half drunk as a opossum on jimson weed. I better toddle home before I do, or say, something embarrassing. So what are you doing with the rest of your evening?"

Standing, she took her neighbor's arm to steady him. "I'm reading a good murder mystery."

Terry got his sea legs after a couple of steps forward. "I love murder mysteries. Once I went to a costume party as Agatha Christie–gray wig, forties-styled shantung dress, stack-heeled, black pumps. Even carried around one of her books–probably *Murder on The Orient Express*. No one guessed what character I was supposed to be. But it was fun. Went about the party for hours until my fancy wig fell into the salmon pate and someone recognized me. Damn funny. Should've seen me. Quite the queen in my day."

Thinking she'd not heard him correctly, Niki asked, "What did you say?"

"Nothing. Just rambling. Be careful of The Weasel, dear. He's a prick without conscience. And those are the worst sort."

# *Seventeen*

After a muddled sleep disturbed by a dream of wandering lost and panic stricken in a dark parking garage, keys in hand but not able to find her car, Niki was out of bed and dressed by eight o'clock. She sat at the kitchen table drinking coffee heavily laced with half and half, Jack's box with Mavis' unread pages at her elbow. She contemplated going ahead and reading the last pages, but decided she didn't feel up to any more surprises about Aunt Mavis this early in the morning. As she sipped the soothing coffee, Niki closed her eyes, trying to visualize her aunt as a speakeasy owner. No. Her mind would not wrap around the idea.

Wasn't it Aunt Mavis who was fond of telling her, don't live your life by default? Through the morning fog camping out in her brain, she heard Mavis' words from the letter she'd written to her. *As for me, I don't ask for forgiveness. I did what I felt was necessary.* Slowly stirring the rich brown liquid in her cup, Niki turned the words over again. Was Aunt Mavis making a statement about her speakeasy business? Saying she'd chosen that life over one dealt to her by default? Niki considered the question. Movies, documentaries, and magazine articles about the prohibition years played across her mind. The anti-liquor laws made criminals of thousands. After a few years, Congress realized the folly of the constitutional amendment and repealed it. Niki tried again, but still couldn't place Aunt Mavis in the picture with other Prohibition criminals.

Instead, Niki focused on her new writing project. The color brochure for the Georgia Department of Natural Resources would advertise a suburban Atlanta wildlife area located near her old apartment in Roswell. Because the task was somewhat "out of the box" for her, Niki was excited and also nervous about the piece. She wanted the client to love her presentation, and was willing to do what she needed to understand the variety of animals and plants living in the outer edge of suburbia. Niki had no camping or hiking experience; had always lived in an apartment, except for the times at Aunt Mavis' house on Cherokee Place, and her knowledge of wildlife was confined to visiting the Atlanta zoo. Getting up to speed on Georgia wildlife was a challenge.

Nevertheless, Niki was enthusiastic. She'd checked out several helpful books from the library—wood ducks are different from black ducks, they are called Canada geese, not called Canadian geese, and cottontail rabbits and swamp rabbits thrive in the area. White tailed deer know to avoid the poisonous copperhead snakes. Most snakes are shy and are helpful in keeping the rodent population in check. Niki wasn't confident about the shy snakes concept, but decided she would visit the area to check her facts, and to get a feel for the location. All in all, writing a brochure for the DNR felt much more challenging than a weed-eater manual or a pamphlet to explain a new drug for psoriasis.

She let her mind wander into an imaginary Georgia forest, spotting a muskrat, or perhaps it was a river otter, then a group of wild turkeys. Maybe Jack would like to go with me to investigate the wildlife area. We could take a picnic. She immediately felt foolish for thinking Jack would care. After all, he'd traveled all over the world and seen many more exotic animals than a Georgia wood duck. Besides, we don't get on well enough to spend an entire day together in the woods. One of us would probably try to drown the other in a beaver pond.

She looked around the kitchen, feeling a heavy quiet. It must be the silent radio, she decided. Usually it's playing music from the oldies station. With one hand trailing across Jack's cardboard box, she got up and crossed to the refrigerator to switch on the radio nesting on top. *The box*, she remembered, I really should finish reading the papers and be done with it. Still, she hesitated, not sure she wanted to know any more about Mavis.

When the radio weatherman predicted rain and possible thunderstorms moving into Atlanta from the Southwest, she decided to drive over to Hastings Nursery before the weather turned ugly. Rummaging for her car keys on the table, she found the sales contract from Rabonette. Four hundred fifty thousand dollars, and maybe more, he'd said. What could she do with her half of so much money?

She poured herself a half-cup of coffee and contemplated the sales contract. Sure, Rabonette was a jerk, but money is money. He was right about one thing. With her half she could buy a very nice house in the suburbs. Though a house in the suburbs probably wouldn't have ten-foot ceilings like the Cherokee Place house, or cherry-wood and tile floors, or three-piece crown moldings around the ceilings. But it would be a new house. One with updated everything. With the prospect of a solution to her dilemma about Jack, it was easy to find fault with Mavis' old house. Niki's mind went about listing the house's shortcomings.

This place needs major remodeling. Plaster from the 1920s is flaking off the walls in the living room and dining room.

Most of the windows need replacing and leak heat and air conditioning like a colander. The kitchen is the only thing newer than a flapper's bobbed haircut. Actually, I love this kitchen. The white tile on the countertops and the black and white tile on the floor–perfect. And the white painted cabinets are real wood, solid panels with pine shelves, not particleboard or plastic. But then, the roof costs a fortune to maintain. Who has terra cotta half-tiles on the roof anymore?

The only bathroom adjoins my room and the hall–unless you count that tiny closet-sized bathroom off Jack's bedroom. I don't see how he even turns around in that shower. And my bath has no shower at all. It's either use the handheld thing or stick my head under the faucet to wash my hair. But I do like the charm of the claw-foot bathtub. I can soak all the way up to my neck.

Of course if we sold, Jack and I could each go our separate ways. No more arguing, or trying to be considerate. Truly, Jack Rainwater is driving me crazy with his tidy, tidy ways. He's asked me forty times how long the stacks of papers are staying on the kitchen table. How long? How about as long as I need them to stay? And he has absolutely no appreciation for the garden, or the work I've put into it. I wonder if he'll even eat the vegetables?

The garden. Niki released an audible sigh when she thought of leaving her garden. If I'm not here, who'll weed the spinach and lettuce? Who'll water the daylilies? And what about my peach tree?

Between the choice of selling or not selling, neither sounded satisfactory. Niki poured the remainder of her coffee in the sink, picked up her car keys, dug under the mess on the table to locate the paperback book she'd recently bought titled, *More About Roses,* and left the house under an ominous, cloudy sky.

For the next two hours she didn't think about selling the house or about how to convince Jack to move out. Her mind was on roses: red roses, white roses, queen roses, recurrent roses, Rosa Virginiana, and Rosa Rugosa. When she returned, she carried two Buff Beauty Heirlooms. This particular rose species, bred in England in 1939 to produce double blooms of apricot yellow, grew to about six feet at maturity and promised a strong, musky tea scent. They also required little pruning. Careful to plant them in well-drained soil, with just the slightest bit of mounding, use plenty of mulch–the nursery salesperson instructed. Niki assured her she could do that. The Buff Beauties were in good hands. Niki smiled to herself as she drove back to Cherokee Place. She was happy with her purchase and looking forward to seeing the roses along the fence with her daylilies–apricot yellow roses and rusty red lilies–a perfect choice. Rain sputtered and spit as she made the turn from Ponce de Leon onto Cherokee Place. No matter, she told herself. I'll plant later, after it clears.

Her mood was still upbeat when she pulled into the drive and saw that Jack was back from Athens and had parked past the screened porch, at the end of the drive near the kitchen. She took her time unloading her precious cargo onto the porch for protection–just in case the rain got too rowdy–and then went back to the car for her purse and keys. By the time she let herself into the kitchen, rain had soaked her "Save the Whales" tee shirt and was trickling through her curly hair onto her face and neck.

Once she saw the equipment piled on top of her papers on the kitchen table, she realized why Jack drove around back to unload. What was all this stuff? Two flood lamp things–big, chrome shiny, and spooky looking. Another object easily identifiable as some sort of camera, a couple of black-box-meter-things, and about a million feet of black wires capped with heavy plugs. Jack's back was to her, but she was sure he was fairly drooling over the pile. Man toys, no doubt about it.

"I take it you bought your friend's camera equipment?" Niki said.

Jack turned and half smiled, then caught the smile and said nonchalantly, "Oh yeah, I did, part of it, but not all. He wanted too much for the Nikkor AF." Niki's duh-look told Jack she didn't have a clue what he was talking about. He explained, "The Nikkor AF is an auto focus lens. Lost the one I had on my last trip out. Well, I mean I didn't actually lose it. It was damaged…whatever. Anyway, it's for portraits, detail commercial shots."

"Oh, okay," Niki returned, "sorry you couldn't make a deal on it." She felt his eyes on her wet shirt and pulled it away from her chest. "Rain. Unloading roses." She reached for a paper towel to dry her face.

"Roses? You mean more garden?"

Niki dumped her purse on the counter and walked past him. "Yes, more garden. Thought I'd plant roses along the fence to keep the daylilies company. I better get a dry shirt."

While she was out of the room, Jack inspected his purchases and moved them off the table and into his room. When he returned to the kitchen, Mavis was looking out the upper glass of the kitchen door into the bad weather. After a moment of worry, she turned and asked Jack, *Have you had a good day?* There was a low rumble off in the distance. She shivered and turned her back to look outside again. Another shiver rippled along her spine. *I was out in the garden. I'm beginning to like what she's doing out there. At first the rain was coming down in lazy drifts, wetting Niki's plants but hardly bending the tender spinach leaves.*

*It's heavier now. I don't like this one little bit. Little rivers are flowing between the vegetable rows. Thunder off in the distance. Storms coming this way. Hope you remembered to roll up your car windows, Jack.*

She spun around to face Jack again when he cursed, "What the fuck?" He'd found Rabonette's sales contract lying atop the cardboard box.

*Oh dear,* Mavis muttered. *Talk about a storm. This ought to be a good one.*

Jack moved to the kitchen door, holding the paper up to the scant light filtering in from the outside. He was standing so close that she could have smelled the clean, woodsy scent of the Irish Spring soap he'd showered with that morning–if her sense of smell would only return. Mavis bent and kissed him lightly on the cheek. He seemed not to notice.

*Now Jack, calm down before you leap to all sorts of horrid conclusions....*

Niki walked into the kitchen before Mavis could finish her statement. Jack jerked around to Niki, eyes squinting, mouth puckered. He waved the contract at her like a Viking with a head on a stick.

Mavis chuckled. *Oh, dear, too late. I'm afraid the boy has leapt.* She lifted herself up onto the kitchen counter to watch the fireworks.

Jack stammered with anger. "What is this? This...this... never mind, I know what it is. I suppose as soon as I was out of sight, that...that..."

Niki finished his sentence. "Weasel. You mean, that weasel."

He looked more confused. "Weasel?"

"Yes. Terry Spiegel calls Ham Rabonette *The Weasel.* Seems to fit."

"Guess you're delighted about him offering so much money?"

Niki wasn't sure yet how she felt about the contract, but so long as Jack was making a fool of himself, she felt compelled to nudge him on down the road. "Well, four hundred and fifty thousand dollars is a lot of money, and…"

Jack interrupted. "The hell it is. I can't believe you let him talk you into this while I was gone. That…that…"

"Weasel. I thought we established he is a weasel."

"Whatever. He doesn't have enough money to get me to sell." With that, Jack crumpled the contract and threw it against the far wall. White he was at it, he grabbed a handful of old bills from the table and threw them against the wall.

Jack's tirade was no longer amusing. Niki took a step closer and gave him a decided poke in the chest. He looked down at the spot she'd touched as though she'd thrown a snake at him. "You hit me. I can't believe you hit me."

Mavis laughed and clapped her hands. *Yes, she did. I can't believe it either.*

"Oh stop it Jack. I didn't hit you. It was a poke. You're hollering and acting crazy. Rabonette hasn't talked me into anything. I didn't even want to talk to the guy. He just showed up in the driveway. Terry's told me about his daddy trying to buy Aunt Mavis out. I don't know why he wants us to sell, but honestly, don't you think we could at least talk about the offer like two sane people?"

Mavis shook her head sadly. *Oh Niki, you don't understand, dear. It isn't that easy.*

*There's no sane way of talking about a Rabonette having my house.*

Jack whirled around away from Niki, nearly losing his balance, and then leaned against the counter for support. His bad leg was throbbing like he'd been shot with electricity. Niki saw the pain in his face. "Jack, you look pale. Sit down and I'll make you a glass of tea. We don't have to talk about this right now."

His response was almost inaudible. "Hamilton Rabonette isn't the solution. You have to trust me on that."

Jack sat at the kitchen table nursing a fresh glass of tea while Niki made grilled cheese sandwiches with tomatoes and mayonnaise. The subject of Hamilton Rabonette was apparently closed, at least for the moment. Mavis sat beside Jack for a time, but when she heard a nervous Abelard chirping from her bedroom, she sensed he was frightened by the building storm and disappeared to keep him company. By the time Jack and Niki finished lunch, whips of high lightning followed by thunder rolling overhead brought another spring downpour.

When the phone on the wall rang, Jack wasn't sure if it was a call, or if the lightning had jumped the wire. He waited for the second ring before he leaned over and picked up the receiver. "Hello." Pause. "Yes." Pause "Okay, I'll hold." Long pause. "Yes sir. What's up?"

Niki heard only Jack's side of the conversation. He told someone it was raining like a son of a bitch in Atlanta, and then listened for what seemed like a long time before she heard him ask, "When? How long?" He reached for a pencil and pad on the table and wrote down something Niki couldn't see. There was another long silence when only the storm outside spoke, then Jack said, "I *am* thinking about it. What about the insurance thing? You said back in the winter that you couldn't get me covered because of the accident. Without insurance it's a no-go."

The person on the other end of the line talked and Jack wrote something else on the paper. He ripped the page from the pad, folded it, and then took out his wallet and slid the paper inside. Niki watched the wallet disappear back into his jeans pocket as he said, "Yeah, I know the Sully. On Rue St. Antoine. Whose team?"

After the person on the line replied, Jack hesitated for about three seconds, then said, "Okay. Tell him I'll be on the 7:30 flight out of Atlanta tomorrow morning. I suppose you know what time I get to Paris since you made the reservation." Niki heard the other person laugh. Jack frowned, said, "Ciao," and hung up. Niki watched him stand silently by the phone, worrying his chin with the fingertips of his right hand. He looked like a man making a to-do list in his head.

Even with hearing only one side of the conversation, Niki would've bet her last dime she knew what Jack was about to say. She closed her eyes and waited. Finally he told her.

"That was the magazine. They want me to go out one more time. Things are heating up again in Bosnia–something about the peacekeepers going in. They need someone who speaks French to mesh with the Paris crew. We'll hook-up at the Sully Hotel in Paris and get a hop over. I need to get my stuff together."

"I thought you were retired?"

Jack looked at her as though he was trying to make sense of some non sequitur she'd said. "I thought I was, but they want me."

"They want you? Sounds like a piss poor reason to get back into a war to me. Seems like I got married twice just because someone wanted me…big mistake, trust me. What about your leg?"

"My leg? Oh, it's healed. Besides we aren't going in under fire. The war is supposed to be over. I shouldn't have to…" He stopped and didn't say what Niki was thinking: that he usually had to shoot his photographs and then run like hell to stay alive.

"Come on, I've watched you walk. You're in pain most of the time. You're on the edge of needing a cane just to balance. What if you do have to run like hell? Then what?"

He didn't answer and Niki knew she was wasting her breath. Still, she had to try. "Answer me Jack. Then what? You told me yourself, you're fifty-two years old. Too old for jumping out of helicopters."

"I have to do this." Jack's raised voice brought Mavis out of the bedroom. She stood in the doorway waiting for one of them to say what was going on, and why the fighting, again. "For Christ's sake, Niki. We argue about every damn thing that comes along. No wonder we can't..." He stopped in mid-sentence, exhaled, and said more quietly, "Did you hear me say we meet at the Sully Hotel in Paris? That's where you can leave a message for me in case of emergency. I'll only be gone a couple of weeks."

Mavis looked from Jack to Niki. When she spoke to Jack, her voice was strained with worry. *Did you say Paris? Is that where you're going? No. I absolutely forbid it. You can't...you can't go back. You can barely walk.*

Niki and Jack walked past Mavis as she reached out to hold Jack by his shirtsleeve. Jack jerked his arm free and headed for the front door, announcing as he walked that he had to drive over to Kroger for a few things he needed for the trip. Niki trailed behind nagging that he had the brain of a baked potato and didn't he notice it was pouring down rain.

Mavis followed them out the front door and waited with Niki under cover of the porch while Jack—who'd just now remembered he'd parked at the other end of the driveway near the kitchen—walked back to the rear of the house under the roof overhang, rain splashing out of the gutters and onto his shirt as he went. They heard his BMW engine turn over and watched him back down the drive, swerve around Niki's car, and careen into the street. Lightning cracked across the sky and brought a double blast of thunder. Mavis and Niki flinched and looked up as the glass panels of the porch light rattled.

At almost the same moment, Mavis saw something bolt from under a camellia bush in the neighbor's yard and run into the street. She yelled to Jack, *Stop. Stop.*

Jack hit his brakes, the metallic squealing sound of German engineering screaming over the hard rain.

Niki cleared the three front steps in one jump and ran into the rain, screaming Jack's name over the storm. Before she reached his car–now sideways in the street after he'd jammed into park and stalled the engine–a maroon Cadillac screeched to a stop, missing a collision with the BMW passenger door by inches. Terry Spiegel exited the Cadillac carrying a huge green golf umbrella. He startled as lightning streaked overhead, then took Niki under cover of his umbrella and waited for thunder to roll past.

"What happened? Why did Jack stop in the middle of the street?"

Before Niki had time to answer, Jack got out of the car and stood in the rain beside them. His voice was high, quivering, his arms flailing in the air. "Did you see what I hit? Shit, shit, shit. I only got a glimpse in the side mirror. Where did it go?" He grabbed Niki by both arms and pulled her from the cover of the umbrella. "Did you see it? I tried to brake, but I felt the back tires…oh shit…I know I hit something."

"I know, I know, Jack. Calm down. I saw something run into the street. That's why I yelled at you, but I think I was too late. A dog, I think. Kind of small, tan, shaggy. But I'm not sure."

Terry walked around to the back of the BMW and Niki and Jack followed. "If you hit a dog it could be underneath." He bent down over the rear fender. All three leaned down over the BMW's low rear end, but were unable to see underneath because it sat so low to the ground. Realizing that she was the most agile of them, Niki got down on her knees, then down on one elbow, and eased under the bumper. Nothing was trapped underneath.

Over the pelting rain, Mavis called out from the porch. *Not under the car. Do you hear me? I saw the dog roll from under Jack's tire and run down the street. Look down near Terry's house. He can't have gotten far.*

Niki got to her feet and wiped rain away from her face. "Nothing. I've heard that when a dog is hurt, panic takes over and he may run for safety, even if he's badly injured. Maybe that's what he did." Niki tried to think. Where could a dog hide? Surely he couldn't run very far. She squinted into the rain, to the end of the cul-de-sac and Terry's house. "Terry, is there any shelter between here and your house? Think. Where would Winston go if he were hurt? Where could he hide?"

Terry didn't have to think, he knew. Taking off down the street at a fast walk, he called back to them from under his umbrella. "Concrete pipe. The city storm culvert. Come on. We have to hurry. It fills with water."

# *Eighteen*

Terry, standing at the rim of the ravine, still held his green umbrella against the blowing rain, though his pants and shoes were soaked and only the back of his navy Polo golf jacket felt dry. Niki was far beyond having any part of her dry when she followed Jack and slid down the bank to the muddy bottom of the ditch. There they slogged about thirty feet to a concrete culvert. Water was already collecting from the street above them, gushing out of the mouth of the pipe, and pooling on the ground where they knelt to peer inside. About twelve feet into the opening they saw bloody matted fur, and a shaggy tail.

Niki gasped. "Oh my God." At the sound of her voice a wet, mottled tan head lifted slightly then dropped back to the concrete. Niki thought–prayed–his head was resting out of the water on the sloped side of the pipe. She stood and faced Jack, who by now was bent over, hands on his knees, breathing heavily. She hoped he had a plan.

Jack was sick to his stomach with guilt, and on the verge of bawling like a five year- old. He got his breath, straightened up, wiped the rain from his face with both hands, and willed the pain in his leg to shut up long enough for him to do something useful. "I can't reach him from here. I'll have to crawl into the pipe."

Niki shook her head. There was no way Jack could crawl into the narrow pipe and back out again with the dog, not with his bad leg.

Terry called out from the top of the bank. "Find him?"

Jack answered, "Yes." Then he called directions to Terry. "We need something stiff like a wide board and something to cover him. Can you…" Before Jack finished his sentence, Terry was trudging across the soggy grass toward his house, his umbrella bobbing along above him like a large, green toadstool suddenly given the gift of walking.

Niki looked up into the rain, letting it wash across her face. She heard Winston's happy bark. Terry must be letting himself into the house. She turned back to Jack. "Why the board?"

Jack was in emergency mode; his voice was clipped, yet calm. "Trauma. Possible broken bones. Need to keep him immobilized to avoid further injury."

His words sounded like a Red Cross manual. Then she connected why. Jack had probably sat through a hundred training sessions on battlefield injury, just in case he, or any of his journalist buddies, got caught in the crossfire. The word, crossfire, suddenly had new meaning. Was that what happened to Jack's leg? Had he been caught in the crossfire? Niki realized that she'd been so defensive about everything else that was going on–the house, and her own life–that she'd not asked how Jack had injured his leg. She'd assumed it happened because of his work, but how exactly?

Would Jack tell me the details, if I asked? Niki guessed no. He wouldn't. He would probably respond with some blasé comment that gave up no real information.

Her mind clicked back to the injured dog. Time to act. She ducked into the pipe before Jack could argue and scooted along the rough concrete on her forearms. When she was even with the dog's hind legs, Niki saw what she thought was a jagged piece of bone protruding up through the flesh. She swallowed hard and willed herself not to throw up.

Jack's voice came from behind her. "Tell me he's alive."

When she twisted her body around to answer, Niki realized that she could almost sit up in the pipe. From a hunched sitting position she inched forward and gently raised the dog's head. He made a sorry attempt to bare his teeth, and then relaxed his head into her hand, exhausted. Niki gauged the water was up to his shoulders, rising to his neck, but his head was not yet lying in a river of rainwater. Niki eased his head down, and sat with her back against the concrete, shivering.

Jack called to her again. "Talk to me, Niki."

"Alive. Barely. Some blood. At least one broken bone. Shock, I think."

"I'm sliding a board in to you. Can you get him on it and push him to me?"

She had no idea if she could or not. Chances were he would attempt to bite her when she tried to move him. But she knew she had no choice. They had to get him out of the culvert and to a doctor. A hard object pushed against her leg, and she reached around to grasp a legless ironing board, one meant for quick pressing on a bed, or table. On top of the board, dry in a plastic garbage bag, were a wooly blanket imprinted with black Scottie dogs–no doubt borrowed from Winston–and a handful of brightly colored neck scarves. *Terry, you are brilliant.* Niki wanted to hug him.

The flow of rain in the pipe was slowing, reminding her of a bath shower after you're done, short rivulets running for the drain. The storm must be moving on. Niki leaned over the injured dog. "Okay little guy," she said softly and rested her left hand on his bony shoulder. He didn't lift his head, though his eyes opened and darted back and forth. She took that as a show of at least marginal trust. She stroked his shoulder and spoke to him, "Hold on little guy. I'm going to slide this board under you and we are going to get out of this pipe."

He offered a weak growl as she cupped both hands under his wet body and slid him onto the ironing board. That done, she quickly covered him with the blanket, and then wrapped his body to the board with scarves. The last two scarves went to secure his head to the narrow part of the ironing board.

So far so good, she thought, until she realized the pipe was too small for her to climb over and push him out of the pipe. She'd have to back out the way she'd crawled in, pulling dog and board along in front of her. Slowly, ever so slowly, Niki pushed herself backwards on her stomach and pulled. The dog whined when he realized he was moving. "It's okay. Hold on. Just hold on," she soothed, not sure if she was talking to the dog or herself.

At the same moment Niki's lower back cramped with a sharp pain from tugging the weight of dog and board, she felt her feet, then her lower legs, in open air. She was out of the pipe. She wriggled her body free and stood in the mud, waiting for the pain to subside, while Jack pulled the dog the rest of the way to the mouth of the pipe.

"Now what?" She asked Jack.

"Terry went for the car. Can you get the other end of the board as I slide him out? It'll take two of us to get out of this ditch without dumping him over."

They went up the slope sideways, trying to synchronize steps to keep the board stable, pants and shoes coated with red Georgia mud when they reached the top of the ravine. The rain had slowed to a drizzle. Terry was waiting for them, engine running, and came around to open the rear passenger door of his Cadillac. "Y'all are doing real good," he reassured. "Hold him just the way you've got him. Try not to jostle him. Dr. Jim isn't far."

Niki hesitated. "Terry, we'll ruin your upholstery."

"Get in. Get in. It's time I traded this old bat anyway."

Mavis, waiting on the front porch, waved to the Cadillac as it drove past. She saw Niki and Jack in the back seat, Terry driving, and surmised they'd found the injured animal. She sighed with relief, and sadness. *Poor little dog. Poor Jack. Ellis would say snake eyes came up on the dice roll for both of them.*

As much as she wanted to wait for them to come home and talk about what happened, exhaustion coursed through her, drawing her away from the porch, away from the house. She felt herself fading, drawn to where the sea rocked gently, giant globes of lights on the water's surface marked her passage, and whales spoke to her in dreams of sweet sleep. In the park across the street, out of the rain washed sky, three crows landed on a spindly pecan limb causing it to bounce as they stretched wings and cawed. Then as a rainbow arched high over the noisy birds, Mavis vanished.

The Cadillac drove north on Briarcliff Road. Terry was speeding through the light Sunday afternoon traffic, and their patient was either cooperating, or had fainted, if that's what dogs do in trauma. Niki wasn't sure. Panic flared when she realized what day it was. "Terry, where are we going? It's Sunday."

"I know. Don't worry. I called Dr. Jim at home."

"Your vet will meet us on a Sunday? He must be very dedicated."

"He is. He's also my nephew—my only living relative. Treats Winston like a king, or rather a prime minister. The boy probably thinks he'll inherit my house on Cherokee Place one of these years. And I guess he will. Why not? He's a good boy. How's our patient?"

Niki tucked the blanket closer around the dog. "I can't tell. His eyes are open again, but they looked sort of glazed. I don't know. Jack, what do you think?"

Jack sat beside her, as stiff as the ironing board, holding his end of the made-do stretcher with both hands and staring out the front window. When he didn't respond, Niki tried again. "Jack?"

Still no answer. She nudged him gently. "Jack, are you all right?"

He turned his head slightly, not meeting her eyes or looking at the dog in his lap. "Sure," he said. "Sure."

Niki doubted that but didn't argue with him.

# Nineteen

With the rain spent, late afternoon sun shimmered on puddles in the parking lot. Niki rested her forehead against the glass separating the vet's office from the outside, waiting, and wondering if the pungent lemon-ammonia smell permeating Dr. Jim's office was always so strong. Perhaps the cleaning crew had just left? Perhaps the odor was strong because the office was devoid of people and pets? Except for us, she was thinking. We're here. It seems like forever. I should wear a watch. Why is it taking so long?

Through the picture window, she watched a family leave Denny's Restaurant next door and navigate around watery traps to a Ford mini-van parked near Dr. Jim's office. A small, dark haired girl with two missing top teeth grinned and waved as she jumped up into the Ford's rear seat. Niki managed a weak smile but hadn't the energy to wave. She was freezing from the office air conditioning blowing like a nor'easter on her wet clothes and rubbed her hands together to warm them.

When the Ford pulled out of the parking lot and onto Briarcliff Road, Niki turned away from the window to the waiting room. Jack had not moved from the chair he'd taken when the vet and Terry rushed the injured dog through swinging doors to the examining room. He sat, back rigid, both hands clasped tightly atop his left knee, knuckles pale, looking straight ahead. Niki followed his stare to the opposite wall where a coffin sized fish tank housed small, blue, feathery-finned creatures swimming among larger golden fish. On the bottom of the tank, green diaphanous fronds swayed with currents born from the pump gurgling air into an otherwise silent world.

Niki watched Jack. She couldn't swear she'd seen him blink. Oh my God, is he holding his breath? She left the window and took a chair beside him. He continued to stare ahead. "Jack." No answer. She rested a hand on his. Cold. Just as cold as hers. "Jack, please talk to me. Say something."

Jack looked down at her hand covering his as though he'd never seen anything like it in his entire life. After several seconds he exhaled. "I'm so sorry. I was rushing. Angry you questioned my going out one more time. My fault. All my fault." He paused. Niki waited.

A door down the hall opened. Terry, arms swinging at his side, and doing an over eighty-year-old man's version of the fast walk, approached them. "Listen up children. Dr. Jim will be out soon. Won't be long now." He frowned when he noticed Niki shivering and retraced his steps down the hall, opened a closet, and returned with a technician's lab jacket. "Here. Put this on. It's thin but maybe it'll help." After a manly pat on Jack's shoulder, Terry disappeared back down the hall into the examining room.

Niki slipped on the jacket and reached down to button it. When the blue teddy bear and alphabet block pattern registered with her, tears filled the corners of her eyes. She was back in the hospital nursery again, rocking her baby, her tiny baby whose heart needed repair. She felt, rather than heard, her baby exhale–more like a sigh. Then no inhale. There would never be another inhale. How long is never? After the nurse took her baby away, Niki slipped from the rocking chair down onto the rug–a rug printed with blue teddy bears and alphabet blocks. Lying on the floor, Niki tried to make herself small. So small she would disappear.

Anne. The letters of her baby's name formed in perfect rounded script in her mind. Anne, Anne. Jack's voice brought Niki back to now, and she wiped the tears with her still muddy hands.

"…you know what I mean? I've lived my life trying to do the right thing. Walking the safety line, being careful, and not taking risks. Stay on the narrow path and you won't get lost. Isn't that what they say? Be careful and you can't fuck up. But it isn't true. You fuck up anyway. Something bad is always out there waiting to jump. Waiting for the slightest mistake. Then you ask: What should I have done?"

For one split second Niki thought they were taking about her baby dying. For years, she'd gone over and over what she should have done. Even made a list. Should she have asked for another doctor's opinion? Should she have gone to another hospital? Insisted on more tests when she was pregnant? But she was so healthy during her pregnancy. Everything seemed fine, so normal–until…

Niki felt the urge to put her hands over her ears to block the noise in her head. *Blame and sorrow, blame and sorrow.* Blame from her ex-husband and sorrow that would last a lifetime. *Blame and sorrow.* Her sane self–the one who had survived–spoke up to tell the other to stop playing the blame record in her head. She forced the record image to flip to the other side, conjuring a slick, black, 45 RPM in a 1950s jukebox.

Life is a crapshoot. Sometimes we don't get to choose. Snake eyes happen out of the chaos. Where did I hear that? Who said that to me? Niki shook her head to bring herself back to Dr. Jim's office, her mind struggling to process Jack's ramblings.

She blurted out, "What are you saying?" And then she cleared her throat and tried to speak more calmly. "Jack, listen. What happened was an accident. A terrible accident. It was the rain, the thunder, and terrible timing to be backing out of the driveway at the same time the dog ran out. But we all take risks. Every time we get in the car to drive, every time we…anyway, you take huge risks when you fly into a war zone to document what's happening with photographs. People die every day doing far less risky things than you do. So don't tell me you live your life not taking risks."

Jack looked at her as though she was speaking a foreign language. "No. No. I'm not taking about that. Not about me. Not my work. Don't you see? The risks I take with my work can only hurt me. Only me."

There was something important in what Jack was saying. Niki could feel it, but the tragedy of the day had worn her out; she was having difficulty connecting his words to that one extraordinary thought hovering just outside her understanding. She settled with groping for words she thought would comfort him. "It wasn't your fault…"

Niki's head shot around with a start when Dr. Jim threw open the examining room door, sending it ricocheting off the wall with a whack-sound. She noticed he peeled off surgical gloves and tucked them in a pocket as he trotted down the hall. Did he mean to hide the blood on his gloves–the reminder of the pain he'd just left behind the closed door? She and Jack stood to face him. Niki took a shallow breath, wishing she had a warm hand to hold for comfort.

"Okay. Here is where we are," Dr. Jim began confidently, "Mr. Rainwater, I understand you have agreed to pay the costs to help the patient, and I appreciate that, but we have a serious decision to make here. Which one of you is actually the owner of the dog?"

Jack's jaw dropped in silence. Niki spoke. "It's complicated. He…well…that is….he is a male, right?"

Dr. Jim frowned at her. "Of course he's a male. Don't you know that already?"

Jack seemed to regain his composure and tried to explain. "Thunder frightened him. He ran into the street and I hit him. We don't know who the owner is. What about ID tags, a collar? Maybe Terry's seen him in the neighborhood."

Dr. Jim groaned and squeezed his eyes closed for a second. When he opened them and spoke again his voice was sad, defeated. "No ID tags. No collar. Doesn't look like anyone takes care of him. My guess is he's a middle aged stray who's never had a home." Dr. Jim paused, his silence punctuating the terrible meaning of the word, stray. Niki felt herself biting down on her lower lip as she waited for him to continue.

"Probably been evading the county animal control truck for most of his life. Surviving on garbage by the looks of him. I mean, don't get me wrong, I think the little guy is cute, but he's probably not Cherokee Place pedigree. And he is an older dog. Not very adoptable as a rule. Most people want puppies. You understand, with no owner I'm obligated to do the humane thing and put him out of his pain."

Niki broke in. "Wait. I want to adopt a dog. Can I claim him?"

Dr. Jim grimaced. "Well, yes, technically you could. If that is really what you want to do. But the decision we have to make, and make immediately, is what to do about his shattered rear leg. I've taken x-rays of his chest and body area. There doesn't seem to be any internal bleeding—just bruising and surface cuts. His lungs are okay. But the leg is far too damaged. We either put him down, or I have to amputate the leg. You understand Ms. Banks? We can't wait. He's in a lot of pain and I won't let him continue to suffer."

Jack stumbled and folded in the nearest chair. "Amputate? What are you talking about? You can't just cut his leg off like we're in the middle of the fucking Civil War." He pleaded to Niki, "That's crazy. Don't you see? You can't have a three-legged dog. Besides, you said you wanted a puppy. You heard what Dr. Jim said, this guy is middle aged. For God's sake, Niki, just put him down. Put the poor thing out of his misery."

Dr. Jim waited for Niki to think about what Jack was saying. She looked away from Jack and closed her eyes for one long moment, before she asked Dr. Jim, "How would he manage with only three legs?"

"Actually just fine, probably. Because we're talking about a rear leg and most of a dog's weight is on the front legs, he'll get his new balance pretty quickly and do everything he needs to do with three legs. He'll do it more slowly no doubt, but dogs live in the *now*. In this moment. They don't whine about what they've lost or how great it was in the old days. He'll adjust. Sure, any major surgery is serious, with recovery time and extra care required. But I'd say this little guy has a strong will to live. Look at how he's managed so far, being a stray so close to downtown Atlanta for goodness sake. I'd give him a strong chance at pulling through and doing well with three legs. He has a zero chance with euthanasia."

Jack held both Niki's arms like a parent explaining the dangers of bungee jumping to a determined fifteen-year old. "Look. I know you feel sorry for him. I do too. It's my fault he's hurt. But think about what you're considering. All the extra care he'll need for the rest of his life, the risk that he might not even make it through the surgery."

Niki was thinking about all of that. She was also thinking about the teddy bears on the lab coat she was wearing and about baby Anne. "Jack," she finally said in a small, quiet voice, "every little thing deserves a chance, even if it means taking a risk."

Jack winced, remembering the secret he held about Niki, and wondered if she was thinking of the child she'd lost. Maybe later, sometime, he should ask her about what happened with the baby–maybe she wanted to talk about it. Maybe. Except he knew he didn't want to talk about it. There were a lot of things that he didn't want to talk about. But a baby who died? Maybe that was different. Maybe you had to talk about that. He thought of releasing the vice grip he held on her arms and hugging her–if only his hands weren't frozen in place. He couldn't seem to relax his fingers. And if he could, there was the risk that Niki didn't want…

"Okay folks," Dr. Jim broke into his thoughts. "What's it going to be?"

The office door opened with a *swishing* sound and a chunky young woman dressed in pale green scrubs ran into the office. She flung her beach-bag sized purse over the reception counter, landing it perfectly on the desk chair, and stood with her hands on her wide hips. "Got your message, Doc. Do I prep for surgery?"

Jack finally released Niki's arms and they answered together, "Yes."

Dr. Jim smiled and gave the young woman a thumbs-up just before she trotted down the hall. He followed close behind her, calling over his shoulder that he would send Uncle Terry out, now that reinforcements had arrived.

# Twenty

When they were alone again, Jack and Niki retreated into silence. Niki resumed her position in front of the window; Jack reclaimed the chair across the room to stare at the fish. When he was sure she wasn't looking his way, Jack watched her. Who was this woman who had survived the death of a child and two failed marriages, and had the guts to crawl inside a nasty concrete storm pipe to rescue an injured dog? He wondered what he would have done had Niki not been there today. Would he have crawled into the pipe? Would he be agreeing to take on the responsibility of a three-legged dog? Probably not.

He thought if the idea of a three-legged dog weren't so tragic, it would be funny. Like in some old Disney cartoon, the dog hobbles along with the aid of a walker, while a bunch of cats hang on the fence throwing fish bones at him because they know he can't chase them. Who in their right mind could love a three-legged dog? He studied Niki's face. She looked tired. Of course she had a right to be tired. At forty-six she should do other things with her afternoon rather than slog around in the mud. Jack almost smiled. I'll say one thing for her. She has grit.

Niki was tired. Her back ached. Her arms ached. Her knees felt like she was seven years old again and had fallen off her bike and skidded across the driveway. She looked down at the knees of her jeans, checking for frayed spots where she'd scrubbed along the concrete pipe. Knees, she thought. Jack's got one bad leg, and the little guy has one bad leg. Well, at least Jack's is still attached. Her mind wandered along without logic or pattern. She was too fatigued to keep it still. Each of them having an injured leg seemed ironic. Or would the proper word be coincidental? If not a coincidence, then were the two events orchestrated? Like Jack had said: there is always something out there waiting to get you if you strayed off the path. Was Jack right? That would mean someone, or something, caused the accident. A God person with a plan? Niki closed her eyes and tried to stop thinking. Obsessing about the why of accidents wouldn't get her anywhere. She tried to concentrate on the cars in the parking lot emptying of families, walking hand and hand into Denny's Restaurant for dinner. But then when she thought of families, she asked herself: Who is my family? The answer to that question was more disquieting than thinking about accidents and a God with a plan.

Niki'd never really believed in a God with a plan. At least not the God confined within the churches she'd attended with her mother. Her mother's religion made no sense to her. They talked about "The Good News" of salvation and going to heaven, then preached we are all terrible sinners, so horribly flawed that chances are we can't get there from here. No, the scientific theory of cause and effect made more sense. God, if there were such an entity, would not spend eternity meting out punishment for sins. Surely God would have better ways to pass the time. Create a new species of peach tree. Make roses bloom all year. And certainly no benevolent God would allow her baby, her Anne, to die.

Niki's mind wandered back to Jack and the dog. She did believe that the universe operated with some sort of order and not out of total chaos. There must be rules. She just didn't know what they were. And if she didn't know the rules, how could she...this was where her efforts to understand always derailed. Without knowing the rules, she worried that winning was unlikely, if not impossible.

Terry came through the door of the examining room and padded down the hall to the waiting area. When she heard his slow footsteps, Niki turned and waited. He looked old, rumpled, damp from the earlier rain, and worried. His usually carefully combed, gray hair tufted up on his head in several places and he'd made no effort to smooth the disheveled strands into place. His Italian, leather loafers made a wet, squishy sound with every footfall.

Jack rose from his chair. "What's the word, Terry?" he asked.

Terry sucked in air through his open mouth. Niki took a step closer to him, thinking he needed support. He held up an open hand to her. "I'm okay," he said, "just tired. We are over the worst of it. The little guy is stable and surgery is proceeding as expected. The leg is gone and Dr. Jim is doing what he needs to do with the wound—you know, pulling skin over the place where the leg used to be so it can heal, making sure muscles are okay, that sort of thing. Jim is encouraged. The little guy is tough. Of course he'll be sore and disoriented for a few days, and we have to be careful about possible infections. But Jim is...like I said...encouraged. He recommends we go home, take a hot shower, and have some dinner and a stiff drink. He'll call when the patient is awake."

Jack looked from Terry to Niki. "That sounds good to me. There's nothing we can do here. I vote we go home. What do you think?"

Niki considered how anxious Jack seemed to leave. Then remembered. Of course he wants to leave; Jack has things to do. There is a plane ticket to Paris with his name on it at the Atlanta airport, and his magazine is expecting him to be on his way to Bosnia.

She felt her stomach roll, free-fall. What if there was another accident–a plane crash? More snake eyes? Jack was waiting for an answer to his question, but all she could think to say was: please don't go. And she wouldn't say that. To go was what he wanted to do. Niki crossed her arms and pulled her hands up inside the sleeves of the thin, cotton lab coat. She was still cold–needed a hot cup of coffee, not a stiff drink. "I think I'll stay here until he gets out of surgery. You two go on home."

Jack grimaced. "Somehow I thought you'd say that. I'll go next door to Denny's and get you a hot coffee. Heavy cream, right? Terry? You want coffee?"

Terry shook his head no and Jack was out the door.

While they waited for Jack, Terry and Niki agreed on a plan. She would stay at Dr. Jim's. Terry would drive Jack back to Cherokee Place where he would move his BMW out of the street–that is if the police hadn't towed it away by now. Jack could run his errands for his trip and collect her later. Terry would rest at home. By the time Jack returned to pick her up, the little guy would probably be awake. Once she had a full report on how he was doing, she would call Terry.

The little guy, Niki repeated the words to herself, the little guy. "We have to come up with a better name than *little guy*. Any ideas?"

Terry shook his head and rubbed his right temple with the heel of his hand. "Headache coming on. A name? Yes. Oh, I don't know. Something courageous. I'm too tired at the moment to be creative. I suspect the right name will come to you."

"What breed do you think he is?"

Terry snickered. "You mean what breeds, don't you?" His emphasis was on the plural. "How about spaniel, corgi, Border collie, and maybe a little dachshund thrown in for good measure. I haven't a clue really, except I hope he's a grateful breed. You are certainly making a monumental commitment to a good life for him. Honestly, as much as I love dogs, I'm not sure I would take on the responsibility."

Niki considered the word, *responsibility*, and concluded that a sense of responsibility wasn't what she felt. That word seemed extremely heavy. It could crush you, if you weren't careful. No, she was feeling something much lighter; hope was closer to the word. Yes, she felt hopeful. At least the little guy had a chance.

# *Twenty-one*

By the time Jack returned to Dr. Jim's office: sans mud, dirty, sodden shoes replaced by nearly-new leather loafers, and wearing clean jeans, Niki had visited with her dog. Though he was still in a deep grog from the anesthesia, and barely opened his eyes when she stroked his head, she assured him that he was going to get well. "We'll have a good life together. I promise. No more scavenging for your dinner. You're my boy now. I'll take care of you." She was sure he grunted his agreement.

"Do you want to go back and say hello to him?" she asked Jack.

Jack thought for a moment and then answered no. He'd wait until the little guy felt better, probably not a good idea to upset him with too many people. Niki didn't press the issue, though she suspected Jack was thinking of himself getting upset and not the dog. "By the way," she mentioned casually, thinking she'd lighten the moment, "I thought I'd name him Bingo."

"Bingo?" Jack said, a little too loudly. "Why that? I had a pony named Bingo when I was a kid."

"I know. I like the name. It seems to suit. You know, lucky-bingo-game and all that."

"Yeah, I get it. But don't you think you should have talked to me about the name before you settled on Bingo?"

Niki let out an exasperated groan. "Well Jack, for good-ness sake. It isn't as though you *own* the name Bingo or any-thing. What's the big deal? If it really bothers you, I'll think of something else."

Shoving his hands in his jean pockets, Jack turned away from her and went over to the fish tank where he could grumble to himself. Why the hell would anyone want fish in an office anyway? Crappy life for a fish. Swimming around and around. Day after day. Never getting anywhere. Fish be-long out in a coral reef somewhere–the Virgin Islands, maybe Belize. Is there a coral reef off Belize? Why the hell should a name bother me? Who cares? It's only a name. Holy Christ, the pony was forty-five years ago.

Niki followed him, stood beside the burbling water, and watched him staring at the fish. So this is how the man avoids conflict–tune out—go off to la-la land–stare at a fish? Little wonder he is still single. With considerable effort, she spoke kindly. "Sorry, I didn't imagine it would upset you. I'll think of another name."

Jack noticed a small blue fish glide over and casually take a bite out of the dorsal fin of a brother blue. "You bastard," Jack swore under his breath, and shook his head with disgust.

"Hello, hello, earth to Jack."

He turned to Niki, giving her an oh-hi-who-are-you look. "No. No. It's okay. Really," he insisted. "You're right. It's no big deal. Bingo's a great name for the little guy. You ready to go?"

It was almost nine when they arrived back at Cherokee Place. Jack offered to fix bacon and eggs, but Niki declined, saying maybe she would have a banana and a piece of toast after she'd cleaned up. Abelard trilled fretfully when she went into her bedroom. She paused in front of his cage, told him he was a pretty bird, and apologized for leaving the bedside light on.

When she covered him for the night he seemed grateful for the peaceful darkness, and settled down to sleep. Niki ran a bath in the claw-foot tub and peeled off her muddy clothes. Twenty minutes later she sat on the side of the bed in a baggy tee shirt and soft gray pajama pants, her hair towel dry, unruly curls tucked behind her ears. She told herself that she'd just lie back for ten minutes, then find Jack and talk to him about the Rabonette contract. The whole selling idea really needed to be discussed before he went flying off to the far edge of the world.

She also wanted to thank Jack for offering to pay Bingo's vet bill. As she lay back on the warm comforter, she agonized over just how to say thank you. She was sure the words would stick in her throat when she tried to sound grateful–though she truly was grateful. Why should a simple thank you be so hard? As she relaxed on the bed, the afternoon played back. It all seemed so unreal, yet the accident was very real. She knew Jack was bent low by what happened. Felt guilty. Still, she had to give him credit. He took care of business. Came up with a plan to get Bingo out of the pipe, and out of the muddy ravine.

In that still space between awake and sleep, Niki was thinking the situation with the house would be easier if she disliked Jack, or at least could muster indifference to him. If either were true, she thought she could be more aggressive, more insistent, that he move out. As it was, the man was annoying, though also a bit charming. And then there was the memory of a teenage crush, recurring like the unexpected aftertaste of Bittersweet chocolate. With the bedroom lamp still on, Niki surrendered to sleep.

Jack knocked softly on the bedroom door. No answer. He knocked again–still no answer. Noticing light spilling under the door, he eased it open. "Niki? Are you okay?"

She was curled up on top of the down comforter, its soft white folds gathered to her chin like a puffy nest. A single coil of damp hair, reminding Jack of a question mark, lay across her cheek. He stood in the doorway listening to the even rhythm of her breathing. It occurred to him that she looked at peace. He knew that he should close the door and walk away, but he didn't.

I don't think I've ever photographed anyone at peace. I could frame a shot just the way she is, use black and white to play up the contrasts. I would need to get closer, maybe shoot from above. She'd probably wake before I could get my camera. I can't believe how young her face looks. Like when we were teenagers. I was such a major shit back then. Trying to be Mr. Cool. Pretending to ignore her. Screw the photograph. What I'd really like to do is lie down beside her. Just lie there. Not wake her. I wonder if her hair has that lemony smell I noticed in the room when I got the box from her closet?

When Jack realized he was doing his old childhood thing of grinding his teeth, he concentrated on relaxing his jaw and looked away. What's wrong with me? I'm acting like a peeping Tom. He debated whether or not to wake Niki–he really wanted to talk to her about Rabonette's contract–but couldn't bring himself to disturb her. Instead, he tiptoed to the bedside table, turned off the lamp, and left her to sleep.

When Niki woke the next morning she was stiff and achy. It took her a few minutes to wash her face, brush her teeth, and absorb the fact that the clock was telling her it was eight-thirty. She checked again. Yes, it was eight-thirty. She uncovered Abelard and made her way through the quiet house to the kitchen. An empty feeling expanded in the pit of her stomach when she realized Jack was gone. She'd missed saying goodbye. On top of the coffeemaker, she found a note. *I'll call from*

*Paris. Take care.* That was all it said. Never mind there was no signature. Of course Jack wrote it. It was just that there was so much unsaid, by both of them.

By nine o'clock Niki had her second cup of coffee and was on the phone with Dr. Jim's office. When the receptionist gave her the okay to visit, she was dressed, out the door, and at the vet's office in forty-five minutes. Dr. Jim walked with her to what he called "the recuperating room" where Bingo was resting, and talked about the next stages of the little dog's recovery.

"I want to keep it simple for you today. When you have other questions, just call me." He opened the gate latch to the chain-link pen and motioned for her to follow. The area was about ten feet wide, with a concrete floor. At the far end was a metal door, now wide open, separating the pen from a fenced outside yard. Niki looked up. A skylight directed morning sun down onto the concrete floor and the blanket where Bingo slept. A food bowl and water bowl sat near.

Bingo lifted his head and growled. "Hey there Mr. Bingo," Jim said to him, "you've got a visitor." Dr. Jim stretched an arm in front of Niki to prevent her from going closer. "Let's just stand here for a moment and give him a chance to relax. He's still pretty disoriented and might bite."

Niki was surprised. "Bite? Has he bitten you?"

Dr. Jim smiled sheepishly. "Well, I should have known better…only a small bite. No problem. We gave him his rabies and other shots while he was under for the surgery. But here is the thing: he doesn't trust people yet. It may take you awhile to become friends. But trust me, he'll come around in time."

Niki wasn't totally sure what she'd expected, but being bitten wasn't it. Still, she felt foolish realizing that she'd assumed the dog would somehow know she cared about him and would instantly love her. She knew now that was unrealistic, though she was still deeply disappointed. "It's okay. We'll work it out. Time is something I have plenty of these days. You were telling me about his recovery."

"Yes, I was. Basically we need to monitor the wound, make sure it drains properly and heals from the inside. It will leak some fluid and maybe a little blood for a few days. Can you see how I pulled the skin at his hip up and over where the leg was attached?"

Niki nodded. The sight of the surgery wound made her stomach do small whirls and flips. She swallowed hard, pushed the nausea out of her mind, and concentrated on what Dr. Jim was saying.

"That skin flap will heal and eventually the area will have hair, hopefully, and the hip will be nicely protected."

"He looks sort of wet all over."

There was another sheepish grin from Dr. Jim. "Yeah, well, he had fleas and was wicked dirty. I decided to clean him up a bit and he objected–thus the small bite. I should have waited."

Niki nodded again, hoping bath time would not always be bite time for Bingo. "I see kibbles in his bowl. Has he eaten?"

"No, probably not. Not yet. We'll be watching him to make sure he finds his balance and can get to the food and water, and to make sure all his plumbing works. Being able to go poop and pee is the number one criteria for him going home."

Niki thought about the food for a few seconds. "He's probably never eaten dry dog food. Maybe we should give him something more familiar."

Dr. Jim quipped back to her. "You mean like garbage and maybe a dead squirrel?"

Niki frowned. She hadn't meant to be amusing. "No. I mean maybe I could bring him some scrambled eggs, or cooked ground beef, or something."

A doctor-knows-best tolerant look replaced Dr. Jim's humorous one. "Here's another place you have to trust me. Unless you want to continue to cook people food for Bingo, you need to give him a chance to accept the kibbles. The dry food has everything he needs–and is lot healthier than what he's used to eating."

"Hmm." Niki wasn't convinced about the kibbles.

The intercom overhead interrupted, asking Dr. Jim to come to exam room four. He pointed up at the speaker, gave Niki an apologetic look, and let himself out of the pen. As he closed the latch leaving Niki on the inside, he asked, "By the way, are you current with your tetanus shot?" Because she looked puzzled, he added, "You know, in case he bites."

For the next half-hour Niki and Bingo played a step forward, growl, stop game. She would move one or two tiny steps closer to him until he raised his head and growled. Then she would stand still. He would stop growling and rest his head back down on the blanket. She would wait, and then move another few steps closer until he raised his head to growl. This went on until finally he raised his head appraising her, no growl, only a stern stare. She remembered reading somewhere that it is best not to look a frightened dog directly in the eyes, so she averted her gaze. He slowly rolled his body over until his front paws were forward, his good leg poised underneath.

Oh no, Niki worried. He's going to attack. She remained still and watched him from the corner of her eye. His body didn't appear to be tensing up to spring at her, and he was not baring his teeth. Maybe that was a good sign. In fact, she decided, he seemed more curious than angry. She took a chance and eased herself down on the concrete floor. It was hard, and cold, and she wondered how difficult it was going to be to get back up again. As she sat cross-legged on the floor, another worry came to mind. If he attacks, there is no way I can get out of here before he rips me to hamburger. She let out a little whine sound and Bingo's ears perked up.

Oh well, in for a penny, in for a pound, Niki decided, and tucked her hands in her lap. While she looked up and studied a waterfall pattern of dust motes riding down the sunlight shaft from the skylight, Niki spoke softly. "When you are better, we'll go home to Aunt Mavis' house. You'll like it. We have a big, fenced back yard with squirrels and rabbits to chase. You'll be friends with our favorite neighbor, Terry, and his Winston. Winston is only slightly smaller than you–a little pompous, but a sweet dog.

"And of course, there is Jack. Jack is… I'm not certain what Jack is. Aggravating for sure. You see Aunt Mavis left us the house together. I have no idea why, but she did. So Jack and I have to work out who stays, and who moves out. And there is this crazy business about The Weasel wanting us to sell. Then we could each buy newer houses. But a new house wouldn't be… it wouldn't be Cherokee Place. You'll see. There is something special about Aunt Mavis' house. When I was young, Aunt Mavis would go from room to room singing an old song. 'Kiss me once, kiss me twice, and kiss me once again. It's been a long, long time.' That's the way the song goes." Niki stopped. Odd, she couldn't remember the rest of the words to the song.

She thought of another important bit of information to share with Bingo. "We have a peach tree planted in the back yard. It's only a baby right now, but just you wait…"

Bingo cocked his head left and right several times during the one-sided conversation. A time or two he yawned. But mostly, he listened.

# Twenty-two

After errands to the bank, dry cleaners, and then to the garden center to buy proper clippers to trim the new roses, Niki stopped by the grocery. There she bought chicken breast strips and two pounds of ground beef to cook for Bingo. She had a plan. When she visited him again she would take a few chicken morsels to offer. She wouldn't try to touch him; she would only slide the juicy pieces close enough for him to reach out and take them. And then, each day she would move closer. And each day he would associate her with the yummy chicken treats.

Once she was home, the beef went into portion-sized bags and into the freezer for later. She sautéed the chicken in a little olive oil, divided it into plastic bags, and stacked it in the refrigerator. Niki was ready for tomorrow. After she cleaned up the kitchen, she was so pleased she felt she deserved a treat herself. She would check on the vegetable garden, water her daylilies, and then dig the holes for the rose bushes.

Mavis was in the garden, standing before the peach tree in the filtered light of the late afternoon, inspecting several unfurling, fuzzy green leaves. *Niki, dear,* Mavis said to her niece as she walked past carrying the shovel, *did you know that the peach tree is not indigenous to our area? Well, it isn't. An English colonist imported them. I don't know what they were called when the*

*Chinese cultivated them, but when they came to Georgia the story is that someone named the tree after the Native American word sounding like 'pitch tree'. The 'pitch tree' was probably a common pine, nothing like this flowering, fruit tree you are babying out here in the garden. Imagine that: the lovely name was just a confusion of language.*

*I don't know, though, I have my doubts about that story. It seems more likely to me that the tree was originally called a pit tree because of the pit in the center of the fruit. Then some Georgia Cracker with a Scots-Irish accent as solid as a stick of cold butter flavored the English word, pit, and we end up with a peach tree. What do you think, Niki? Perhaps you should write an article for Atlanta Magazine about the peach tree. Clear it all up, once and for all.*

Niki was diligently digging the first hole by the time Mavis stopped talking about peach trees and joined her. She rested her hand on Niki's shoulder. *I'd love to know what happened with the poor little dog. You seem happy today, so I'm thinking he's going to recover. I suppose Jack has left for the war of the week? You know, I learned a long time ago that Jack is like a summer head cold. You just have to let it run its course.*

Niki dug into the second hole, being careful to space it far enough away from the first to give the roses room to spread out. The freshly turned earth was fragrant and moist from yesterday's rain. Niki breathed in deeply, wondering why she'd been an apartment dweller all those years.

When a healthy breeze blew out of nowhere to stir the full skirt of Mavis' silk shirtwaist dress, she laughed, twirled around with the little wind, and began to sing: *Kiss me once, kiss me twice. Kiss me once again. It's been a long, long time.*

On the second refrain, as Mavis' throaty alto voice rose into the wind, Niki thought she heard the phone ring. She stopped digging, listened, released the shovel, and ran for the house. Just as she picked up the receiver, the call ended and the message light blinked on the answering machine resting next to the phone. She hit the playback button and Jack's voice filled the empty kitchen. "Hey. I'm in London waiting for my flight over to Paris. It's raining ropes, as the French say, instead of cats and dogs. It's eleven-thirty Paris time. I think I told you I'm at the Sully Hotel. I left the phone number on a Post It note on the mirror in my room. Because of the bad weather, don't know when we'll make the hop over for the shoot. I'll try to call tomorrow. Take care."

Mavis breezed inside to stand beside Niki just as Jack's message finished. *Oh, no. I missed it. Play it again, Niki. I want to hear his voice.*

Niki pressed playback on the answering machine and listened to Jack's message a second time before she hit the save button. She and Mavis sighed, one sigh sounding like the echo of the other. Both were sorry that Niki had missed Jack's call.

Outside again, the tangle of vines and thorny bushes humping over the glass potting shed at the far end of the yard occupied Niki's attention. She wondered if perhaps Terry had a gardener he'd loan out for a day to clean up the shed. After a shower, she would call Terry and ask. She wanted to thank him again for yesterday, anyway.

While Niki was in the bath struggling with the hand-held shower, and vowing to install a large walk-in shower if she stayed in the house, Hamilton Rabonette–also known as The Weasel–knocked on the front door. Mavis flew to the foyer, and when he stepped closer to leave a business card in the door, she got a good look at him through the glass sidelights. *Pity. Looks just like his father.*

A shadow moving across the glass startled Rabonette. He stepped back too quickly and tripped on a loose tile, tangling on his own feet. Once he regained his footing, and took a quick look around the neighborhood to make sure no one had seen his pratfall, The Weasel retreated to his car, limping.

*Poor Baby. He seems to have hurt his leg. Well, one can only hope the pain is lasting.* Mavis heard the phone ringing again and flew back to the kitchen where the machine had just rolled over to answer. After the caller identified himself, Mavis recognized the voice as an old friend of Jack's, a fellow photojournalist. He said he was going to Paris; heard Jack was there, and wanted to get together. Could someone please call him and let him know where Jack was staying in Paris? Mavis smiled. *How fortuitous.* She looked down at the row of five buttons on the answering machine, deciding which might do what she wanted done, and pressed one.

A setting sun painted the Atlanta sky coral, pale blue, and white. Niki sat on the screened porch drinking iced tea with lemon. She'd phoned Terry. He would report for gardening duty, along with a pair of helpers, the following morning. Once she got the worker bees busy with the shed, she would take the chicken bribes to Dr. Jim's office and visit with Bingo. All in all, Niki felt it had been a good day, except for finding Rabonette's card in the front door when she went out to collect the mail. No matter, she told herself. I don't have to talk to him. Bingo is going to mend, Jack is safe, at least for the moment, and I have this glorious sky.

Mavis took up her favorite spot on the wicker chaise. *I see you're drinking tea. I'd give a pretty penny for a double scotch right now. You know, years ago I used to smoke those thin French cigarettes. I can't recall the brand name, but they were extremely satisfying. Stopped smoking though. Martin was determined the habit was unhealthy. I guess he was right.*

A fly buzzed against the screen and Niki got up to swat it with her shoe. The fly fell dead into one of the rose pots, a reminder that she needed to finish the rose planting project she'd started earlier. *I feel so good tonight, if it weren't getting dark, I'd plant the roses now. But it's too late.* Another unfinished project came to mind—the remaining pages in Jack's cardboard box.

After Mavis kicked off her shoes and wriggled her toes, her right hand went up to touch her pearl earring. When she felt her left, naked earlobe she sighed. *A missing earring is a terrible tragedy. If I'd misplaced both, I could put the loss out of my mind, know they were gone forever. But one gone missing? Then there is always hope for its return. Silly, I know. Wait. Niki, I just thought of something. Maybe my matching pearl is in Jack's box with the papers. Why don't you go fetch the box and take a look?*

Niki rose from the chair, thinking she felt good enough to handle the rest of Mavis' story, and retrieved the box from the kitchen table. As twilight gathered and crickets woke for the night, Niki turned on the table lamp on the porch and began to read. She picked up where Mavis was writing about finding the Baker Street house.

*When Ellis and I first looked at the three-story, red brick house, we felt the only sane course of action would be to burn it down and start over. It was a wreck.* The two bay windows flanking the front door were sagging like some old dowager's face. The trim hadn't been painted since Peachtree Street was a dirt road to the boondocks, and what paint remained was a nasty brown. When you stepped into the entry hall, the smell of wet, rotting garbage almost knocked you over and when you made your way to the front rooms, forty years of abandoned mouse nests—and God knows what all—were hidden about in piles of newspaper. And we won't even talk about the kitchen.

Noticing Niki had picked up the papers from Jack's box, curiosity got the better of Mavis and she left the comfort of the wicker chaise to look over Niki's shoulder. *Oh, you're reading about us remodeling the Baker Street house. That was a very long time ago, but I remember it vividly. It was fun, actually. Having red velvet drapes custom made for the parlor, ordering Italian tiles for the new fireplace surround, shopping the estate sales and auctions for furniture. That's how I met Martin Book, you know. We kept running in to each other at auctions; bidding on the same items. He was an excellent physician, but buying and selling antiques was his passion.*

When Niki felt air whispering across the back of her neck, she shuttered and reached around to fluff her hair away from the collar of her shirt. Then thinking she would be more comfortable, she left her chair and stretched out on the wicker chaise to read.

Mavis planted her hands on her slim hips. *Well for heavens sake, Niki. You've taken my favorite place to sit. Move over and I'll sit beside you.* Niki didn't move and Mavis stifled a yawn with the back of a hand. *Oh, never mind, dear.* She picked up her shoes from the floor beside the chaise. *It's okay. I think I'll let you read in peace and go back to the bedroom and visit with Abelard. Besides, I know the part about Baker Street by heart anyway. Don't forget to check for my pearl earring in the box.*

With a little wave, Mavis left the porch and crossed the living room, her stocking feet silent on the tile floor. By the time she walked through the foyer and shadowed across the carved birds mirror, she was fading. By the time she stood at the canary's cage and spoke to him, she felt the draw of the rocking sea and saw the lights welcoming her.

Niki herself yawned. It had been a busy day and she still felt tired from yesterday. Was it only yesterday that Jack had run over Bingo? Only twenty-four hours ago? She tilted her head, listening, thinking for a moment that Jack might phone again. Then she remembered the time difference between

Paris and Atlanta and knew he wouldn't. Niki picked up her aunt's papers and read on.

Mavis continued to describe finding the house on Baker Street in terrible disrepair: The upstairs was not as bad. Though half the ceilings were falling down in soggy clumps due to roof leaks, most of the garbage seemed to have been moved to the first floor. We were actually encouraged by the second floor, and I remember Ellis remarked that the wide plank pine floors weren't buckled from the water, yet. The house was sad really. Spacious rooms, once occupied by a wealthy Atlanta family, had been partitioned and re-partitioned to make a rabbit warren of tiny rooms to rent. And, the one and only bath was located on the first floor. Nevertheless, on the positive side, the house was quite large, in a prime location, and very cheap.

I can't say I ever loved the Baker Street house, certainly not the same way I adore 24 Cherokee Place, but after we took a contractor over there and he came back to us with a reasonable plan for renovation, I could see the wisdom of mortgaging our lives to purchase the grand old dame, That's what Ellis always called the house–the grand old dame. I wonder now if Baker Street didn't remind him of houses he knew in New Orleans as a child. I do wish I could ask him.

Anyway, with our renovation plans in hand and wearing out best business suits, Ellis and I called on several Atlanta banks about a loan. All turned us down. Of course, the country was still cash short and suffering terribly from the depression in the late thirties, so even with our large down payment, I can see why the banks were skeptical. We couldn't very well give them a business plan based on illegal whiskey and gambling, now could we?

Interestingly enough, when the idea of going over to Auburn Avenue and approaching Mr. Herndon at Atlanta Life

Insurance dawned on Ellis, they were happy to make us the loan. Now that I look back on it, I think Mr. Herndon was sold on the location of the property, and not on us. Being a savvy businessman, he knew if we couldn't make the payments a foreclosure would net him a renovated property on a potentially high traffic commercial street. Then Atlanta Life would own an instant office building in a white neighborhood without him trying to buck the white system. Yes, Mr. Herndon was a smart man.

It took eight months to put the house to right, but the contractor was a magician with wood and plaster. It was his idea to build the wraparound porch from the rear of the house along the left side and all the way across the front. After he rebuilt the bay windows, they tucked under the porch roof as though they looked out on Baker Street from shaded eyebrows. There were two rooms on either side of a sitting room at the rear of the house. That's where Marie and I lived. We shared a large bath. The kitchen was huge and we took most of our meals at the long, pine farm table under the windows. The formal dining room, living room, front parlor, billiards room, and sunroom were located on the front and sides of the house. Ellis and Jack had a new apartment over the three-car garage in the rear. Most guests parked back there, climbed the three steps, and walked around the covered porch to the front door.

It was a simple plan, really. We were known as a private club where a small, elite membership could play cards, have a special dinner prepared, and trade gossip. Each member paid a monthly fee. That fee guaranteed access to the downstairs front rooms and game rooms –the public rooms. Our excellent cook, Little Flora, kept the guests happy with crab canapés, cinnamon sugared pecans, or some other delicious treat. Special private dinners, drinks, and added services were billed by the middle of the month. Members paid the tab by the first of the following month.

All members understood the house added a percentage onto their bill. If someone didn't like the arrangement, they didn't join. Members were accepted by recommendation from another member, and always invited as guests initially so that Ellis and I could decide their suitability. Judge Benny Renfroe, an old customer from the Moody Street days, was our first member. He helped us work out the details and we had no problems filling the membership. If a tab wasn't paid in thirty days, membership was withdrawn and Ellis would politely deny that gentleman access until the account was settled. In fifteen years, I can only recall one member who left owing us money, and he died of a heart attack in his sleep, bless his heart, so I don't fault him.

Baker Street was about successful men having a comfortable place—away from the couples dominated country club—where they could socialize. It was also about making a comfortable living for us. And it certainly did that. We paid off the mortgage in five years. If members played gin rummy, poker, or bridge for higher stakes than pennies, I made it my business not to know about it. If members discussed business or politics, or formed financial alliances, we were a private house with a staff that had no interest in knowing the nature of their business.

Of course, I knew about the business of untaxed liquor Brother Frank sold us and we, in turn, sold by the drink to the members. But you know, before the war it all seemed like a fairly innocent way to make a living. And when, during the war, President Roosevelt went on the radio to announce a new tax levied on earnings to raise money for the war effort, we felt it was our duty to make sure the amount we paid in taxes was our fair share. Ellis even enlisted in the army, for goodness sakes.

Niki rubbed her eyes. She was tired of reading and a little bored by Mavis' commentary on the Baker Street house. This part didn't sound very different from the business at Moody Street. Grandfather Frank provided the whiskey; Mavis and Ellis provided a comfortable place to serve it. Since Terry was coming over with his gardeners early in the morning, Niki decided to go to bed, finish Mavis' story another day.

# Twenty-three

At a little before seven the next morning Niki was dreaming it was summer. Another Atlanta day in the nineties, but it was her tenth birthday and she didn't care about the heat. Aunt Mavis was taking her to the Atlanta zoo. She was excited about seeing the gorilla called Willie B. again. He was her favorite. In her young girl's heart, she was sure that the huge creature's sad eyes saw into her soul, and understood she would set him free, if only she could.

Niki woke to the smell of gardenias and thought, in her shallow wakefulness, that Aunt Mavis was standing over her bed telling her it was time to get up. An exciting day deserved to be savored. Of course, she told herself, Mavis was not there, and it wasn't her tenth birthday, but she got up anyway, thinking to get a head start on the day. After she dressed and took her coffee out to the porch, the sight of the cardboard box and knowing she had only a few pages left of Mavis' story, prompted Niki to sit and read.

*The upstairs rooms at Baker Street were rented to young women whom we felt were, for lack of a better word, acceptable.* No drinking was allowed upstairs. Any drugs and you were gone as soon as a taxi arrived. Fern lived in the largest bedroom on the second floor. Five other bedrooms were split between the second and third floors. All girls paid identical rent. Baker Street had been a boarding house since around 1900, when it was not un-usual for an establishment to cater to young, working women. Back then it wasn't considered safe, or respectable, for a young woman to live alone. In our day, it was more a matter of eco-nomics. A room in a boarding house rented for a lot less than an apartment. And since women were paid less than men, no matter what job they did, many single women were forced into boarding houses until they married.

The upstairs at Baker Street was reached either by the "grand" staircase from the foyer or by an outside stair at the rear of the house. Only Ellis and I had keys to the door to the outside stairs. Ellis made his office in the butler's pantry tucked in the foyer, under the grand staircase. He always knew who went upstairs, and the arrangement was that each mem-ber would speak to Ellis on his way down again. All members knew better than to abuse the privilege, lest those privileges be withdrawn. As I said, it was a simple plan.

It's unfortunate we didn't withdraw Ham Rabonette's priv-ileges long before that night. Perhaps if I had not been worried about other things, I would have seen it coming. The Atlanta mayor was under a lot of pressure to give the police chief carte blanche to crack down on gambling and illegal whiskey in the city. Then there was a bribery scandal in the police department and many of the old, trusted faces were gone.

Rumors about corruption and an impending sweep of sus-pected illegal businesses ricocheted all over town. We began to think that we were operating on borrowed time, especially af-ter Senator Kefauver's hearings on organized crime saturated the news. I think that was around 1950. Not that we had any-thing to do with organized crime, but when the hearings were broadcast every day on the radio, the public followed them like soap operas. Then everybody was jumping to conclusions about the mob operating in Atlanta, and turning over every outhouse looking for gangsters.

Even our clients who'd previously laughed off the idea of a citywide sweep, and knew they had sufficient political clout to assure a phone call in advance–if a sweep was planned–felt uneasy. Ellis and I talked about converting the downstairs into a fancy restaurant. We could have imported a chef from New Orleans, hired a jazz trio, and allowed the customers to bring in their own whiskey in a brown bag–perfectly legal in Atlanta. But we didn't. I don't know why.

It seemed that our energy was spent looking over our shoulders and dealing with one drama after another at Baker Street. Between Marie's excessive drinking and my hauling her to one "dry-out" hospital after another, and a kitchen fire that closed us down for two months, I had my hands full. Then, just when I thought we were back to calm waters, one of the girls somehow got into the office safe and walked away, or should I say drove away, with a little over three thousand dollars, plus my emerald necklace. It was just one thing after another.

By the end of 1952, the Baker Street years were over. But I'm getting ahead of myself. I was talking about Hamilton Rabonette. When a respected member brought Ham to Baker Street just before 1950 dawned, he was fresh from a national tennis tour, his fair face smiling and confident on the cover of Colliers Magazine. In his mind, at least, he was a celebrity. Ham was brashly charming, some said handsome, glib, and exuded an air of aristocratic slumming. I disliked him on sight. A month or so after his first visit, he returned as a guest at our annual masquerade party held annually on December 21. He was dressed as Bluebeard the pirate. What else? That should have been a big clue.

By the time the party was in full swing he and Fern were goo-goo eyeing each other; by the end of the evening they had left together for parts unknown. By New Year's Eve, Ham was a regular at Baker Street and a regular with Fern.

Niki looked up from Mavis' words, wondering if she had understood correctly. Ham? Is Mavis talking about our Hamilton Rabonette's father? The Weasel's father–a regular with Fern–Jack's mother? Niki's eyes went back to the typed pages.

I knew Ham was engaged to Ada Atherton, the youngest daughter of another real estate family in Atlanta. But what could I do? You couldn't tell Fern anything. Good Lord, she was twenty-three by then and had a five-year old son. You'd think she was fourteen the way she carried on about Ham. I remember even Marie tried to talk some sense into her. After all, Marie knew from her own experience of being dumped years ago by Bucky Mitchell–another Atlanta society brat–that boys like Ham like to play in your backyard. But they don't come through the front door and marry you.

Atlanta society brat? Niki's stomach lurched. Now she was sure Mavis was writing about The Weasel's father. *Does Jack know this story? Is that why he dislikes Rabonette?* Niki read on, now with more concentration, and greater speed.

Truthfully, Fern acted that way about anything she decided she had to have. She only thought of herself; never considered the consequences. Then when the adventure was over, she moved on, leaving the battered hearts for someone else to mend. Just like she did with Ellis, and just like she did with Jack.

I loved Fern, I really did, but well, Fern was Fern. Her selfishness saddened me for a long time. She broke Ellis' heart even though he didn't talk about it. And I know Jack was certainly shortchanged for a mother. As good a daddy as Ellis was to Jack, there was no making up for the fact that Fern pretty much ignored him. She wouldn't even nurse Jack when he was born. Said nursing would ruin her figure.

Niki frowned and looked up from the page she'd been reading, wondering how badly Jack had suffered from having Fern as a mother. She knew Mavis had loved him, but…

A knock hammered on the back door and a voice called out, "Ms. Banks. Ms. Banks. You up yet?"

Oh crap, I wanted to finish this, Niki muttered, and put the papers back in the box. Must be Terry and the gardeners.

Two young men stood on the back patio. Both wore tight, faded jeans and white tee shirts, rolled up at the upper arms to expose tan and well defined muscles. Niki looked at one, then the other. Although the man on the left had bright yellow, dyed hair spiked up in front like a rude pointing gesture, and the other man's head was crowned with dark brown curls, they looked remarkably alike.

"Hey," said the yellow haired young man. "I'm Ed. This is my brother, Ward. And yes ma'am, we're twins. Mr. Spiegel sent us over."

Niki opened the door and stepped out onto the patio. Twins. Her mind flashed to the fact that Mavis and Marie were twins, though not identical like these guys. She wanted to get them working and go back inside to finish Mavis' story about Baker Street.

"Nice to meet you, Ed, and Ward. Is that right?"

Now the darker haired man spoke up. "Yes ma'am. He's Ed and I'm Ward on account of our parents had five girls in a row before us, and our mama wanted to name the first born son after our daddy." He paused, looking at Niki. When she didn't offer a reply, he continued. "Daddy's name is Edward."

After a half stroke silence, Niki got it and smiled. "Oh, I see. Edward. Right."

The yellow-haired Ed shook his head several times. "He tells that stupid story to everybody we meet. Embarrasses the hell out of me. Terry said to tell you he had something he had to do first thing this morning but he'd call you a little later. What was it you needed us to do for you?"

They walked back to the shed and Niki explained, "I'd like all the vines and stuff cut away and hauled off. You can keep any snakes you find."

They smiled as though they'd heard that joke before. Many times.

"Then I'd like to… sort of…maybe look at whether it can be repaired. I know there are broken panes of glass in several windows, and I'm not sure if the roof is sound. Can you clean it up for me so I can decide about the repairs?"

"Yes ma'am. No problem. We'll get our tools out of the truck."

"Wonderful, thanks." After Niki was back inside the house, she realized she hadn't asked Ed and Ward about their hourly rate. She considered turning around, going back outside and asking, then decided against it. She would talk to Terry and pay Ed and Ward what he paid them. Or, she would ask them later about the hourly rate. At the moment, she wanted to pour herself another cup of coffee, finish Mavis' memoir, and drive over to Dr. Jim's office to visit with Bingo.

# Twenty-four

Settling back in a wicker chair on the screened porch, Niki picked up the last of the charred pages. She hoped they weren't burned beyond reading because she was curious about what else Mavis wrote about Jack's mother, Fern. And about what kind of mother could ignore her son. Did she not love him? Niki was also curious about what else Mavis would say about Fern's relationship with Hamilton Rabonette. So far, it seemed that Mavis wasn't fond of Rabonette. And what had Jack's dad thought about this other man coming to Baker Street to see Fern? Niki reached back in her memory, trying to recall if Fern and Ellis had been married. She thought not. But still, he couldn't have been happy about Rabonette hanging about Baker Street.

Niki's thoughts bounced to The Weasel. Why did he bring his aging, sick father to Mavis' funeral? Why would his father want to be there? When Niki began to read again, the story seemed to have jumped ahead. The first page began:

*Atlanta Woman Dies in Freak Accident. That's what the newspapers said. But that is not what happened.* It all started back in June. Ham Rabonette had been to the house on Thursday night to see Fern. In fact, he was there most of the night. Then on Sunday morning Fern opened the morning paper to the society section. Half of the front page was filled with wedding pictures of the

Atherton-Rabonette garden wedding. According to the following article, the wedding had been held the afternoon before at the Morningside Golf and Country Club, and was attended by most of the crème de la crème of Atlanta society. Marie, Ellis, and I were having coffee in the kitchen when Fern slammed the Sunday paper down on the table. I noticed that in the obligatory photograph of the happy couple, Ham looked smug and handsome in his wedding tuxedo. He seemed to be gazing into the eyes of the homely little Ada with adoration, though I suspect it was really avarice for her daddy's money. Ada looked grateful and demure. Poor Ada. She was a lamb to the slaughter.

Marie, never the speechless sister, gibed at Fern, "Well, Fern honey, would y'all look at that. It's a fucking wonder the prick didn't ask you to be maid of honor."

Fern went berserk, screaming and raking everything off the kitchen table. When she reached for dishes to throw, Marie, Ellis, and I headed for the back porch, out of the line of fire. Before she wound down, Fern had shattered every plate, cup, and saucer in the kitchen cupboard, and broken two of the ladder-backed, kitchen chairs. I'm glad we kept the good china locked in the pantry. Ellis watched her from the porch through the windows. When she started slashing the cushions on the chairs with a butcher knife, he went back inside and took the knife away from her. She hit him, kicked, and cursed, but finally she calmed down enough to let him sit on one of the unbroken chairs and hold her. Poor Baby Fern. She was crying so hard her whole body shuddered. Broken dishes and broken dreams everywhere.

On Tuesday, the Queen of Hearts Florist delivered two-dozen red roses to Fern. The enclosed card read: Don't believe what you read in the funny papers, Sugar Pie. You're my girl. H.R.

If Ham had delivered the flowers in person and I'd had the butcher knife, I might have killed him where he stood. Three weeks later Ham returned from his honeymoon and slithered his way back into Fern's bed. I'm not certain what he told her, but I can almost hear his lying mouth swearing he really didn't love Ada, never made love to her, and would divorce her just as soon as it was "financially" feasible. Marie was right. The man was a prick, plain and simple.

All through the summer and fall Ham Rabonette made sporadic appearances at Baker Street, usually drinking too much and shooting his mouth off with one crass remark or another. No doubt he and Fern fought about his marriage to Ada. Fern was sullen, not sleeping well. Ham was just simply obnoxious. Marie was drinking heavily. Ellis was like a cat waiting for the rocking chair to land on his tail. Thank goodness Jack was away at camp for part of the summer, and then by fall, he was busy being a new first-grader.

I would never have put up with Ham Rabonette's behavior from a regular customer. About the only person he didn't insult was Brother Frank. Ham was a fool, but he wasn't stupid enough to cross Frank—not with Frank's quick temper and the pistol he usually carried in his belt. Then too, I knew by then that Ham's daddy was Frank's money partner, so I figured the two of them were bound together, like it or not. Or so I thought.

Late one Friday morning Ham showed up at the house unexpectedly and let himself into the kitchen. I was busy writing out the grocery and supply list for Ellis and certainly didn't care to be disturbed by Mr. Rabonette. He poured himself coffee and had the nerve to sit at the table with me and start some kind of nonsense about him buying into the business. The way he talked, he hadn't a clue that Ellis and I were partners—the man was blind as well as dumb. He went on and on about how he'd made valuable contacts down in Cuba, and had a plan to increase our profits five hundred percent.

I probably looked at the man as though he had lost his mind, but refused to respond to his overtures. What was wrong with him? Didn't he read the newspapers? We were worried that the mayor would sell us out for an election year headline in the Sunday edition of the Journal, and this fool was talking about some hair-brained plan that would make us more visible than we already were. And Cuban contacts at that. Yes, I could just see the New York mob's accountant, Meyer Lansky, stopping off at our house for dinner on his way back from checking on the casinos in Cuba. What world did Ham live in!

About that time Fern bounced into the kitchen. "Oh Ham honey," she sang in her sweet little voice, "I didn't know you were coming by. What a nice surprise." She glided across the room and perched on his lap, nuzzling him with a kiss under his jaw as she settled in. A puppy greeting her owner, I was thinking as I watched her.

She parted his jacket enough to get her arms around him and then rubbed against his chest as she cooed, "And look at me. I just got out of the tub and my hair is soaking wet." Fern extracted a well-manicured hand from around Ham's waist and patted her damp curly hair. "Do I look just too, too ugly? Like a drowned rat, I bet."

That was it. If I sat at the table and watched them any longer I would surely throw up. I got up just as he separated her robe front and casually traced her right breast with his hand until his index finger rested on her nipple. She shivered with delight and playfully scolded him to stop that in front of her sister.

I busied myself at the sink and tried to ignore them. It was impossible. Ham cooed back to Fern, "Sugar, you don't look like a drowned rat to me. I'd say you look more like a wet pussy."

Fern giggled and they left the kitchen for upstairs. I should have cracked his head with a cast iron skillet right then. Ham had no respect for Fern, or any other woman.

It was December eighteenth when it happened. The whole house was in a flurry making plans for the annual masquerade party scheduled for the twenty-first. The florist and caterer occupied my time most of the afternoon. I remember they argued over whether red poinsettias would be the best accent for the roasted chicken stuffed with walnuts and currants, or if we should go with simple green holly. Finally they compromised, deciding to use some of both and left congratulating each other on their mutual creative talents. I was left with a splitting headache and wishing I'd not hired either of them.

Ellis was in the cellar, taking inventory of the liquor and wines. Marie and the other girls were probably upstairs primping for the evening. Ellis' Aunt Evangeline, from the French side of his family, had recently visited us and taken Jack back home with her to New Orleans for a holiday before Christmas. I'm grateful for that. Martin and I were in the study. As I recall we were sharing a laugh about the costumes he and his friend, Terry Spiegel, were planning to wear to the party, and having a brandy before we moved on to discuss business.

By this time, Martin, Ellis, and I had formed a partnership to import and sell antiques and art. We were doing quite well, probably because Martin was knowledgeable and had made excellent connections in Europe after the war. That particular evening we discussed a deal we'd recently completed: the purchase and subsequent resale of six, eighteenth-century,

Chippendale dining chairs. Martin was interested in rolling our proceeds into another venture, and my attention was on several photographs spread out on the coffee table showing an ornate, Dutch court cupboard. I remember Martin was explaining the symbolism of the intricate hunting scenes carved into the cupboard's door fronts. I didn't even realize Ham Rabonette was in the house.

When I heard a sound like glass breaking above our heads, and then the sound of something fairly heavy smashing against a hard surface, I left the study to check on the noise. I remember Martin stayed; probably thinking whatever was going on was harmless. The next sound was furniture sliding across the wood floor and slamming against a wall. That's when I took off at a run for the stairs. I heard Ham Rabonette yelling, "You little cunt. Tell me who. Whose are they?"

Ellis passed me going up, taking the steps two at a time. I heard more sliding furniture sounds, glass breaking, a thud, and then nothing. Marie and the other girls were in the upstairs hall when I reached Fern's door. Ellis was banging on the door with his fist. When he didn't get a response, he turned the knob and pushed, but the door was not opening. He pushed again, but it still didn't move.

I shooed the girls back to their rooms, telling them not to come out until I called them. Everyone except Marie retreated. Poor frightened Marie stood horror stricken against the opposite wall of the hallway, gripping a curling iron in one hand and a brush in the other, as though to fend off the violence behind Fern's door.

Ellis put his shoulder to the bedroom door and I heard him grunt like a bear when he forced aside whatever was blocking his way. The door opened enough for him, then for me, to squeeze through. The room was a battlefield. The reading chair and lamp were overturned and lay cocked against one wall; a drape was torn from the window; the green paper window shade hung down by one bracket; bedcovers were stripped off the bed and piled on the floor; several dresser drawers were pulled out and thrown against the wall. Fern's vanity mirror was broken into crazed shards.

For a moment, I thought the room was empty, until I saw the reflection in the broken vanity mirror. I turned to my right–two bodies crumpled in the corner beside the dresser. Ham was face down–no shirt or shoes–atop Fern. He moaned; tried to stand. Ellis had him by his belt jerking him off Fern before he could get footing. When Ham snarled in a drunken voice, "Get that high-yeller nigger off me," Ellis slung him off to the side like a sack of potatoes, and he fell to the floor with a groan.

Fern was lying face up, not moving. Her head was twisted oddly to one side as though she was struggling to see something above and behind her. There was a strawberry abrasion marking her right cheekbone. As my mind began to comprehend what I saw, Ellis lifted her out of the corner onto the rug. A smeared trail of blood marked where her head had rested.

I took a pillow from the heap of bedcovers and put it under her head. Blood seeped from her hair onto the white cotton and widened into an arc. I thought of finding Mama years ago; could smell the blood again. Ellis leaned over Fern, close to her mouth, checking for breath. I knelt and felt her neck, then her wrist, for a pulse. There was none.

I don't think Ellis understood at first. He kept saying, "Come on, Baby, get a breath now, come on, breathe for me, Baby. Breathe for me." It seems he said it ten times over and over before he stopped and looked at me. I think I was numb at that point and couldn't feel much of anything. But Ellis, Ellis began to cry. Tears dropped from his face onto the shoulder of Fern's dressing gown. The room seemed suspended in time. All I could see were his tears making one dark circle after another on the pale blue satin.

I have no idea how long we knelt beside Fern's body. It may have been seconds, or it may have been minutes, I don't know. The next thing I remember was Ham Rabonette getting to his feet and jerking me up by my arm. He thrust his fist into my face and mumbled something like, "Tell that little cunt to get up off the floor and tell me whose these are." Then he opened his fist and held out a pair of gold, horse heads cufflinks with small diamonds in each eye. When I said nothing, he thrust them closer to my face, as though the cufflinks would explain everything.

When I grabbed the bits of gold from his open hand and pocketed them, Ham drew back to hit me. I ducked his drunken effort and Ellis came up off his knees and punched him. His nose cracked like a dry twig. Blood splattered into the air, raining across my dress in tiny sprinkles, and then he dropped to the floor, unconscious.

There were voices from the hall and knocking on the door. Marie and Martin were trying to force their way into the room. "Stay outside, Marie," I called. "Don't come in here. Let Martin in. You stay in the hall." The last thing I needed was Marie in the room getting hysterical.

Martin wedged his way through the doorway. I think he had to push Marie back into the hall. I could hear her crying. The next few seconds were filled with the horror of what had happened, and the realization of what it could mean for all of us. Martin felt for a pulse, and then tried to revive Fern–more for our benefit, I think, than for hers. Martin was a good doctor. I'm sure he knew by the twisted angle of her neck, and the blood, that she was dead even before he checked. I think it was Martin who covered Fern with the spread from her bed, but I'm not sure. I do remember Ellis ripped one of the bed sheets and tied Ham's hands and feet so he couldn't cause any more trouble.

What did we do next? As I recall, Marie continued crying outside the bedroom door and I went out into the hall to comfort her. The rest of the house was quiet. When I finally let Marie into the bedroom, she stood against the far wall shivering. Ellis, Martin, and I talked in short half sentences.

We agreed there was no reason to hurry an ambulance. She was dead. When we called the police, who would come? Did we have any friends on duty? Would they believe Ham had killed her? Intentional or not, he killed her. He would lie to the police. His daddy would fix it. Yes, his daddy. He'd say it wasn't Ham.

"You know," Martin said thoughtfully, "Ham despises Ellis—can't stand the thought of him and Fern together. He'll say Ellis killed her."

I went over to Marie and hugged her to me, told her to pull herself together. "Sister," I told her, "stop crying and go call Brother Frank. Tell him we need him over here right now. Don't accept any excuses and no details over the phone—just tell him to come. If he balks, tell him his partner's son has stepped in enough shit to bury us all."

By the time Brother Frank arrived, December sleet blew sideways against the windows, pinging and popping as it hit the glass. I'm not sure who thought of the plan, but we all agreed—all except Ham Rabonette. He didn't get a vote. I insisted Martin leave Baker Street immediately, so that the police wouldn't ask him about the incident, and he wouldn't have to lie about what happened. He resisted, being the gentleman that he was, but finally did as I asked. Frank washed the blood off Rabonette's face and shoved him and the rest of his clothes in the back seat of his car to sleep off the booze. After that, Ellis and Brother Frank carried Fern to the steep outside stairway that descended from the upper floors of the house to the back parking area. The ground at the bottom was turning to slick, red mud as the freezing rain pelted the warmer ground. The wood steps were already glassy with ice.

It wrenched my heart to leave her there in the mud, but it was the only choice. Rabonette would have hung us all for Fern's death. And here is the irony. When we called the police, neither the coroner nor the Atlanta PD questioned why Fern would go down the back stairs in the freezing rain, dressed only in her silk dressing gown.

I told them I'd found her when I went around to lock up for the night. They didn't question that explanation either. They simply filled out the proper forms, carried her away in an ambulance, and left, eager to be where it was dry and warm. To them Fern was only one more whore, dead in the freezing rain.

Brother Frank drove Ham Rabonette, and his car, home and took a taxi back to Baker Street to pick up his own car. He left again without coming into the house. I don't know what he said to Rabonette as they drove. I never asked. The next day a small paragraph appeared in the Atlanta Journal about an unfortunate accident that had claimed beautiful young Fern Banks' life. The following Sunday, in the society section, there was a two-column piece about Mr. and Mrs. Hamilton Rabonette's upcoming second honeymoon cruise to Havana. The couple wanted to get away, the article said, to enjoy each other's company before the expected arrival of their first child.

I've often wondered if Ham told Fern about Ada's baby that night and about the trip they were taking to Havana. Maybe that's what really started the argument. We'll never know. And then I've also wondered how Ham explained his broken nose to the blissfully happy Mrs. Hamilton Rabonette. No doubt, the story must have been a good one.

We closed the house that night and didn't open again until after the first of the year. The girls complained, of course, because the Christmas season was always a busy time when money flowed easily, downstairs and upstairs. Our annual masquerade party was cancelled, much to the disappointment of our members. And in fact, there were no more parties at Baker Street after that night.

Fern was buried in the Banks' family plot at Oakland Cemetery with only the family present. After the funeral, Ellis drove down to New Orleans to bring Jack home. Then the day after Christmas, Marie, Ellis and I took six-year old Jack up to the mountain cabin in Cashiers—a trip Jack and I would make again, two years later. The child only asked about his mother once. Ellis told him she went to live with the angels in heaven. Jack looked puzzled, as though he couldn't imagine why she would want to live with angels. Or perhaps he was puzzled that angels would want her to live among them.

On one bitterly cold night in Cashiers, we sat on the porch bundled in coats and blankets, looking across the valley to dark humps of mountains beyond. Except for the lamp burning behind us in the cabin, there wasn't a single light to break the darkness until we looked up. Above us, the canopy of night sky hung low, encrusted with brilliant, uncountable stars. Atlanta seemed far away.

And the gold, horse head cufflinks? There were times I wanted to throw them in Brother Frank's face, but I didn't.

I saved them. When he died, and was laid out in his fancy mahogany casket at the funeral home, I slipped the cufflinks into the breast pocket of his suit. I hope those cufflinks weigh like a grindstone on his heart for every single second of eternity.

# *Twenty-five*

The kitchen clock chiming half-past eight brought Niki back to the screened porch. Her mind felt cloudy, confused by what she'd read. She must be misunderstanding what Mavis had written. She understood the part about Hamilton Rabonette killing Fern in a drunken rage about something, and them moving Fern to the bottom of the stairs. In the mud. Oh my God, how horrible. The mud. Niki remembered what old Rabonette had said at Mavis' funeral, "Ferns in the mud, ferns in the mud." Now she knew what he meant. He was thinking of that night, where they left Fern. Was he trying to say he was sorry? Is that why he came to the funeral? Or was he there to gloat because he'd outlived everyone who could accuse him of murder?

Then there was the rest of Mavis' story–about the Baker Street girls–which she didn't quiet grasp.

Niki dropped the papers back into the box, deciding she needed to change clothes and get to Dr. Jim's before they brought Bingo's breakfast. Maybe her plan of using the chicken strips to entice him to trust her would work. She hoped so. She would read Mavis' memoir again later. Clear up her misunderstanding.

On her way out to the car Niki waved at Ed and Ward, who were hacking away at Virginia creeper and honeysuckle vines engulfing the shed. Ed waved and trotted over. "Ma'am, did you know you got electrical running into your shed?"

"You mean like lights and wall plugs?"

"Yes, Ma'am. There's a conduit running up that back wall and feeding into the building. It's a good thing we found it before we cut it with a machete. Man-o-man, Ward and me would be lit up like a Christmas tree. The concrete floor looks fine in there, and as near as I can tell, the roof isn't leaking. You got six broken windowpanes. Want us to replace those while we're here?

"Yes, please. If you can."

"What are you going to do with the shed once we get it all cleaned up?"

Niki thought about that for a second. What would she do with the shed? Store garden tools? Start seedlings over the winter?

Ed didn't wait for an answer. "It's a real nice room in there. Plenty of light. Kind of like a little playhouse. What with a little work and all, you could even make it into a guesthouse. Add some running water–maybe even a half-bath."

Niki frowned. Guesthouse? Who would visit? She had no family, unless you counted Jack. Did she count Jack? Was Jack family? No, not really. It appeared they were not really second cousins, as she had always thought. Or maybe they were, by the crazy Banks marriages and alliances–a cousin once removed kind of relationship–but maybe not. It was all too confusing. She let go of Ed's possibilities for the shed and told him she would be home by late morning. The shed would have to wait. She was in a hurry to get to Dr. Jim's and make friends with Bingo.

On the drive to the vet's office, Niki's mind played back Mavis' words about Jack when his mother had died. "The child only asked about his mother once." That's what Mavis had said. How strange. The idea of a little boy so bereft of his mother's love that he didn't seem to miss it, made for a haunting, sad, image. For another block or two in the slow moving morning traffic, Niki contemplated if having Aunt Mavis to fill the gap left by his mother could have been enough for Jack. Then she thought of herself.

She had her mother when her father was no longer a part of her life, though she remembered missing his hugs and his laughter when he danced her around in his arms. After the missing part there was anger because he wasn't there. Then she became aware of a hole inside herself. There the question of why didn't he love her enough to come home lived. And finally there was the day-to-day growing up time, moving into a place of not thinking of her father, of no longer asking the question because she knew it had no answer. Is that what happened to Jack? Did he no longer think of his mother? Niki couldn't imagine asking him that question, or that he would ever answer it, if she did.

Bingo looked up when Niki entered his pen. No indication he was poised to bite her. Then he lowered his head to the blanket again and ignored her. She waited for the right moment to offer him chicken bits, speaking to him softly and slowly.

"Dr. Jim says you can go home in a couple of days. I'm making a list of some things you might want. What do you think? A cushy bed with a tan cover? Or maybe navy blue?" She paused. "Yeah, I agree. Tan is better. Won't show hair as badly. And of course you'll have your own dinner bowl. I found one in the cupboard. Nice heavy pottery that won't tip over. It even has USA stamped on the bottom. Cool huh? Speaking of dinner..." Niki took the plastic sandwich bag from her pocket. It made a slight rustling sound when she opened it. Bingo watched closely. She took a chicken morsel from the bag and held it up for him to see. "Yum. This chicken smells pretty good. Want a piece?" She offered Bingo the morsel. He looked interested, though wary.

Maybe she could stand and give the chicken to him. That plan didn't work. As soon as she was upright and moving closer, he growled. She sat down again, held out the chicken, and scooted herself a little closer to him. He sniffed and scooted a little closer to the chicken. And that's the way it went until Niki was finally able to push the chicken close enough for him to reach the first piece. He quickly snapped up the food. Did his tail wag? Yes, Niki was sure she saw him wag his tail. Just for a second. But nevertheless a wag. She wanted to get up and do a victory dance. By the time the bag of chicken was empty, Niki sat close enough to Bingo to touch him–though she didn't. No future in pressing her good luck and upsetting him–or being bitten.

She sat on the concrete, eying him from a lowered gaze, pretending to ignore him. Soon, the little guy fell asleep. There was a comforting rhythm in his breathing in and out, in and out. The sound whispered: I… live. I… live. I… live. Niki closed her eyes and decided to put his bed next to hers when she got him home.

Later, after she'd stopped off at a new pet superstore at the corner La Vista Road and Briarcliff and filled two large shopping bags with all things dog related, Niki was feeling relaxed and hungry. She went home, unloaded Bingo's new bed and other necessities, and had her peanut butter and banana sandwich prepared before she registered the fact that the twins, Ed and Ward, were gone. Deciding they were off to buy replacement glass for the broken windows, she took her sandwich into the back garden and ate it as she surveyed the work they'd done on the shed.

Ed was right. The small building was more like a miniature house. In addition to removing overgrown vines and bushes, the brothers had washed the two walls of windows, scrubbed down the two wood walls, and cleaned the terracotta tile roof to shine in the sun. Niki ran her fingers over the blistered wood siding. *Needs a good coat of paint, but I can do that.* When she gave the rotted door to the shed a push, it dragged across the cement floor as it opened. She made a mental note to ask Ed about hanging a new door. Inside, the shed smelled of moist earth but was reasonably clean. Niki decided with a few days of airing out, a little paint, a new door, and new overhead lights, the shed just might be suitable for something other than storing tools. The ringing phone sent Niki running. She managed to pick up just before it rolled over to the answering machine. She was glad to hear Terry's voice, but disappointed it was not Jack's.

Terry was short, but pleasant. "Hey Niki. You all right?"

When she assured him that she was, he asked if he could stop by about four o'clock. "Sure. I'll make the martinis."

"Atta-girl. I'll see you then," he replied and hung up.

Niki had over two hours to tidy up her Bingo purchases, have a bath, and make Terry's drinks. *And I need to plant those roses,* she reminded herself. She poured a glass of milk to wash down the peanut butter and took it to the screened porch. Most of Mavis' papers were stacked on the floor beside the wicker chaise, leaving the box nearly empty. When Niki picked it up to move it off the chaise, she heard an object roll to one side. She opened the top, and fishing underneath the papers, withdrew a single pearl and diamond earring. She turned it over in her fingers, feeling the warmth of the almond- sized pearl.

How in the world did I miss this in the box? I must have seen Mavis wear these earrings about a thousand times over the years. Niki tilted the box several times. Nothing else rattled. No second earring. She wondered what had happened to the mate for the pearl, and then dropped the single earring back in the box.

Niki decided to read the last few pages again, slowly. Maybe the confusing details would become clear. She reclined in the chaise lounge and imagined Aunt Mavis sitting beside her telling the story of the Baker Street years. After pausing several times to consider Mavis' choice of words, and recalling how her aunt's straightforward personality would have framed her story, Niki was certain she understood. She didn't like what she read, but she understood.

*Girls upstairs were charged rent…members only allowed on the first floor…unless…Ellis always knew who went upstairs…members got a bill for extras…Hamilton Rabonette was a regular at Baker Street…Grandfather Frank helped cover up Fern's murder…the gold, horse head cufflinks…*

Niki added the twice-read pages to the stack on the floor, and wished Jack had let the papers burn. Why would Mavis write all that down after so many years? Jack's note said he thought she meant me to have the memoir. Why? Why would Mavis want to taint the memory I have of her by revealing she and Ellis operated a house for illegal whiskey, and prostitution? I can't believe she would want me to know that. And does Jack know it? He was a child then, but surely he knew something was going on. Well, maybe not. Jack was only about six when his mother was killed, and Mavis says she closed the house two years later when Jack's dad died.

Niki's fingertips went up to press against her eyelids. Suddenly she felt a headache thundering like buffalo hooves up the back of her head and spreading across her forehead. And what about Grandfather Frank? What was that business about Fern having his cufflinks? Why would she have his cufflinks? Niki flushed with anger, then disgust at the possibility. *No, I cannot believe that Aunt Mavis would want me to know that. What if Jack decided to read the papers after all?*

Her head pounding, Niki hefted the stack of papers in one hand, the box in the other, and stalked out to the kitchen. There, she stuffed Mavis' life story into a garbage bag and raked the old sales receipts and paid bills still sitting on the kitchen table into the box. She tied the top of the garbage bag to seal it, and then tossed the garbage bag in the kitchen pantry and headed for her bathroom to find something for her headache.

As she walked past Jack's closed bedroom door, Niki hesitated. Then unexplainably, she opened the door and stepped into the room she'd considered off-limits since Jack arrived. The wood blinds were half-closed. Thin slats of sunlight filtered into the room and danced in and out of the motion of the ceiling fan. It was cool in there. Cooler, Niki realized, than her bedroom on the back of the house. The blue and white pinstriped comforter was pulled up on the double bed. No clothes left about, a pair of worn brown slippers beside the dresser. Niki smiled, remembering catching Jack before dawn on the screened porch, slippers wet from the sprinkler spraying his feet.

She noticed a yellow sticky note on the mirror, just as Jack had said it would be in his message. The phone number for the Sully Hotel in Paris was printed neatly across the square piece of paper. He hadn't called back. Maybe she should call him. No, she decided. She wouldn't call Jack. After what she'd read in Mavis' papers, she was afraid her voice would give away how she felt. But how did she feel about Mavis' story? Anger squatted in the pit of her stomach. Who was she angry with? The entire Banks family? Just Mavis? Was she angry with Ham Rabonette for getting away with killing Fern, and with Martin Book, whom she'd always respected, for helping cover up the murder? What else did she feel? Shame? Humiliation? Inside her head, a firestorm raged.

Niki took a step closer to the mirror and Jack's note. She noticed a smiley face drawn below the hotel phone number. A smiley face? That was a surprise. A smiley face seemed too spontaneous for Jack, just didn't fit. Like learning to play the Irish flute. Who would think Mr. Knife-Pressed-Jeans with the fancy haircut would play "Danny Boy" every night before bed. The same tune every night, for God's sake. How weird is that? Niki looked around the tidy room again. There was a lot she didn't know about Jack. They were little more than strangers really. It occurred to Niki that Jack was like Bingo. If she moved closer, he growled. Even with a headache, the vision of Jack growling brought a smile. She closed Jack's bedroom door, knowing with certainty what to do with Mavis' papers.

# *Twenty-six*

After two ibuprofen for her headache and a thirty-minute lie down to help them work, Niki carried the prized Buff Beauty roses from the screened porch to the fresh holes she'd prepared for them near her daylilies. Her shovel, along with the plastic garbage bag of charred papers, waited.

Ed and Ward sauntered from the back of the garden carrying tools and a bill. Mavis walked behind them, treading lightly in her high heels on the soft grass and brushing several hitchhiking leaves from her silk, shirtwaist dress. She walked past Niki and looked down at the papers spilling from the open garbage bag.

*I see you have been reading while I was away. My memoir? No doubt. Something tells me you aren't thrilled with my life story. Hmm. I suppose I shouldn't be surprised. And I can't blame you. Jack meant well, I'm sure, but honestly I do wish now that he had left well enough alone.*

Ward handed Niki a bill. "The windowpanes are listed separately at the bottom. Also the glazing compound we bought to put the glass in place. The rest of the compound is out there in the shed, in case you need it for something else. Ed and I sure hope you're happy with the job we done. Call us again, if you need something else."

Mavis patted Ward on the back. *Good job, young man.* He smiled, and Mavis spoke to Niki. *The shed looks wonderful, dear. It hasn't looked that clean since 1953. You know, you could do a lot with that little house. It would make a wonderful studio.*

Niki replied to Ward that she was very happy with the job they'd done, and went inside to get her checkbook. While she was gone, Mavis rifled through the papers in the garbage bag, sending several pages swirling up into the afternoon air. When she was satisfied the papers were all there, she let them fall back into the bag. Ed and Ward looked at each other, puzzled. Ed whispered to Ward, "Now that's a weird wind, ain't it? Nothing blowing but those papers. Hey, I smell gardenias. You smell 'em?" Before Ward could answer, Niki returned and handed them a check. They were gone before she could ask them about replacing the shed door.

Niki knelt on the ground and went about pulling papers from the bag and tearing them into small pieces. She groused as she ripped. "I don't have a clue why Mavis would want to tell me all that stuff. Didn't I have enough crappy memories of my father's side of the family?"

With both hands planted on her hips, Mavis leaned over Niki. *Well, Miss Prissy. You are the one who wrote to me and asked all sorts of questions about the family. I guess you really didn't want to know after all.* A bee, newly arrived to the neighborhood and curious about the rose bushes, made a pass over the two women, then circled back to pause in Mavis' hair. She swatted the bee on his way and tidied hair back into her French twist. *I'm sorry Niki. That remark was unkind and uncalled for. I certainly didn't write down my life story to shame you about the Banks family. But really dear, everything that happens around you isn't always about you, you know.*

With most of the papers torn into unrecognizable bits, Niki sat down in the dirt, exasperated. She wished she could call Mavis on the phone and ask her why she would write it all down. *I always thought you were…* Niki paused, searching for the right word.

Mavis finished her sentence for her. *Perfect. Is that the word? Niki dear, you are smart enough to know none of us is perfect. I'm sorry I've upset you. I never meant to do that. But as for my life, I made my choices and lived by the consequences every day—as we all do. Writing it down? I don't know that I can explain to you the need to write it all down. That part is confusing, even for me.*

Niki covered her face with her hands, determined not to cry.

"Niki? Are you all right?"

When Niki looked up, Terry Spiegel stood beside her.

Mavis smiled at Terry. *Oh, good. I'm so glad you are here. I can't seem to make her hear me. Maybe you can talk some sense into her. Get her to understand all of this is not about her.*

Niki got to her feet. "I'm fine. Just a little headache, that's all."

"Niki, I was a good attorney. I know when I'm being lied to. What's wrong? Our little guy hasn't taken a turn for the worse, has he?"

Niki made an effort to sound upbeat and chatty. "Oh no. Nothing's wrong. He's doing great. Dr. Jim thinks I can bring him home in a couple of days." As she talked, Niki picked up the shovel and turned the dirt over a few times in the holes she'd dug for the rose bushes, making the space big enough to bury the contents of her garbage bag. "I'm visiting with Bingo every morning. We're becoming friends. Did I tell you I named him Bingo? Hope you don't mind if I put these roses in while we talk?"

Mavis nudged Terry and he stepped sideways to keep his balance. *Terry, she's lying about there being nothing wrong. Ask her what's in the garbage bag.*

Terry stepped forward and picked up the black plastic bag. "Is this shredded paper some new idea for mulching?"

Looking down at her digging, Niki replied too quickly, "Yes. Mulching. Latest thing." She took the bag from Terry, divided the paper scraps between the two holes, and gave him back the empty bag.

Mavis laughed and nudged Terry harder. He stumbled again and cursed the fates for old age, and himself for too many martinis the night before. As Niki worked the paper into the dirt, a "gotcha" smile settled on his face. "Well, if you're mulching, my dear, I think the mulch goes on top around the rose bush after you plant, not in the hole before you plant. Now fess up, and tell me what's going on?"

Mavis crossed her arms in front like a cigar store Indian and waited beside Terry for a reply. Niki was silent for a few, very long moments, planting first one rose, then the other. When both rose bushes were tamped in and she was satisfied the proper amount of dirt was covering the tender roots, she watered the plants down with the hose.

Terry waited, shifting his weight from one foot to the other to keep the circulation going. He cleared his throat. Mavis cleared her throat. He brushed wisps of gray hair off his forehead. Mavis tucked back errant light auburn strands. Niki continued to water the roses in silence.

Finally, Mavis trailed a hand lightly across her neighbor's shoulder. *I think we are wasting our time, Terry. She is not going to own up about the papers. I'm going inside and visit with Abelard.* She fluttered past him in a warm breeze; leaving him thinking he smelled a familiar perfume.

Niki leaned on her shovel and offered Terry a strained smile. "I'm done. Why don't you sit on the patio and I'll bring out martinis."

Terry knew when to retreat. "Great idea."

Shortly, Niki and Terry sat side by side on the patio in folding lawn chairs, a tray of martinis on a small round table separating them. Terry sipped his drink and held the glass out to Niki in a mock toast. She returned the gesture with the glass of white wine she'd brought out for herself. "Before I forget to tell you—The Weasel left a card in the front door yesterday. I guess I was in the bath when he knocked. Can't say I'm sorry I missed him."

Terry nodded and sipped again before he put his glass down on the tray. "And before I forget…" He reached into the pocket of his rainbow-hued Hawaiian shirt, took out an envelope, and handed the envelope to Niki. "Jack left this for you."

Niki opened the envelope, extracted the single sheet of paper, and looked down at the official looking document. "I don't understand."

Picking up his martini, Terry swallowed the last of the drink and poured himself another. "It's a warranty deed for this house. Jack signed his half over to you. You are now the sole owner of 24 Cherokee Place."

A quiver stirred in Niki's chest, like a curtain suddenly caught by the wind. "What? Why would he do such a thing? When did he do it? Was it Sunday? He's probably just upset about running over Bingo. Feels guilty. He can't mean it." A horrible thought squeezed her heart. "Or does he think he isn't coming back from Bosnia? Is that it?"

Terry shook his head. "No. I don't think that's it. He gave me the deed on Sunday and asked me to record it for him at the courthouse. That's where I was this morning when the

SING ME AN OLD SONG

guys came to clean up the shed for you. Apparently, he had the deed before the accident with Bingo. I think he got it drawn up when he went to Athens the other day. Anyway, he certainly didn't indicate to me that he thought he wasn't coming back from Bosnia. Besides, if Jack died, God forbid, you'd inherit the house anyway. Those are the terms of Mavis' will. No, this isn't about Jack thinking he's going to die in Bosnia. I thought you would know the reason for the deed."

Niki continued to frown and stare at the deed. Terry gave her a few seconds to gather her thoughts and then continued. "Oh come on, Niki. You know I am a hopeless busybody. What is really going on? First the deed, and now you hiding a pile of half-burned papers under the rose bushes–this has to be a good story. You have to share it with me. After all, what are friends for?"

Not knowing where to start, but feeling the need to start somewhere, Niki drank the last of her wine and considered where to begin. A small black-capped bird flitted from limb to limb in the dogwood tree, chirping. When he flew away, Niki tried to explain. "I really don't know why the deed. Jack and I argue more than we talk, so he wouldn't have mentioned it to me." She hesitated, collecting thoughts that might be relevant. "Neither of us wanted a roommate. Jack's a person who travels alone–literally and figuratively. And I guess I'm somewhat jaded from past relationships, used to being by myself."

"Did you say somewhat jaded?"

Niki gave him a don't-go-there look. He smiled and toasted her again with his fresh martini. "So what's with burying the bag of papers?"

Niki breathed in deeply and then exhaled. "Ah yes, the papers. Right. Can we just say I learned more than I wanted to know about parts of Aunt Mavis' life?" She hesitated again before she said, "In case Jack doesn't know, I buried the evidence."

Terry raised an eyebrow to Niki. "I assume what you mean is you found out about the Baker Street house?"

"You know?"

Reaching over with a liver-spotted hand to pat her knee, Terri answered, "Yes, dear. Remember I told you that I met Martin Book when he bought this house. He was older, but a grandly handsome man—a good man. I loved Martin; he loved Mavis. Mavis adored me as a friend. I adored her, as a friend. Strange triangle, but we remained friends. Martin would ask me to go along with him to call on Mavis at Baker Street. I would have followed Martin anywhere, just to be in his company. And to be honest, I enjoyed being with Mavis and Martin and watching all the, shall we say interesting, shenanigans at Baker Street. My Lord, it was like a real life soap opera. I am a busybody. Guilty as charged. Besides, I'd led a somewhat sheltered life up until that point. Certainly, I wasn't interested in any of the girls, but it was fun to be with Mavis and Martin, to be part of the "insiders". And truthfully, I did meet an interesting man, or two, there." Terry stopped and studied Niki's face. "Why Niki, you look shocked."

"I am shocked. I guess that's the correct word. Yes, it's a shock to learn your favorite aunt ran a whorehouse in Atlanta during prohibition—and then kept it going until 1952, or 1953, whatever."

Terry narrowed his eyes at Niki. "Hush your mouth, young lady. Baker Street was never a common whorehouse. It was...well it was more like a gaming house, a club—yes, a club with extra privileges. A whorehouse? Indeed. You should know better. And besides, aren't we being just a little sanctimonious?"

Niki rolled her eyes. "Maybe. But if I had to choose a life career, I would hope I'd choose something other than being a madam selling illegal whiskey."

Terry leaned closer, holding Niki's eyes with his. "I would *hope*. Is that what you said? *Hope?* But you don't know, now do you? None of us really knows what we'll do until we stand on the edge of the cliff, now do we? Be careful you don't fall off that cliff on your self-righteous butt."

Niki smiled at Terry's comment. He had a point there. His next comment wiped the smile from her face. "I'm fond of you, Niki," he said with as much sobriety as a man whose had three martinis in the afternoon can muster, "so please don't think me unkind if I question whether your anger, or disappointment, or whatever it is, at Mavis might have more to do with yourself, than her. Maybe you're asking yourself what the Banks' blood running in your veins makes you? For that matter, maybe you're asking what kind of person Baker Street made Jack?"

Niki frowned but didn't answer. Terry finished his speech. "Mavis would say none of it makes a damn bit of difference. We are who we strive to be. The key is the struggle. She taught me that. Your Aunt Mavis was a caring, and honorable human being. She was worthy of our respect and love. She earned it." Terry waved his free hand into the air. "Okay. I'm finished pontificating now. Pour me another martini."

Niki obliged Terry with a fresh drink, thinking he may be describing Aunt Mavis accurately, but not her grandfather Frank, and probably not to her father. Banks blood? Her blood? Her legacy? Terry was probably right.

They sat in silence, watching the sun riding lower on the horizon and listening to the afternoon traffic humming along Ponce de Leon Avenue. Now and again a bus whined, or a heavy truck ground through gears pulling itself up the hill in front of the old Sears building. Everywhere in the city it was going home time.

Niki finally spoke. "What should I do about the deed? I won't take Jack's half."

"You could sell to Hamilton Rabonette. Be done with it?"

"Never."

"Never? Well done. Mavis would be proud of you. She always said you were tough."

At that moment Mavis strolled out of the house to the patio and stood beside the pair. *I've been listening to the radio inside. Did you know they've found mass graves in Bosnia? Maybe thousands of bodies. Genocide, they're calling it. My God, sounds just like Hitler in World War II. How can anyone do that? I do hope Jack is safe. I remember him saying that part of the world is becoming just like Vietnam. You can't tell the good guys from the bad guys. They'll offer you a smoke one-minute and shoot you the next. Terrible, just terrible. I want Jack home.*

With no reply from either Niki or Terry, Mavis shook her head with frustration until she noticed the sweating pitcher of drinks on the table. Then she fussed. *Oh lovely. The world is going to hell in a wicker basket and you two are having cocktails. Terry, Terry, you and your martinis. Actually, right now I'd love a double scotch. What were you two talking about? Why would I be proud of Niki? I'm already proud of her.*

Terry's remark about Mavis being proud made Niki uncomfortable, though she couldn't say why. "Well, whatever. We won't sell the house to Hamilton Rabonette. I can tell you that."

Mavis kissed Niki on the top of her head, yawned, and then ambled out into the early evening of the yard. *Of course you won't dear. I never thought you would.* By the time Mavis had walked between the rows of spinach and kale, to the bench under the dogwood tree, she was as diaphanous as a dragonfly wing. In another breath she was gone.

Terry moved his chair a little to the left to catch a better view of the last of the pink sundown hovering over an oak tree at the edge of the yard. "What makes you think Jack doesn't know about Baker Street?"

Niki had a quick reply. "He'd never have given me the box of papers if he'd known what was in it. I'm sure of that."

"Hmm. Maybe Jack thought you already knew."

"No. I don't think so. And he can't know everything Mavis wrote. Not everything. He just can't."

When Terry raised a questioning eyebrow, Niki wondered, Can he?

# *Twenty-seven*

When the bedside clock's illuminated digital face rolled over to 1:17 am, Niki was awake staring at the ceiling. The anger she'd held toward Aunt Mavis had partially dissipated. Terry was right. Who was she to judge? She'd not been seventeen years old during the Great Depression or an orphan with two sisters to support. And truth be told, it was her Grandfather Frank who haunted her from Mavis' memoir. He was the one who seemed to taint everyone he touched. Niki was sorry she'd read the memoir and sorry that she couldn't take a pill and forget it. As tired as she was, she could only toss and turn in her bed, replaying scenes from Mavis' world before Cherokee Place.

Grandfather Frank smuggling whiskey in through Savannah harbor—yearly masquerade parties for the club members at Baker Street. Fern acting like a common…I don't want to have that picture of Jack's mother in my mind. I still don't understand why Mavis would write any of that down. I would think she'd want to forget those days. She had a new life with Martin Book. A good life. A respectable life.

If she felt she had to talk about the past, why didn't she confide in a friend? No, she couldn't do that. I wouldn't either. But why write it down? Maybe she wanted to write it out of her head. I know what that feels like. That's the way it was when I wrote the story about Anne dying. I'm glad the agent rejected my story. It was the writing I needed, not the publishing. Is that the way Mavis felt? Is that why she decided to burn the papers?

Niki fluffed her pillows for the tenth time and rolled over to the opposite side of the bed. Maybe Mavis was trying to rid herself of the memories by writing down what happened. Or could there be another reason? Niki thought back over what Jack had told her about finding the papers.

He said she wrote the memoir during the last few weeks of her life–about the time she'd replied to my letter. Why did I even write that letter? Childish. My father was a distant memory by then. I know was unhappy with Lyn–knew I'd made a mistake by marrying him. I was probably thinking there was something wrong with me, or looking to blame a bad marriage on my genes and not bad judgment. Did my questions about my father prompt Mavis to write her memoir? In her letter to me she said she wished she'd told me more about my father. But when I think about what Mavis wrote in the memoir, she says very little about my father–but a lot about her Brother Frank. Of course, many of the pages are burned too badly to read. There could have been more.

Grandfather Frank, what a piece of work he was. But I am my mother's child and nothing like Frank Banks–except I do admit to a small tendency to selfishness. Okay, maybe not so small, sometimes. Grandfather Frank must have been the most selfish of men. What was I, ten, maybe eleven, when he and my father died? I can't remember if Mother went to the funeral. I don't think so. What would have been the point?

And then there's Jack. What does he remember about living at Baker Street? How much does he know about his mother? He seems to remember his father as a strong and loving man. Yet Ellis was half of the partnership with Aunt Mavis. He certainly knew everything that went on at Baker Street and at Moody Street. I can't think about this any more. I'm giving myself another headache.

Niki finally gave up on sleep and got out of bed. She walked around the house in her bare feet, peeking out one shuttered window after another into the sleeping neighborhood, noticing which houses rested in the safety of a porch light left on, and which houses crouched in total darkness. She went to the foyer to make certain she'd left her own porch light burning, and remembered the day she'd come home to find Jack's suitcases stacked on the marble floor.

Oh, Jack. You are truly a difficult man. God help us both, but I think I miss you. Please be safe. Why go to Bosnia? Are you trying to prove you can still 'run with the big dogs?' Or are you running from Cherokee Place? From me?

In the middle of the night, standing in the dark foyer, the house felt large, and empty, as though not a piece of furniture, not a mirror, not a painting, not a rug, remained. Niki had a prickling sensation that if she spoke, her words would echo in the nothingness, then be swallowed by the plaster walls. The heavy silence almost made her wish for Jack's flute, squeaking out "Danny Boy" for the millionth time. Navigating her way in the dark to the comfort in the kitchen, Niki turned on the overhead light and made a cup of herbal tea. After a second cup, drunk while reading several chapters of a book on Georgia wildlife, Niki crawled back into bed and dropped into a fitful sleep.

She woke tired; her aching arms and legs missing the lost hours of rest. Her first thought was to get up, get dressed, and be on her way to Dr. Jim's. After washing her face and brushing her teeth, Niki felt better, more together, excited about seeing Bingo. She removed Abelard's night cover, thinking to give him fresh food and water before she made her coffee. The bird was not on his perch. Niki felt a rush of panic. Had he gotten out of his cage? She raised herself up on tiptoes for a better look inside. Abelard was on the newspaper-covered floor. On his side. Eyes open. Not moving. She opened the cage door and touched him lightly with her finger. "Silly bird. What are you…" There was no need to finish the question. Niki realized Mavis' beloved canary was dead. She closed the cage door and stood transfixed by the sight of the small yellow body, and the impossibility that while she slept, his life had simply ceased to be.

When the random cruelty of death seized Niki, there was no holding back the tears. She cried long hard sobs that shook her body and wrenched her stomach. She cried all the tears she'd swallowed on Sunday when Jack ran over Bingo, when she'd seen the bone pierced flesh of his small leg. She cried all the tears wanting to be shed after she read Mavis' story of Dell Ritter's passion and disappearance, and all the tears stored up for the loss of her baby.

When she was too weak to stand by Abelard's cage and cry, Niki folded onto the bedroom floor like a damp towel and cried until there were no more tears. Then she slept. At a little after nine, awake and her face swollen from crying, she made coffee and called Dr. Jim's office to tell them she would be late. Before she left, Niki nestled Abelard's body in a pair of fuzzy, purple mittens she'd received years ago as a Christmas present, and buried him beside the rose bushes.

Thirty-minutes later she was at Dr. Jim's watching Bingo make a brave attempt at walking around the outside exercise yard. With each step forward his one back leg hopped to right itself with the front legs. A vet technician, tethered to him by a loose lead, was telling him he was good boy and encouraging him to take a few more steps. Niki approached slowly. She said hello to the young woman and then knelt down at a safe distance to speak to Bingo. "Good morning, little guy. I certainly didn't expect to see you playing in the yard so soon." Bingo gave her a slight wave of the tail.

"I think it's okay for you to come closer," the tech told her. "The amazing thing is that he seems all calm and cool with us touching him as long as we are outside. Dr. Jim thinks maybe Bingo feels more in control being outside, thinks he can always run away if he feels threatened."

Run away? Niki repeated the words to herself. Would he ever be able to run again? It broke her heart to see him struggling so, just to walk. Niki squeezed her eyes shut for a second to compose herself. No more tears, she told herself, no more tears today. She stood up and fished a chunk of cooked chicken from a plastic baggie in her pocket. Bingo's tail moved faster and he offered a muffled, "Ouff. Ouff."

When Niki held out the chicken and walked slowly up to him, Bingo gingerly took the meat from her hand and looked expectantly at her. More tail wagging. She held out another piece of chicken and then a third.

The tech handed Niki the lead. "Go ahead. Walk him around. You just have to go slow cause he's still getting his new balance."

Niki stared at the lead, hanging limp across her hand. Then woman and dog stared at each other. She had no idea what to do next. Bingo seemed to be waiting to see if she was up to the task. After a few seconds, Bingo took two tentative steps closer to her and she was so overcome with joy that she knelt and hugged him around his shaggy neck. All her worry about being bitten disappeared. All his worry about this human being not being one of the good humans disappeared. Niki got a slobbery kiss on the ear as a reward. When she stood up, Dr. Jim was standing beside her.

"Congratulations, Niki. I believe you have made a friend." Niki grinned. "Bingo is doing great. We still need to monitor his surgery recovery. Watch for infections and all that, but I believe you can take him home tomorrow."

"Really?"

"Yes, really. It's like I told you before, dogs live in the now. Little Bingo here is not worrying about what he lost. Four legs or three legs, he's moving on with living. Are you ready for him at home? "

Niki thought for a second or two. "Yes, I'm ready." She leaned down again to give Bingo another hug. "What about you, little guy? You ready for a home?"

Later that afternoon, Niki went out to the vegetable garden to do some much needed weeding and watering. Pulling weeds was relaxing, but it didn't stop her mind from bouncing about. What to do about the deed Jack had signed? How long would Jack be in Bosnia? Are they still fighting over there? How is Jack managing with his injured leg? Should Bingo have a second bed in the kitchen so he won't have to walk all the way into the bedroom to lie down? Jack was about six or seven when his mother was killed. How much could he possibly remember?

Niki looked up from her weeding when she heard a familiar jingling. With Terry in tow, Winston pranced across the yard, bouncing the metal ID tags on his collar. She stood up to take in the whole of her neighbor's appearance. Today's dress was definitely not plaid Bermuda shorts and sandals. Today Terry wore black, tassel loafers, a steel gray suit, red pinstriped shirt, and a Jerry Garcia tie that captured the colors of an Amazon rainforest. Niki knew the tie was a Garcia design not because she was a fashion maven, but because she'd recently written a small advertising piece for the manufacturer. Her amusement grew as she considered Terry, who didn't seem like the Grateful Dead type, wearing anything inspired by the iconic band's guitar player. "Great tie," she said to him. "You'll surely shine in a crowd."

Terry stroked the silk lovingly. "Trolling bait for meeting new friends tonight. It's a Jerry Garcia design."

"Yeah, I know. I like it."

"Do you really?" Niki nodded and offered a small smile. Terry returned her smile and a look of newly minted kinship passed between them. "I didn't figure you for a fan of the late Garcia's guitar genius or his art. Are you a design savvy kind of girl, after all?"

Winston jumped up on Niki, asking to be petted. She obliged. "Hey, my boots are L.L. Bean."

Terry dismissed her remark with a wave at the air. "Oh please, sturdy and style are not necessarily the same thing."

They both laughed. Niki was struck with how much she enjoyed Terry's company and how grateful she was that she'd gotten to know him. She wanted to tell him about Abelard but something stopped her, something that wasn't ready to share the sadness. "True," she replied. "Hey, guess what? Bingo is coming home tomorrow."

Terry wrapped his arms around Niki and Winston insisted on getting in the middle for a group hug. "Wonderful. Are you ready for him?"

"Funny. That's what Dr. Jim asked me. Yeah, I think so. Jim said something interesting about dogs."

Terry brushed Winston's paw dirt from his trousers. "What's that?"

"He said that dogs live in the *now*. Isn't that interesting? *Live in the now*."

Terry's lips tightened as he considered Niki's comment. "Hmm. Sounds like good advice. Jim's a smart boy. Takes after my side of the family."

Niki smirked. "No doubt. How come you're all dressed up?"

"Theater tonight. *Porgy and Bess*. Wouldn't miss it." Terry sang out a couple of lines from "Summertime" and Niki clapped. "Thank you, thank you," he replied and made a mock bow. "I just wanted to come over and make sure you weren't angry with me for shooting my big mouth off yesterday. You know, about Baker Street."

Removing her gardening gloves and tucking them into her jeans pocket, Niki shook her head no. "I'm not angry with you. Just trying to work it all out in my mind."

"Work it all out?" Terry made a *pshaw* sound and Winston's head jerked up at the noise. "Well let me know if you do. Even at my age, I haven't worked anything *all* out."

"You know what I mean. Work out what to do with the information about Mavis' life at Baker Street."

"Well, you buried the papers in the rose garden. What else can you do?"

"I guess… I mean …I don't know. It's just that I have trouble separating the Aunt Mavis I knew from the one who lived on Moody Street and then Baker Street."

Terry looked puzzled. "Why would you think you could?"

Niki didn't have an answer. She wished she could talk to Jack about Baker Street; ask him what he remembered. Maybe his memories would soften the hard words Mavis' had written. But no, she wouldn't chance hurting him by stirring up a stew of old memories.

Winston pulled at the lead and Terry inched forward to let the dog know he was to get his walk after all. "I'll trot along now. Give old Winston his exercise. Then too, I like to be early for the theater. Watch all the hoity-toity Atlanta elite as they parade in."

Terry turned to leave; Niki stopped him. "Wait. Do you have time to answer a couple of questions?"

He stopped and faced her again. "Sure, if I can."

"I'm not clear from Mavis' memoir if her sisters, Marie and Fern, actually worked in the Baker Street house. You know what I mean?"

Terry rolled his eyes dramatically. "Yes, dear, I understand. Marie and Fern may have taken money from various boyfriends, but from what Martin told me, they pretty much lived on what the house made. Mavis and Ellis owned everything. The other sisters depended on Mavis." Terry paused, thinking back forty years.

"Although, I do remember Marie had a small beauty shop in the house. But honestly, as heavily as she drank, I don't see how she made much with it. I knew several of the girls upstairs who entertained club members at night—Janna Leigh especially. When Mavis sold the house Janna moved to New Mexico. Opened a dress shop, I think. Most of the girls upstairs had day jobs—shop clerks, office workers. Women's salaries were pitifully low back then."

A flush of uncertainty receded like a sea tide in Niki's stomach. Her mother was a shop clerk at Rich's Department Store. Terry read her mind. "No, Niki, your mother did not work at Baker Street. Though, I do think that after your mother divorced your father, Mavis helped her financially."

Niki nodded her head in agreement. Yes, she'd always thought so. After her mother died, Mavis had paid her college tuition that last year. In fact, now that Niki thought about it, Mavis had probably paid her college expenses all along.

"Just one more question. Mavis had very little to say about my father in what she wrote. Did you know him?"

Terry was quiet for a few seconds, remembering events that happened a long time ago. When he spoke it was as though he'd reached back to recall a list of admissible evidence for court. "Frank Banks, Junior. Played poker. Drank a lot of bourbon. Jack Daniels brand. Handsome man. Reddish hair. Freckles. Quiet. When he said something, it was often funny. Always seemed to be watching his father. I couldn't tell if he was truly interested in the man, or trying to gauge if he needed to get out of the line of fire. Mavis' brother, Frank, had a mean temper."

"Yes, I gathered that from Mavis' memoir. Did you ever see his temper set loose?"

Terry studied the ground, his mouth twisting left and right. "Well, there was one time I remember well, but I'm not sure you really want to hear the story."

"I asked. Go ahead and tell me."

"All right. If you're sure. In my mind the story plays like an old movie. It was fall. Baker Street. Dogwoods were red and gold. The parlor windows were open, a crisp breeze billowed white sheers at the front windows, and the late night traffic moved lazily up Baker to Peachtree Street. Mavis, Martin and I were off to one side of the room playing canasta.

"Ellis' voice carried into the room from his office under the stairs. He was talking on the phone with the caterer about a party they were giving. 'No,' he's saying loudly, 'no quail. This is a barbecue crowd.' Frank sat at the game table. The coat to his white linen suit hung across a curved chair back. Not a hair was out of place. He sipped a whiskey over ice; a white handkerchief wrapped around the sweating glass, and studied his poker hand. Another player was to his right. A man called Yancey was to his left. Yancey was youngish, tall, sallow-skinned–always drank milk because he had a sour stomach from the war. I think it was Marie who told me that his daddy died and left him a meat packing business in south Atlanta. The sausage king, Marie called him.

"Every time Yancey thought he had a winning hand, Frank got lucky. Every time he lost Yancey cussed, complained about his cards, and leaned back to balance his chair on the back legs and whine about going home. I could tell by the way Frank adjusted the cuffs on his shirt and flexed his shoulders that Yancey was getting on his last nerve.

"Then the other man at the table knocked over his drink–whiskey all down his shirt and onto his pants. Frank came up out of his chair and backhanded him across the mouth. He didn't move, didn't say a word. Then Frank stepped out and kicked Yancey's tilted back chair out from under him, landing the fool flat on the floor. Frank stood over Yancey and said something like: I can't think about my game with you running your mouth. Then he stood up, giving Yancey an eye full of the pearl handled pistol in his belt.

"After several seconds, Frank turned to the other man–the one he'd slapped–and told him to help the gentleman up so they could play cards. The poker game went on until Frank won all of Yancey's sausage money." Terry stopped, frowned, and looked off into the distance as though he'd just remembered something else about that night.

Terry's story and his deep frown registered with Niki, but she didn't respond. It wasn't that Grandfather Frank's actions surprised her; she just didn't know what to say. At first she felt she should apologize, say she was sorry. Suddenly, she knew that the other man at the poker table–the one Frank had slapped–was her father. That's why Terry frowned. He'd just now remembered who the man was. A flush of humiliation sang in her ears. She made herself busy fishing for her gardening gloves in her pockets.

Terry came back to the moment. "I just remembered a conversation between Mavis and Martin about your father landing a job as a reporter for the Decatur newspaper. Mavis was very pleased."

"He was a writer?"

"Well, yes, I guess. I know that's what I remember them discussing. Maybe that's where you inherited your writing abilities. Look, I'm sorry, but I have to run. We can talk later, if you like. Take care."

As Terry walked away, Niki managed a wave. A reporter? How could I not know that? Of course, he was such an alcoholic he probably kept the job about a week. But still, the paper must have thought he had some abilities, or they wouldn't have hired him.

Terry was rounding the corner of the house when Niki called out, "Have a good time tonight. Good luck with the Jerry Garcia tie."

# Twenty-eight

At dusk, Niki left her gardening and went inside to rummage in the refrigerator for something quick to warm for supper. Nothing looked appetizing, and she didn't want to cook for just herself. Finally she chose a chunk of pale fontina cheese and a beer. Crackers, good cheese, and a cold beer sounded good.

As she shut the refrigerator door, a bell tinkled from somewhere in the house. Because the sound —Abelard swinging from colored beads in his cage while pecking at his bell— was so familiar, Niki didn't fully register the noise at first, not until she opened the cupboard to find crackers and heard the jingling sound again. She paused, reassured herself that Mavis' canary could not be in his cage playing with the bell. He was buried beside the roses.

Niki stood still and listened, waited for the bell to sound again. Silence. After a long few seconds, she chided herself for letting a noise that wasn't there frighten her, and walked out of the kitchen to her bedroom—Mavis' old bedroom.

When she flipped the switch beside the bedroom door, bright overhead light chased shadows into corners. Once she was satisfied the room was empty, Niki switched off the brash ceiling light and crossed the room to turn on the bedside lamp. Abelard's cage still hung from the white wrought iron stand, just as it had for the past fifteen years. It was empty. Of course it is empty.

Just as she turned away from the cage to leave the room, the bell tinkled again. Niki flinched and then heard another familiar sound–traffic on Ponce de Leon Avenue. The vehicles sounded too close. She crossed to the French doors leading to the back yard and pulled back the drapes. One door was slightly ajar. She was sure she hadn't opened the door. Now this door is opening and closing on its own, just like the kitchen door, she told herself. After she closed and locked the door, and switched off the bedside lamp, Niki felt a twinge of sadness as she covered Abelard's cage for the night. "Old habits die hard," she whispered to the empty cage.

Jack phoned during her cheese and beer supper. She was surprised at how glad she was to hear his voice.

"Hey, Niki," he said, sounding chipper. "What are you up to?"

"Eating cheese and crackers for supper. How about you? And where are you?"

"Actually we are still in Paris. The weather is better but we are still waiting on clearance to get into Bosnia. It seems mass civilian graves have been found and everybody's too busy pointing a finger at the other guy to process our paperwork."

"Yes, the reports are is all over the NPR news. It's terrible. Just terrible." Niki didn't know what else to say to something she couldn't even imagine one human being doing to another. "So what are you and your crew doing while you wait?"

Jack laughed. "Good question. The other guys are working their way through the copious wine list in the bar. I've been swimming. The hotel has this amazing heated pool covered with a glass greenhouse sort of dome. I can swim and watch the rain slide down the outside of the glass, watch all the

Parisians stroll down the avenue with their chic umbrellas. The most fashionable color this season is purple. Or, as the French say, 'cramoisi.' I think that's the word for purple."

Niki echoed, "Swimming? Is that what you said? Does swimming help your leg?" Once the question was out of her mouth she worried that Jack would be angry because she mentioned his injured leg. He didn't sound angry at all.

"Yeah, it does," he replied. "I am amazed at how good it feels to be in the water. I think I'll join a gym with a pool when I get back."

Get back. Niki repeated the words to herself. Two thoughts collided in her mind. The first was that she wanted him to come back. The second was that he sounded as though he wanted to come back.

There was silence from Jack's end of the line and Niki wondered if he was waiting for her to say something. She stuttered a couple of *uh, uh, oh goods,* and then blurted out without thinking, "The house is so empty I'm hearing things."

Jack sounded genuinely concerned when he asked, "What kinds of things?"

Sorry that she'd said anything and not wanting to bring up the subject of Abelard's death, Niki tried to blow off her remark. "Oh, nothing really. It's just an old house. Haunted by the past and all that, I guess."

There was another silence on the line before Jack answered, "Yeah. I guess we all are. Are you okay? I mean are you frightened, or anything?"

How nice it felt to have someone ask if she were okay. "No, no, I'm fine. Really." And at that moment Niki really did feel fine.

"Good. Hey, I can't talk long. This is costing a fortune. All the umbrellas on the avenue reminded me of last Sunday–Terry and his big green golf umbrella. What's the latest on Bingo's recovery?"

Niki's mood elevated. Jack was actually asking about Bingo. "Oh, he is doing so well Dr. Jim says he can come home tomorrow."

"Vraiment?"

"Whatever that means."

"Sorry, the French jumped in. Really?"

"Yes, really. I spent a fortune at the pet store on beds, bowls, leash, collar, treats, and all those doggie necessities, so we are ready for the little guy."

"Hey, that's great. I look forward to seeing him."

"Vraiment?"

Jack laughed at her attempt at French and said, "Yes, really. Listen, I have to go. Someone is knocking on my door. Take care."

Jack hung up before she had a chance to say goodbye, leaving her standing in the kitchen holding a silent phone and her mood deflated. Why didn't I mention the deed? I should have said something, told him I can't accept his share of the house. I wanted to tell him about the two guys cleaning up the garden shed, fixing all the broken windows. Too bad the shed isn't big enough for an indoor pool. Still, Ed is right. The shed is bigger than it looked with all the vines creeping all over it. At that moment, what to do with the shed came to Niki with perfect clarity.

By eleven the next morning Niki was back home with Bingo. She'd taken one of his new beds for him to ride on in the back of her Honda and that had worked out fine. He sat up, watching out the window as she drove, looking as though he was perfectly confident all would be well. Once home, Niki lifted him out of the car and took her time walking with him from the driveway through the gate and into the back garden.

Bingo sniffed at the grass. Niki walked him over to the side yard and into a pine straw area she hoped would be his new potty spot. When the dog half raised the hip where his missing leg used to be and peed on the pine straw, Niki felt like cheering. She reached down and gave him a long rub around the ears and told him he was a very good boy.

With that success, they walked around the yard for a while with Niki explaining about the garden she'd put in since she moved into the house. When they reached the hosta bed planted nearest the glass garden shed, they paused and Niki looked back at the house. "This was Aunt Mavis' house, Bingo," she explained. He cocked his head and listened. "She loved it, and I'm beginning to admit that I love it, too. I feel like I can depend on this house. You know what I mean?" Niki knelt to hug Bingo. He accepted her hug and snuggled closer. "Just like Aunt Mavis could depend on it. Aunt Mavis loving this house and sharing it with me–that's what I'll remember."

After a light lunch of a chicken chew for Bingo, and a ham sandwich for Niki, the two returned to the garden. Niki wanted to measure the shed to see if her idea might work. Was it big enough for a photography studio? How about heat and air conditioning?

Bingo made it as far as the patio before he circled around a few times in a sunny spot and fell asleep. When Niki completed her measuring, she reclined in the chaise beside him and relaxed, the sun warming her face and her dog's comforting breathing as company. A phoebe bird in a nearby oak tree called out for her mate and Niki dozed. She dreamed she was standing on the shore of an unknown aqua sea, shading her eyes with both hands and watching hundreds of pumpkin-sized globes floating atop gentle waters. In the rhythm of the rocking waves, each iridescent orb caught the low afternoon sun in diamond lights of blue, gold, and violet before scattering it high into a cloudless sky.

# Twenty-nine

Later in the afternoon Niki was in the kitchen serving Bingo his first supper at Cherokee Place. She felt rested, happy, and tuned the radio on top of the refrigerator to the oldies music station while she watched Bingo eat his chicken mixed with dry kibbles. Suddenly, Bingo lifted his head from his new red bowl and turned to face the door to the foyer. He stretched his neck, poised to listen, whimpered, and then looked at Niki. She knelt to reassure him that what he'd probably heard was traffic along Ponce de Leon Avenue–perhaps the squeal of a car's brakes. After a couple of seconds of listening, ears pricking, Bingo went back to the important business of supper.

In the bedroom, Mavis stood in front of her canary's cage. She removed his night cover, saw the cage was empty, and inhaled a sharp breath. When she cried out, her voice carried like a wolf's wail on the night wind. *Oh no. Not Abelard. Please, not Abelard.*

Bingo's head shot up again. This time he barked one strident note. Mavis turned. *What was that? A bark?* She replaced Abelard's night cover, kissed a finger and touched it to the cage. *Good night, sweet prince*, she said and followed the sound of the bark.

Bingo sat at attention facing the foyer doorway. When Mavis entered he stood and barked again. "What is it, little guy?" Niki asked. He turned his head to Niki, waiting.

Mavis leaned down to the dog. *Well, I should have known. You are the little dog from Sunday's terrible accident, aren't you?* Bingo wagged his tail. Mavis laughed and the tea cups in the cupboard rattled.

Niki heard the clatter from the cupboard and assumed the vibration was one of those infrequent airplane noises. She opened the cupboard to check for breakage. Finding none, she turned back to Bingo and patted him reassuringly on his head. "It's okay Bingo, just a little airplane boom. Don't be frightened."

The newcomer to 24 Cherokee Place, but old hand at what is scary and what is not, gave Niki a tolerant you-have-so-much-to-learn stare. She misinterpreted the dog's expression and told him he was a good boy. That was fine with Bingo and he licked her cheek in thanks.

Mavis watched the exchange between woman and dog with amusement. *So, here you are. And it's Bingo, is it? Cheerful name for a dog, or a pony. I like it. Your pedigree looks to be in question, but I have to say you are cute. I'll tell you one thing, though. You are not to soil my white carpet. Always wipe your feet when you come inside.*

Bingo wagged his tail and barked again.

Niki watched Bingo as he wagged his tail and stared at the empty doorway. "What in the world…" Before she finished her sentence, the kitchen door opened and Jack came through carrying his worn leather duffle bag. Bingo immediately turned and hopped over to Jack, who reached down and rubbed the dog behind both ears.

"Would you look at that?" Niki said, "It took me several days and two pounds of chicken to make friends with him."

Jack smiled and shrugged. When Mavis brushed past Niki to kiss Jack on the cheek, a breeze closed the kitchen door. Both Niki and Jack looked at the closed door. Neither mentioned it.

Satisfied he'd done the proper greeting, Bingo left Jack's side, veered around Mavis, and hopped over to lie down on his bed by the pantry. There was an awkward silence before Niki said, "What happened to the Bosnia trip?"

Jack tossed his bag into the foyer and took out the cold pitcher of tea from the refrigerator. "You know, you can't get iced tea in Europe." He leaned against the counter, poured a glass, and took a long swallow.

Niki poured herself a glass and quipped back, "Fascinating. But what happened to Bosnia?"

"Bosnia's still there. I just decided not to go."

Jack received skeptical looks from Niki and Mavis. After a long enough pause to give Jack an opportunity to elaborate, Niki gave up and said, "Okay. Okay. I can tell this is going to play like twenty-questions. I ask and you give yes or no answers. Don't do that to me. Just sit down and tell me the long version."

She must have been smiling because Jack replied playfully, "May I assume you are glad I'm back?"

After a couple of beats with no reply from Niki, Mavis pushed them both to sit at the kitchen table and leaned in close to Niki's ear. *Don't let this chance pass you by, dear. When today becomes the past, its possibilities are as lost as rabbit tracks in a snowstorm.*

Niki reached over and rested her hand on top of Jack's. "You may assume." She hesitated, then added, "I realized while you were in Paris that having the washer and dryer to myself isn't all it's cracked up to be."

"Ah, I see. Okay, good enough." Jack left Niki's hand on his.

"So, Mr. Rainwater, what really happened in Paris?"

Mavis lifted herself up on the kitchen counter to listen. *Yes, Jack, what really happened to change your mind about going to Bosnia?*

Jack drank his tea and seemed to be picking his words carefully from a jumble of possibilities. "As I told you last night, bad weather and no clearance papers grounded us. Swimming laps in the hotel pool gave me a lot of time to think. And then last night while we were talking, the knock on my door was an old friend, another photographer. He said he'd called here and someone played him my message–you know, that I was at the Sully Hotel in Paris. So I guess you talked to him earlier in the week."

Niki had no idea what was Jack talking about. She was sure she hadn't talked to anyone on the phone about him being in Paris. Yes, she'd saved his message about being at the Sully, but hadn't played it for anyone else.

Jack caught the puzzled look on Niki's face. When she didn't say anything, he continued. "So, my friend mentioned he was between assignments–and he speaks French. He was fine with taking my place with the crew.

"They got clearance papers late last night so everything is a go. He's happy. I'm happy. The magazine is happy. I snagged a seat on the midnight flight to Gatwick and connected from London with a flight to Atlanta. That's the long version, except I need a hot shower and a nap."

Leaning back in her chair, Niki thought of several questions she wanted to ask. Why the cheerful mood from someone who'd spent the better part of a day, and night, on an airplane? What was he thinking about while he swam in the Sully Hotel pool? What changed his mind about having to go out one more time for the magazine?

She forced herself to sound casual and asked just one question. "Okay, but why didn't you want to go on to Bosnia?"

From her perch on the counter, Mavis crossed her legs and smiled. *My, oh my, this is really getting interesting. Yes, my sweet Jack, why didn't you want to go on to Bosnia?*

Jack's reply was slow and deliberate. "I realized I wanted to come home."

Niki's response was also slow and deliberate. "*Vraiment?* Is that the word?"

Jack smiled. Such was a sweet smile, Niki thought. She wondered how she'd not noticed before now that his dark brown eyes were sprinkled with gold flecks.

"Yes, that's the word. It means *really*," Jack replied. "I think the word can also be used for the English word, *sincerely*."

The thin metal cleats on the heels of Mavis' ivory leather pumps made a click-click sound on the tile floor as she slid from the counter top. *I know that song. Great old tune. Was it the Andrews' Sisters who recorded it? Let me sing it for you.*

At the moment Jack repeated the word, sincerely, Niki's heart raced ahead a few beats like a tap dancer ending the routine on a flourish.

Bingo raised his head from his after supper nap, listening as Mavis sang out, *Sincerely. Oh, oh yes, sincerely…I'll do anything for you…If only you'll be mine.*

When the kitchen door blew open, Mavis stopped singing and walked over to look out into the twilight. *Well, my stars. This is a day of surprises. Jack, Jack, turn around. Look out in the garden. You will never guess…*

Jack was occupied with helping Niki carry tea glasses and snacks to the screened porch and did not look outside. In the kitchen, Bingo closed his eyes again to nap. Mavis checked her lipstick in a pocket mirror she kept in a kitchen drawer, and fluffed up her hair a bit. Then she stood tall, took a deep breath, and walked through the open door out to the bench under the dogwood tree.

# *Thirty*

"Well, I have to say, I've sat on that bench several times the last few weeks, but I never expected to find you there."

Ellis looks up at Mavis with a pleased, half-smile. "Is that a fact? And here I am. A day of surprises to be sure. Come and sit with me. It's going to be a crackerjack evening."

She sits down beside him and feels the familiar, solid presence that is Ellis, the way he grounds everything around him with confidence, the comforting clean soap fragrance of his skin. *Clean soap.* Realizing she can smell again, Mavis sits back with a start and then closes her eyes to breathe in all the grassy, freshly turned earth, new plant richness around her. *Amazing. Truly amazing.*

"It does smell good out here. That Niki girl has been working hard."

"Yes, very hard. She may be Brother Frank's granddaughter, but she isn't afraid of hard work. I'm very proud of her, and of Jack. Have you seen Jack?"

"Sure, I've seen him. I've been watching for a while now. He's grown into the fine man I knew he would be."

"Do you want to go inside and sit with them on the porch? I think they are finally beginning to ..." Mavis lets her sentence trail off. She isn't sure what Niki and Jack are beginning, but she knows it is something stronger than what they'd had when she arrived back at Cherokee Place.

Ellis releases a roll of deep laughter that escapes into the air sounding like distant thunder. "No, Mavis. No spying. They'll work it all out."

Mavis crosses her legs and studies her right foot as she bobs it up and down. "I don't know what you are talking about. I never spy."

"Lord, woman. Who do you think you're talking to? I know better."

She feigns a coquettish smile, knowing Ellis really is the one person who does know better. She wonders though... "Ellis, what are you doing here?"

"The question is: What are *you* doing here?"

Mavis worries her one pearl earring with her right hand, thinking. "I'm not totally sure. I think I'm here for Niki and Jack."

"That a fact? Well, that does make you important, now doesn't it? Got to hang around the house to make sure other folks get their lives in right order. That it?"

The foot bobbing stops and Mavis sits erect, pressing out imaginary wrinkles in the skirt of her dress with her hands. "You are making fun at my expense, Mr. Rainwater. I don't appreciate that at all." She looks back at the house and sighs. "Abelard. My sweet canary...he died. Did you know that?"

Ellis takes her pale hands and covers them with his. "Yes, I did. I'm so sorry."

"Do you think I'll see him again?"

"Lord, Sugar, I don't know. I really don't know. One thing I do know is I've missed you, Mavis. Can't tell you how good it is to sit here and talk like old times."

Mavis feels a stiff muscle in her neck begin to unwind, each breath unbuckling tension she hadn't known was there. "I've missed you, too. It was so hard without you."

"You know I would never leave you and Jack on my own accord. I wanted to be here for my son, and for you. Though, I must say, you did a fine job raising the boy. And I'm grateful to Martin Book for his part in Jack's growing up. Martin was a good man."

"Yes, he was a good man. But then so are you."

"Well, we did have our moments, didn't we Miss Mavis. Through it all, you know I always loved you."

"You never said so."

"No, I guess I didn't. I know I messed up big time when I got back from the army and let myself get fooled by Fern's flirting. I should've known better–known I was nothing but a few afternoons of entertainment. Lord knows I paid for those two weeks of foolishness for the rest of my natural born life. But it was always you I loved. From that first night you came to Aunt Mae's house, it was you."

"You could have told me that a long time ago. It may have saved us both a lot of heartache."

Ellis laughs again. "Now there you go, putting it all on me. If you felt the same about me, you could have let me know. All those years, seems like you were always either in love with someone else or getting over someone."

Mavis has to admit Ellis is right. After Dell she was particular about who shared her bed, but never lacked the opportunity. She feels for her pearl earring and thinks of Dell Ritter. Dell was so long ago. Only one page in the book of her life, really. Martin was a sweet chapter. But Ellis? Ellis filled page, after page, after page. "So you think it was just bad timing with us, eh? Ships that pass in the night and all that?"

"Something like that, I guess."

"When Fern died, you held her hand and cried over her body. I was sure you loved her. I remember your tears made spots on her silk dressing gown."

"Did I do that? Lord have mercy. I probably did cry over that girl. Such a waste. I'd hoped she would wake up, love her son, and be the mother Jack needed. That didn't happen. But that's all right. You and me, we did right by Jack, didn't we?"

Mavis nods and their eyes meet. At that moment she can see their lives played out in the darkness of his eyes, years of taking care of one another, years of being each other's anchor in the storm. What she'd tried to tell Niki was true—Ellis had always been her best friend. But more than that, she'd loved him longer than anyone else. What else had she tried to tell Niki? Oh yes…to look in the box with the papers.

"Ellis, can you wait here? Just for a minute. There's something I have to do."

"I got nothing to do but wait for you, pretty lady."

Mavis nearly flies back into the house. The cardboard box is on the kitchen table. She shakes the box and smiles. Something rattles inside. She removes the lid and reaches inside. Her fingers shift papers about until she touches her missing pearl earring. She extracts it from the box, attaches it to her left earlobe, and whirls around the kitchen a few times, doing a little two-step. Bingo looks up from his bed, but goes to sleep again when he realizes the breeze in the room is just Aunt Mavis doing a happy dance.

On her way out of the kitchen, Mavis calls to Niki on the porch. *You'll have to get your own pearls, dear. These are mine.*

When she sits down again, Ellis asks, "All done?"

"Yes, all done. Now, what were we saying?"

The Atlanta sun is setting in a canvas of flamingo pink above pillows of blue as they relax on the bench and talk. Soon, twilight lengthens in the garden and brings a family of tree frogs out to sing. A large mottled-brown rabbit, unconcerned with the two whispering shadows sitting in her garden, hops silently into the spinach to dine. Lights go on in the kitchen. Niki passes in front of the windows, and then walks out of view.

Mavis turns her head, just for a second, to catch sight of the rabbit hopping to another row of leafy greens. When she looks back at the house, her heart flutters.

"Ellis, look at the house." He turns to the lighted windows and waits, not knowing what he is supposed to be looking at. "Don't you see?"

Ellis looks back at Mavis and shakes his head, no.

"Look at the porch. It's the old back porch at Baker Street. Look, there's that funny Terry Spiegel dressed like Agatha Christie. Of course Terry's waving a martini glass. And Martin's beside him, dressed like Christie's detective, that Frenchman, Hercule Poirot. Must be one of our masquerade parties. Remember, no one knew what characters they were supposed to be, and then Terry's wig fell into the salmon. Oh my Lord, we all laughed so.

"And there's Janna Leigh saying something to Terry. She's dressed as Marie Antoinette–carrying a ghastly fake head. That girl always had a wry sense of humor. I think she was at Baker Street the longest. When we closed, she moved out west to open a shop. Smart girl. Wonder if she ever married."

The Mad Hatter from Alice In Wonderland, also known as DeKalb County Judge, Benny Renfroe, meanders onto the porch and surprises Janna Leigh with a tickle from behind. She turns and slaps him soundly across his face. He laughs and grabs her for a kiss. Mavis is caught by the irony of the scene.

"This is so crazy. I'd hoped once I wrote some of the stories down, the memories wouldn't haunt me. What about you, Ellis? Does it trouble you to see the Baker Street crowd again?"

Mavis takes her eyes away from the porch and looks at Ellis. "Well? Does it?"

Ellis doesn't answer, but does that teasing thing he sometimes does of sucking air through his front teeth and shaking his head from side to side, as if to say: *I don't know kiddo. You might be losing it.*

Mavis gets right up in his face. "What do you mean by that look? Don't trifle with me you crazy Creole man. Are you telling me you don't see the porch at Baker Street?"

He drops the smirk from his face and stands up. "I'm sorry Mavis. I shouldn't fool with you. All I see is your Cherokee Place kitchen through the windows. Could be the twilight playing tricks, or maybe not. One thing I've learned since that oil rig accident is that time doesn't run straight ahead like some Southern Railway train bound for Baltimore. Sometimes it zigs and zags. I mean think about it, what difference does it make? All we really got is right now anyway."

Mavis is skeptical. "Hmm. Maybe." She looks back to the lighted kitchen. It is her Cherokee Place house again, her home. The word home has not come to mind before now. The word settles in her stomach like warm cocoa on a cold night. Baker Street was an elegant house, but this stucco cottage with its arched windows and dancing light is *home.* As she thinks the word again, she feels lightheaded and grateful.

Mavis walks away from Ellis and touches the tiny, furry buds on Niki's peach tree. She wonders how long it will take to make fruit. "Since I came back to Atlanta…" Her thoughts swirl and refuse to come together. "I wanted Niki and Jack… well, I…"

Ellis goes to her. Cupping his hand against her cheek, he strokes the softness of her skin and she presses his hand with hers. "Mavis honey, you were here today when Jack came home. Don't look for more."

After a moment of stillness, Ellis looks up at the sky. The early evening patchwork made of shadows and half-light is sewn into a dark night, with only a handful of stars sprinkled across the heavens. "Well, you ready? It's getting late. Time to go."

"Go?" Mavis lets his hand fall away. "Where are we going?" She thinks of the times she'd felt bone weary and gone to the resting place beneath the warm sea, where lullabies are sung by whales and welcoming lights seem to know her name.

Ellis offers no answer to her question. They stand in silence a few moments longer, Mavis feeling her heartbeat throbbing in her fingertips and wondering if Ellis has the same sensation. Just as she is about to ask him, he studies the sky again and says, "Uh huh." The sterling sliver of a moon he'd expected is finally rising. "Yeah, we got to get going. Take a good long look around, pretty lady, cause you never know when you'll be back again."

"When you'll be back again? Now I *know* that song. What is it? It's right on the tip of my tongue. It's not from the forties or fifties, though–newer than that. Oh come on, give me a little hint. Is it something to do with night trains? No, no, it's jet planes. Yes, it's something about going on a jet plane."

"Will you stop with the name-that-song-thing, woman? It makes me crazy."

"Crazy? Well, you never mentioned that before. If I was making you crazy, you should have told me."

Ellis throws his head back and erupts again with laughter. She nudges him playfully on the arm, and then eases her hand into his when the laugh is spent. She opens her mouth to say something clever but he places a finger to her lips. "Shh. Listen," he whispers. And they are quiet, waiting for the magic of the night to point the way.

Jack looks up from his chair on the screened porch. "Did you hear that?"

"No. I didn't," Niki answers. "What was it?"

Jack rises. Niki stands beside him. She follows when he walks across the living room and foyer, through the kitchen, and outside to the garden where a thin crescent moon marks the eastern sky.

Because she has eaten one entire row of young spinach and has a full belly, the brown rabbit simply notes their arrival in the garden with a twitch of her nose before disappearing into the flowerbeds.

"Listen," Jack says.

Niki listens; she wants to hear what Jack hears, but there is only the familiar hum of traffic on Ponce de Leon Avenue, and doves cooing from the dogwood tree.

"Someone was laughing," Jack says quietly. "I know I heard it. Sounded just like my dad."

# And Finally

To Readers: thank you for being here, for choosing this book, and giving this story a chance. Mavis has been speaking to me for several years. I hope her story speaks to you.

I am eternally grateful to Annie Laurie Kinsey Blackmon, a lady of kindness and intelligence, who shared her stories of Atlanta with me, and opened my heart to love the city as much as she did. Speaking of Atlanta, please remember this is a work of fiction and all people and places are used fictionally. No offense is intended. Thank you, Dee, for your continued encouragement and wise plot suggestions. Thank you, Karen, for identifying grammar errors and punctuation gremlins. Those missed are totally mine. Thanks also to Sing Me An Old Song's early readers who encouraged me to let Mavis have her say. I also appreciate Roy Lenzo, DMV, who shared his knowledge of canine medicine. And as always, thank you to my sons, daughters-in-law, and to my husband, Rick. You all know I will probably never be rich, or become famous, but you cheer me on anyway. Am I fortunate, or what?

See you next time,
*Morgan*

# *About the Author*

Morgan James called Atlanta, Georgia, and its metro area home for many years before moving to Western North Carolina, where she now lives with her husband and various animals, large and small. Her two previous books, the Promise McNeal mysteries, Quiet The Dead, and Quiet Killing, continue to receive excellent reviews and are applauded by fans as: *everything a Southern mystery should be*. The next Promise McNeal mystery, Quiet Hearts Can kill, will be released soon. Follow the author on www.morganjameswrites.com, and on Goodreads.

Cover photo by RetroAtelier @ iStockphotos.com

Made in the USA
San Bernardino, CA
16 June 2013